ONION SOUP

For my auntie Ne'Ne!
You have been a wonderful mentor
in my times of need. i love you
for all those times & the times to
come.   Love your niece
                    dr.dale
              X

Onion Soup

By d. r. dale

Cover photograph and design by Keith Saunders
Author's photograph by Marcia Parker

ISBN-10: 0-595-30165-7
ISBN-13: 978-0-595-30165-2

Printed in the United States by Morris Publishing
3212 East Highway 30
Kearney, NE 68847
1-800-650-7888

Acknowledgements

Thank you God! No way could I have chosen such a wonderful bunch of people who showed such patient support over the years.

A very special thanks to my mom, Jo-Ann Dale and my Uncle Moses Blackmun for keeping everything I've ever written. Of course Mom, thank-you could never sum it up.

To my Grammy, Selmer Hines, for her consistent prayers, I love you.

Thank you so much to my husband, Remer Lee for believing in my dreams.

I remain grateful to my family and friends for being there for me.

To Sonya, Brandi and my sisterfriend, Tahji; I can't thank you enough for reading all those loose pages! Your friendships have been invaluable.

Thank you to Alyson Blackman for flying to Savannah to keep me sane in the final stages of publication. Thanks also to Janet, Eva, and Terri for being my long distance therapy team. Also to my local therapy team: Andrea, Marcia, Ramona, and of course my cousin Marilyn Smith—Thanks a million! And to Shenita Ferguson whose two words ("change it!") made me believe again, you are sincerely appreciated.

This list would not be complete without the biggest thank-you to my agent, Joyce Parks. See, we were right! It started with us and will end with us!

To anyone that I've missed, please know that it's not intentional. I appreciate you all and I'll catch you on the next go around.

CHAPTER

1 Gwen leaned down to scratch her ankle where the cat circled. She could smell the pies cooking in the oven. In about thirty more minutes they'd be done.

The pies had served as a temporary distraction to the tears she'd been fighting all morning. It was only a matter of seconds before they would finally overpower her. A teardrop rolled from her face, landing right between the cat's eyes. The splash glued a small circle of hair to its skin. The cat meowed loudly and shook its head in confusion.

Walking to the living room, Gwen sniffed back more tears sending the combined mucous and tears down her throat. Her head hurt from the pressure. On the way, she flicked on the Central air unit to cool the house. She hadn't planned to use it; although it was the supposed reason her friend Allison insisted she bake the pies at her house instead of Gwen's own kitchen. The summer heat that Allison incessantly complained of hardly bothered Gwen at all. Gwen did however suspect the true reason for Allison's insistence to be so that Allison could brag on her newly purchased, much larger range. Allison could identify a manufacturer and quote a price in seconds yet couldn't make time to give her cat a name.

On the couch with her feet curled beneath her, Gwen's tears flowed afresh. The cat hopped on her lap and she stroked its back into an arch. The cat gave a lazy purr of appreciation as Gwen tried to ease her mind of her troubles. Instead she concentrated on the celebration of her pastor's anniversary to take place the following day. Of course with Gwen heading the Anniversary Committee, which simply meant she did all the work, there was really not one reason Allison could take any of the credit. Gwen managed a chuckle since Allison could manage to involve herself in anything—small or large. She surely would not be slighted as Gwen received compliment after compliment on her infamous pies. Allison felt that Gwen's use of her oven to bake those pies constituted brownie points for her as well. As far as Gwen was concerned, little of it mattered. She'd baked for countless occasions and this was just like any other. Though she didn't mind the cooking since it just happened to be her thing, it all equaled the same thing— work. Besides, she had reasons of her own for relenting to her friend's nagging and none of it had anything to do with new ovens or air conditioning. Using Allison's kitchen gave Gwen the perfect excuse to avoid her husband, George. She could not stand his expectant eyes following her when he thought she wasn't looking. There went George again, interrupting her thoughts.

Gwen glanced down at the cat napping contently on her lap. "It's just like Allison not to take the time to give the cat a real name," Gwen thought. "I think I will call you Miss Kitty," she said aloud. "Yes, that's perfect. You look like a Miss Kitty." She continued stroking. "I bet I can tell you anything, huh? At least I know that whatever I say will stay between us."

Any other time, Gwen would have felt silly discussing matters of such a personal nature with a cat, yet she found Miss Kitty's company oddly comforting.

"It's just that lately I've been scared see? Sometimes I feel I'm going to lose my footing and when I do fall I'm afraid I'll crack into a million pieces."

The cat's meow encouraged Gwen to continue. "I just don't know what's happening to me. I love George and we used to be so passionate. And now all I feel is dried up. What a pair we've turned out to be. Me crying all the time like a crazy woman and George fussing because I can't. No matter how hard I try, I can't get used to his smell in my nostrils, or his touch on my skin. Oh God how I once craved that smell and his touch. Shoot, I could lay forever under his touch. And now? I cringe if he so much as reaches toward me. All I do is wonder if he's thinking about her."

Gwen relaxed her head against the cushions of the sofa, briefly forgetting her listening companion. Miss Kitty bore claws into her thighs as a reminder. The cat screeched from the force of Gwen's shove.

"Shit! I mean Shoot! Look what you made me do old silly cat! Got me cursing. Some friend you turn out to be! Maybe I really am going crazy."

Gwen settled back, eyes shut tight against the tears. She began to doze with earlier memories of her marriage playing behind her closed lids. George was holding her, whispering something she could not hear. In her dream, she felt a longing for him in that part of her that had fallen asleep. She smiled.

Her nap was interrupted when the smoke detector sounded. The smell of burning apples filled the room. While fanning the smoke away, the dream lingered on her mind. Had it meant what she thought?

Gwen opened all the windows and dumped the burned up pies in the trash. By the time she was done, Allison's kitchen was spotless. Not that her friend would notice since the kitchen was Allison's least favorite place in the world. For that reason, Gwen was glad to have a place where her home cooked meals were welcomed. Many were the days when George carried bags of foiled covered plates from her kitchen. For Gwen, cooking was therapeutic. George often teased that she cooked enough for a small army.

Most dishes were sent to Allison's husband; Malik who so seldom got a home cooked meal that he appreciated Gwen's overzealous cooking. A few evenings of each week, he would call Gwen up just to tell her how much he enjoyed whatever she'd whipped up that day. Gwen would smile in appreciation and George would chuckle knowing how much his friend was starved for those meals. The last couple times George had not laughed with her nor joked how Allison was indeed starving Malik. His thoughts were elsewhere. Like on how he was sure Malik wasn't being deprived in the bedroom. George would have traded his meals for pop-tarts if he could wriggle into his wife and explode passionately together the way they once had. Gwen would be hurt if she could read his mind.

Gwen stood back inspecting her work. Except for the dishes of food she'd brought tucked away in the oven, and the pie left on top to cool, her presence could easily go unnoticed. She checked her watch as if time were going to slow down and two o'clock would never come. Her watch callously reminded her of the forty- five minutes remaining before her appointment. She massaged her temples at the very thought of having to undo then re-sew a brand new bunch of weave into the hair of the pastor's wife. At her last appointment, Gwen had tried explaining to Mrs. Willard that she needn't have the hair sewn in but once every two months, but the conversation fell on deaf ears. The woman ignored her and insisted that one month was the very most she would wait. And so it was, Mrs. Willard came faithfully every week for her wash and condition then on the first day of the fourth week for her re-weave. Gwen had nearly told her numerous times that she wasn't so stupid as to not figure that it hadn't been but three weeks plus one day. Like most times, she held her tongue and bitterly complained to George afterward.

Gwen locked up leaving the key in the designated spot under the counterfeit garden rock then carried the pies to the car. Two o'clock was coming much too fast.

📖

In one year Monica had gone through more relationships than she cared to admit. She lay on her bed facing the door that man number three had slammed as he walked out. The latest, Leroy, had measured up better than the others. She filed him under P for promising when she'd been hoping for the other P word. Perfect. She should have known he wouldn't come close when he introduced himself as LaRoi. Huh! What a laugh, she thought. That Negro knows he grew up with everybody he knows calling him LeeRoy. Not until the brother got himself a good paying job, some new clothes, and a spank brand new Acura that he figured he needed a new name. The thought was as absurd as her cousin, Devita, suggesting that she separate the syllables in her name to sound like Moneeka when it was just plain Monica. With an i.

Monica stuck out her tongue at the door and searched for her padded slippers. She thought briefly about tossing them out with the garbage, but dismissed it. Just because Leroy would no longer be a part of her existence, did not mean she couldn't enjoy the one lovely gift he'd given her. All the rest of his efforts at gift giving had been a flop. Either he'd give her something she had no use for, or something she already owned. At least there would be no more episodes of smiling while she unwrapped useless gifts.

Devita looked up from the morning newspaper to watch her cousin's latest boyfriend try his best to snatch his coat from the unwilling hanger. She tried not to laugh.

"Hi, LaRoi. Bye, LaRoi."

The door slammed.

Monica could hear Devita and dreaded the exchange she felt coming. Devita, who was two years younger than Monica's twenty-nine years, had always been a thorn in her side. They'd grown up together never having much in common. Monica was sure the only reason contact was never broken was because Devita nearly always initiated it. Occasionally Monica would forget a phone number of some relative and need to call Devita to get it. Those times she would hope her cousin would just leave her a voicemail and not deliver the request personally. Devita nearly always appeared and Monica hated it. Just the day before, she'd called Devita to confirm the date of the Maxwell's family reunion when lo and behold Devita came'a knocking. On top of that, Devita's upscale apartment was being exterminated; thus providing yet another reason for her to show up. It had taken three strong drinks and a nerve pill to endure her overnight.

Monica tripped over a box at the foot of her bed. Her blood began to boil when she thought of her yester night. Leroy had come in all smiley faced carrying the box. Her temperature raised a notch when she thought how that idiot had had the nerve to have the box wrapped in frilly paper. With that stupid grin, he patted his foot while she opened it.

Monica relived the moment while staring down at the box. "What the hell kind of gift is this?" Monica asked herself. "A thigh master? I should have taken it and hit his stupid ass over the head with it," she said lifting the box. Suzanne Somers grinned her skinny ass up at Monica. She carried the box into the kitchen with her.

In the kitchen, Devita rummaged through the cabinets. She looked as if she'd stepped from a Wallstreet ad in her summer suit. Her hair was as impeccable as the day she'd gone to the salon to have it styled. Monica nodded a greeting then waited for the snide comments to follow. Devita started right on cue.

"I was wondering when you were going to get up."

"I've been up. I just didn't feel like coming out of my room. Coffee made?" The mention of coffee drew a frown from Devita. "You know caffeine isn't good for you. Not to mention the calories in all that creamer you use."

Monica rolled her eyes and let the box she held fall hard to the table where Devita sat. "Neither is you standing there with your best white lady voice giving me advice I didn't ask for. This is me, Devita. Remember?"

Devita sat down. "Just trying to be helpful."

Monica was tired of her cousin. Devita's trying to be helpful was only her way of letting Monica know how much better she felt she were in comparison. With her so-called helpful hints getting more outrageous, surprisingly she never tired of introducing new ones. Monica thought she would get it after the last time when Devita suggested she lose fifty pounds and invest in a tummy tuck. Monica had laughed so hard that she broke wind and couldn't tell if Devita cracked up laughing with her because of the absurdity of her proposal or the unexpected explosion of intestinal gas.

Devita slid the box aside and started, "You may not need that caffeine if…"

Monica cut her off purposely. "Please no more advice. You know I've never listened to you."

"Excuse me for trying to save you from the lonely woman you're about to become. Judging from the sound of LaRoi slamming the door, I would say that some of my advice might be worthy of taking."

"Fuck you and Leroy, Devita."

Devita faked surprise. "Now, now cousin. That's uncalled for. I was only going to suggest a breakup makeover. I know my stylist could work wonders."

Sarcasm sliced through Monica's words. "Thanks, but no thanks. I like me right fine with my baldhead, jeans, and sneakers. As far as that man goes, good riddance. Besides, his name is Leroy."

"Okay, I'm not saying anything else."

"Good."

"I'm just going to sit here and watch your baldheaded self suck down that poison."

"Don't do me any favors. Better yet, don't you have somewhere else to be?"

"You know my house is being exterminated."

"That was yesterday, and in this day and age no one has to leave home anymore while it's being fumigated. I think it's safe to go back now."

"I was not taking any chances sleeping in my house with all those chemicals."

"You mean your apartment?"

Devita folded the newspaper she'd been reading. "It's a condominium to be exact, but never mind that. You know what your problem is don't you, Monica?" Devita didn't bother to wait for an answer. "You're just too stubborn to listen to anybody but your own self."

Monica hit the start button on the coffee maker. Devita was wearing on her nerves like gritting teeth. She swung around to face her. "And do you know what your problem is, Devita? You're just a well educated, nicely dressed, hoodrat who still believes the whiter you are, the righter you are."

Devita ignored the comment. "Okay, let's not argue. I was thinking we could hang out today. We never spend much time together anymore."

"That is no accident," Monica mumbled under her breath.

"You say something, Monica?"

Monica sat across from Devita and almost thought an outing would be a good idea.

"What do you have in mind? There's this movie I been dying to see."

Devita frowned. "I was thinking maybe we could visit this cute little wig shop I passed yesterday and then go to the gym. You seem to be gaining a little weight."

Monica set her cup down on the table. "What the fuck are you, Devita? A human scale? Tell me what exactly offends you about my size twenty-two body, and my short hair? Is it that you find it so hard to believe that I can have my pick of any man I want? Or is it that you think I should settle for assholes like Leroy because I'm not a size six!"

Devita had nerve enough to look hurt. "I didn't mean it like that."

"You damn well did and you always have. Get the hell out my home."

Devita grabbed her overnight bag. "I'm leaving since it's obvious that LaRoi's leaving is having an effect on your mood."

"No, you're leaving because I put your ass out!"

The door slammed for the second time that morning.

"His name is Lee-Roy, you ignoramus!" She yelled at the closed door.

Monica couldn't wait for the coffee decanter to fill up. She stuck her cup under the stream of coffee. She was so angry that she thought of calling Gwen, but debated if the moment could be considered crucial or not. Since Gwen had told her some time ago that Monica considered everything crucial, she had began to weigh every situation by which were worth stressing over and which others were not. This one rated a big NOT. Monica had seen Leroy hightailing it away from her months before it happened. It was only a matter of time before he tired of her mood swings. During their argument, right before he grabbed his drawers with the red lips pasted all over them, he had told her flat out that he couldn't figure if she were ever going to be his 100% lover or half sex partner slash good girl. He was fed up with the yes/no, yes yes/no no, yes/oh yes baby shit that he had finally blown up. That morning had been one of those yes, but maybe later days. Leroy told her in no uncertain terms that he had his needs while she crossed her legs and informed him just where to put his needs.

To pass the time, the rest of the morning was spent cleaning and watching all the morning soap operas. After her apartment reeked of lemon scented cleaner, Monica decided that Gwen would just have to get an earful. She picked up the phone and dialed the number. Gwen answered on the third ring. "Hello?"

"Hey, girl. You got time to give me a quick cut?"

"Monica, chile, quick is what it would be. You have nothing to cut."

"How about a lining?"

"Lining, my butt. What's up and make it quick? I've got the weave queen in there impatiently waiting."

"Okay, you're on to me. I'll tell you all about it when I get there."

"I'll shape your cut up, but be prepared to sit on the floor while I plant my tired behind in a chair. I am not standing up no more when this chick leaves."

"Eeeoo! You mean I gotta sit on the floor?"

"Yep."

"Well, I guess."

"Bye, Monica."

"Aw'ight, girl. Lighten up. I'm only joking. See ya soon."

Gwen was just finishing up with her client when Monica sat down. Mrs. Willard finished giving last minute instructions while taking in Monica's short haircut as if the number one abomination had just walked in. Gwen looked ready to yank every strand of hair from the demanding woman's head. Monica wanted to jump up and ask Gwen why the hell she was going through that madness. Ever since the particular incident that had caused Gwen to resign from her job, Monica had patiently watched her friend go from one idle hobby to another—the latest being cosmetology. She easily admitted that Gwen was an excellent stylist, but still felt that her training had been a means for paying her way through college to become a teacher. Barbering and such had served its purpose as Gwen had succeeded beyond measure. Three years prior, she'd been appointed Principal to one of the neediest Elementary schools in the entire district. Her presence began to have a positive impact almost immediately.

Monica's attention was drawn to Mrs. Willard momentarily. She snickered at her back as Gwen walked her out. Gwen however failed to see the humor.

"Girlfriend, wipe that stupid grin off your face before I hit you in it."

"Ooh, aren't we touchy today? Was Miss unbeweaveable extra horrid today?"

"Worse. If I hadn't seen all that matted up mess under all that silky straight hair, I wouldn't have believed it myself. Stuff looked more like an afghan than a weave. I had to give a for real 911 perm, and she had the nerve to try to short change me."

"You're just too kindhearted that's all."

"You don't have to tell me. And by the way…"

"What now? What I do?"

"Are you going to take Miss Hill as a client? I told you I was trying to get out of this mess. I'm finding a new hobby."

"Can't you still keep four or five of your clients? I've taken all the rest."

"Didn't you just hear what I just said? I don't want to do this anymore. I'm thinking up another business venture since my sister, Journey is coming home. We've been kicking some ideas around."

Monica asked the next question cautiously. "Will you be going back to your old job?"

Gwen ignored the question as Monica suspected she would. She continued as if she'd never asked. "I'll take Miss Hill, but she's the last one. I guess you're trying to appoint me the next ghetto diva of hair?"

"Why not? You're good, girl."

"Thanks for the compliment, but like I said that's it and no more. I already have half the projects as patrons."

"Don't start with me. You know you aren't but a block or two away from them projects yourself."

"Ouch, Gwen. That was a low blow."

"I meant that lovingly. Now come on over here and bring the clippers off the table on your way."

Monica handed the hair clippers to Gwen then sat on the pillow on the floor. Right in the middle of telling her all about her ended romance, the doorbell rang. Diondra walked in followed by her three children. Gwen greeted the young woman warmly, but Monica cringed inside. The dookie braids she'd painstakingly styled for Diondra as a favor to Gwen were all over her head. She wondered what grand lie would come from Diondra's mouth this time.

Diondra spoke to Gwen and nodded to Monica. She wasn't a pretty girl, but when she tried, she was attractive at most. That day, it was clear that she hadn't made a conceivable effort. Dark circles orbited her eyes and her clothes hung sloppily off her frame. Her nose was running as much as the children trailing her. She wiped it on the sleeve of her shirt. "Gwen, can I speak to you for a minute?"

Monica nudged Gwen to keep her from getting up. "Gwen has been on her feet all day. You can say what you have to say in front of me."

Gwen could not believe Monica's nerve. She clicked off the clippers and stood. Monica rolled her eyes and watched the two of them walk into the kitchen. When they came out, Diondra kept on toward the door without her children. Monica started in before Gwen could turn the clippers back on. "She got you again didn't she?"

"Not in front of the kids."

She could hardly wait until Gwen instructed the kids to watch TV in the den.

"Now what do you mean she got me again?"

"Com'on, Gwen. You know exactly what I mean. Diondra does this every other day. She marches in here with some sad, sob ass story and you fall for it every time. How long is she supposed to be gone today?"

"Just a couple of hours."

"Which means five or six. I'm telling you as a friend, you better stop it now before you end up spending more time with them than they own mama. They already depend on you basically to eat."

"You don't have to tell me anything. I acknowledge that you have a point, and I've considered your argument but…"

"But what?"

"If you let me finish, I'll tell you."

"Why, when I know you'll only make more excuses for Diondra?"

"No, I'm not. I was merely going to inform you that I don't do what I do for Diondra. I do it for her children. She's just a kid herself with three babies to raise."

"She wasn't such a kid when she laid down and shit out two more after the first one. What are their ages? About two, three and four?"

"Watch your mouth and no. They're three, four and six."

"See, that's what I'm saying. Is the gas on yet?"

"No, but that's where she said she was going today."

"Yeah, right. I guess that means they'll be eating dinner here too?"

"I would feed them even if I didn't have to. So don't lecture me because I know you are just a lot of mouth. *You* would do the same because we both know that it's not the children's fault that they have Diondra for a mother."

"You're right, I would. Except for today they'd be out of luck. All I have in my refrigerator is an onion and a jug of water."

"Then you would make onion soup."

"Yeah, I would, but it still ain't right, Gwen. If you ask me, all Diondra needs is a good old fashioned ass whipping."

"Keep your voice down and in case you didn't notice...nobody asked you. Now hold still and let me finish. Besides, you didn't finish telling me about your latest breakup."

Monica blew air through her teeth. "I don't believe I wasted an entire morning tripping on him. I even watched all the soap operas to keep from thinking about him and you know how I hate the soaps. I should have never given him the time of day anyhow. Leroy is all that he could be which is a complete waste of my time."

"I could say I told you so."

"But you won't and I thank you. It's just hard sometimes being single. But I guess I couldn't expect your sympathy."

"I have not always been married, and to tell the truth, sometime I think marriage is even harder."

"Don't say that. Big George is a wonderful husband."

Gwen sometimes hated that she could never be totally open about her and George's problems. Although Monica was truly a great friend, Gwen selfishly wanted to keep George's image untainted for their friends. She missed Journey so much right then. Journey could listen and neither condemn or judge.

"You need to know how lucky you are to have a husband like him. If you ever need reminding, girl, call me."

"For your information, I don't believe in luck. What I am is blessed and what you need is not a man like George. You need Jesus."

"Yeah, I know."

"Then why haven't I seen you in church?"

"Because I figure I don't need church to find Jesus. All the heathens up in the church house done probably ran him outta there anyway."

"Com'on, Monnie. That's a cop-out and you know it. I'm not saying that Jesus is only in the church. I've just missed hearing that angelic voice of yours in the choir stand."

"Maybe I'll go next Sunday."

Sunday is tomorrow."

Monica had to laugh. That's why she loved Gwen the way she did. She was a good person outside of Sunday service. Monica however had begun to question too many things as lately. Some weeks she just couldn't find herself amid the churchy ritual of Sundays. She still continued her prayer life but church was becoming less of what she felt she needed. It was as if the church had lost the healing balm that used to soothe her so. Maybe later she could talk to Gwen about it but not now. For now she would just enjoy her friend's laughter.

The laughter lightened the mood and Monica was glad. She stayed while Gwen warmed food to feed Diondra's kids. They sat at the table chatting while the kids wolfed down two helpings of spaghetti. Monica loved Gwen's spaghetti and had a helping herself. She would have left in good spirits had it not been for Allison's dramatic entrance. Decked out in a sleek, peach pantsuit, her complaints could be heard over the rinse water from the faucet.

Gwen, who could have predicted to a tee, the exchange between Monica and Allison, cut a warning glance at Monica. "Not today. Could you paleeze try to keep your mouth shut?"

Monica faked her best expression of innocence. "Who me? I won't say a word. I'll just stay and dry these few dishes."

Gwen dried her hands on her apron on the way to meet Allison in the living room. Better that her two friends did not make eye contact right away to avoid conflict. Monica had always found Allison shallow and bland. Sometimes Gwen didn't blame Monica's assessment. Allison was and forever would be shallow, but Gwen considered her a friend nonetheless.

Allison stopped short of the kitchen when she saw Monica standing over the sink. She rolled her eyes toward the kitchen then turned her attention to Gwen. "I didn't know you had company."

"Glad to have it too. Monnie is keeping me company while I watch Diondra's kids."

"Diondra must be missing in action again?"

Gwen was tired of explaining Diondra's whereabouts. "She said she'd be back soon. Have a seat."

Allison fanned herself with her hands. "Girl, I think I'll pass. It feels like a cross between purgatory and hell in here. I don't know how you stand it. I just stopped by to remind you that Anthony and Sean are planning to drop by. I just saw them at the bakery and was pretty sure you had forgotten."

"Shoot! That's right. I'm supposed to keep Janelle for Anthony tonight."

"See, I knew you forgot. What would you do without me?" Allison sang.

"Keep living," Monica mumbled under her breath. She did have to admit that Sean's name got her attention. She stuck her head from the kitchen.

"You hear that, Monica. Anthony is coming over," Gwen called.

Monica couldn't care less. "Maybe I'll have time enough to flirt with that fine client of his."

"You mean Sean? Now you behave yourself, you hear? Besides, I tried to hook you up with Anthony. He's the one who needs a mother for his daughter."

Monica disappeared back into the kitchen. "I keep telling you Anthony is gay," she called over her shoulder.

"Monica!"

She came back into the living room. "Well he is."

"How could you say such a thing?"

Monica stood with her hands planted on her hips. "Gwen, when have you ever seen him with a woman?

"So. I've never seen Sean with a woman either, but that doesn't mean anything."

Monica shrugged and peeled a banana. "Both of'em could be gay."

Allison couldn't believe how flippant Monica was about such an accusation. "What an awful comment to make about someone. Just because a man doesn't run around chasing every skirt he sees, particularly yours, does not mean he's gay. You should be ashamed of yourself!"

Monica threw up her hand palm first and made a noise like a screeching car. "Eeeerch! I'm not talking to you."

Allison rolled her eyes to the ceiling. "I would expect such childish behavior from someone like you."

"Explain just what you mean by someone like me."

"You know what they say."

"Who the hell is *they*, and no I don't know what *they* say. I'm more interested in what the hell *you* are saying?"

"I'm saying that you are bitter because you can't find a decent man, and it might be because no decent man is going to attempt to turn a you know what into a housewife. I'm sure you can fill in the blank."

"If you're calling me a whore, then let me just make something clear to you. I'm not a whore, just whore-ish. And since you like filling in blanks with insults, how about here's one for you. I think that you are nothing but a fake, griping you know what. I'll even give you a hint. It starts with a b and rhymes with itch."

"No you didn't."

"Yes, I did."

"Well since you went there. Let me tell you that you are lucky that Gwen tried to match make a harlot like you to anyone."

"Harlot? I bet this so-called harlot can have your man! How much you want to bet?"

Gwen threw up her hands in frustration. "I would put the both of you out like usual, but neither of you are going to run my blood pressure up today. Kill each other if you want. Just do it quietly. I'll be in the den with the kids."

Allison continued the argument. "My man wouldn't have your big butt!"

Monica kicked off her shoes. "How about I just gon' ahead and whip your ass and settle this thing."

Allison took a seat and crossed her legs. "I'm too old for this juvenile display."

Monica stepped back into her shoes. "I didn't think you wanted none of this. You might need to be trying to get home to that husband of yours. After all, you do know what they say about four-legged canines like Malik?"

Allison was on her feet again. "What is that supposed to mean?"

"It means you can't make a dog walk on two legs unless it's begging or humping something. Not necessarily the Master's leg if you know what I mean."

George walked in just as Allison yelled, "You Hussy, take that back!"

George stepped between the two women. "Hey, hey, hey, hey! How is it Gwen left the both of you in a room alone together?"

Gwen recognized George's voice and called to him, "Hi baby."

George looked from the two women then toward the direction of Gwen's voice.

When Gwen appeared, she was unconcerned. "Don't pay them any mind. They act like this every other time they're in the same room. I'm sick of being in the middle."

Allison grabbed her purse and gave George a quick hug on the way out. "See you two tomorrow at church. Gwen, I'll call you after I think you've put out the garbage."

"See you tomorrow, Allie. Thanks for reminding me about Janelle and Anthony."

Amazingly, Monica ignored the comment and sat down in the chair. "Sorry about that, Big George. You know how it is. I try to resist hassling Allison but it is such fun."

George chuckled accepting a kiss from Gwen. To Monica he said, "Allison ain't so bad."

Gwen pulled George by the hand into the kitchen. "I kept your dinner warming in the oven."

Monica busied herself straightening her clothes when she heard a car pull up. She hollered she'd get the door just as the doorbell rang. Anthony's face was the first she saw. Sean stood behind him, next to Janelle. With her baseball cap on, it was like seeing Anthony twice. The resemblance she and her father shared was remarkable. Monica put on her best smile.

"Hi, guys. Gwen's in the kitchen with Big George."

It was Sean's sexy baritone greeting her. "Hi yourself. You look lovely as always."

Monica's witty response was lost in her throat when the screen door swung open. Diondra was stepping inside. The three had gone to the kitchen before Monica could turn her attention to flirting with Sean.

"Diondra's here!"

Gwen stuck her head through the alcove and mouthed the words, "He is NOT gay".

Monica whispered, "Ask him."

At the mention of their mother's name, the kids shuffled out to meet her. Monica watched as she grabbed their hands and started to walk out without so much as a thank-you. She was glad Gwen was in the kitchen and wouldn't hear her confront Diondra.

"I believe the proper phrase would be 'thank you', Diondra.

Diondra seemed shaken that someone was speaking to her. "Oh. Thanks, Gwen," she called out.

Gwen yelled something back, but Monica could barely hear it. Anthony had whispered something in Gwen's ear before they had headed to the den. Sean sat in the kitchen talking football with George. Monica was more curious about the conversation going on down the hall until Janelle sat beside her and asked if she would braid her hair. Monica figured, why not, since she had no one to flirt with.

In the den, Anthony stood looking sheepish with his hands shoved deep into his pockets. Gwen knew whatever he wanted to discuss was uncomfortable for him. She waited until he spoke to look up.

"Gwen, I hate to ask you this, but I don't have anyone else I can trust."

"You know you can ask me anything. Sit down, let's talk."

Anthony sat but continued to squirm on the sofa. He finally locked his hands between his knees since he couldn't figure what else to do with them. "It's Janelle. She's fourteen now and asking a lot of questions. I know she's becoming interested in boys, but I can't seem to bring up the subject of…you know."

There could be a million subjects and Gwen couldn't figure which one was causing such hesitation. When Anthony saw the confusion on her face, he continued.

"Sex."

Gwen tried not to laugh, but couldn't help it. Anthony had whispered the word as if he were cursing.

"That's all?" She asked. "I thought this was going to be about something really foreign."

Anthony laughed nervously then relaxed against the couch. "Well it is sorta alien to me. Since Lena died twelve years ago, I've had to be both Janelle's parents. Most situations I can handle, but for some reason when the conversation veers toward sex…" His voice trailed off.

"What do you want me to tell her if it comes up?"

"I want you to tell her what you know. I mean tell her how important a decision sex is between two people. Of course I wish she would wait until marriage, but I realize she may not. I just don't want her listening to her friends and picking up some extravagant expectations. You know as well as I that some young men are after sex and nothing else. I don't want to see my baby hurt."

"I'll do my best. All I can tell her is my experience and how God intends sex to be between married people."

Anthony stood and breathed deeply. "That's all I ask. I wish I could tell you how much I appreciate having a woman in her life that I can trust. It hasn't been easy rearing a girl child. I'll be back promptly after my meeting with Sean. It should be no later than nine."

"Don't worry. Janelle will be fine."

"I know," Anthony said. And he did know. He knew the first time George introduced him to Gwen that she could be trusted. He needed that since there was no one he could trust with the true reason it was so hard for him to talk to his daughter. The truth was, that it had been so long since he'd slept with a woman that the subject excited and embarrassed him too much to even talk about. For the time being, he knew Gwen would do a good job. She was used to talking to young people. They trusted her as both a teacher and a confidante.

C H A P T E R

2 By the time Gwen and George's house emptied, it was past nine o'clock. Gwen sat on the side of the bed tying a scarf around her hair. George came out of the bathroom drying his hands on his pajamas. He had to bend his 6'4" frame considerably to keep from bumping his head against the top of the door. She was thinking about how odd the two of them had looked in their wedding pictures. At 5'4", she had looked dwarfed beside him.

"You going to bed kinda early tonight ain't you?" George asked.

Gwen faked a yawn. "I'm feeling a little tired. I been baking pies all morning for the pastor's anniversary tomorrow, dealing with Mrs. Willard's head and you saw all the people who stopped over today."

George wouldn't be so easily put off. He sat on the bed beside her and wrapped an arm around her shoulder. Gwen tried to ignore his wily smile as he squeezed her. "I was hoping that tonight we could…well, you know we are married folk."

George couldn't miss the fearful tremble of Gwen's voice. "Maybe another night. I'm tired and I know my feet are swollen."

That was not the answer George had hoped for and to let Gwen know it, he stormed from the room. She could hear him mumbling all the way down the hall.

"That woman can stand on her feet all day cooking pies for church folk, do folk hair, but can't even lay in the same bed with her own husband without trembling. I might as well make the couch my permanent bed since that's where I end up all the time anyhow!"

George flipped through the TV channels until he heard Gwen calling him. He wanted to ignore her but the sorry in her voice beckoned him from the sofa. There were tears in her eyes when he walked in.

"George, don't be angry. I don't want you to go to sleep angry."

George sat next to her and wiped her tears away with his thumb. He measured his words carefully. "What is it, Gwen? We can't keep going on like this. I thought we agreed to try to get through this. Don't you still love me?"

The stony look she gave was what he feared.

"Please don't do that, George."

"Do what?'

"Make me feel as if this is my fault."

"I'm sorry. That's not what I meant to do."

"You know I love you."

"I know, but lately I feel like I'm just part of this house. Like a piece of old furniture or something. You've gotta talk to me, baby. I need to understand."

"You want me to talk, then I'll be honest with you. Sometimes at night when you're sleeping, you smile so hard I think your face will crack to pieces. I can't help but wonder if those smiles are for me or because you're thinking about her."

George dropped his head into his hands. "If I'd known this thing would hurt us so badly, I would have done something so different. I know I hurt you by seeing her, but I swear on everything dear to me that we never had sex."

"I believe you, but still and all. It was almost more than what it was."

"I'm sorry and I'm even more sorry that sorry is all I can say. Too bad sorry don't change shit, huh?"

Gwen hated herself for asking but she needed to know. "Why, George? Why? Is it me?"

George held her hands in his. "No, baby. That was never it."

"Then why?"

"No reason could ever be good enough. I made the biggest mistake of my life and I can't give you a decent enough reason why."

"That's not good enough for me. Try."

"I don't really know why. I guess it could've been because she was young and she made me feel young again. I was so jealous of the time you make for so many people that I looked for someone who'd give me their undivided attention."

"Yet you never said anything to me."

"No, I didn't. I was scared you'd see that it was nothing but jealousy and tell me how petty I was being. Instead of trying to talk to you about the way I felt, I ended up doing something I'll regret the rest of my life."

"Tell me again. How far did you go?"

"One kiss. I promise that's it. That don't make it okay and I know it." George stared into her eyes then fell silent. "If I say anything more it's going to sound like I'm running some schoolboy game on you. I love you too much for that."

"Anything more like what?"

"Like how all I kept thinking was she wasn't and never would be you."

Gwen watched the tears slide down his cheeks and wanted to believe in her husband. "Why did you tell me?"

"Don't you see, baby? I had to. After twelve years of marriage, I owed you that much. I wouldn't be a man if I hadn't."

"You know I want to believe you."

George laid his head in her lap and squeezed her nightgown in his fist. "Please, please believe me. That was the first and only time I ever thought to do something like that. I love you, Gwen. I just wish I could zap things back the way they used to be."

"I don't question that. I know you do."

George lifted her nightgown and fingered the puckery scar on her knee. "You remember when you did this? We were fooling around in that old shed when one of the nails stuck you?"

"Mmhmm."

Gwen closed her eyes and shook her head yes in remembrance while George took off her house slippers. He was happy just being close to his wife.

"You remember when we first got married?" He asked. "This place right here is where you broke your toe on that old table your Nana Sweetie gave us."

Gwen felt the warmth of his lips on her toe and the familiar scratchy of his beard on her leg. Once, she had loved that feeling. She took pride in trimming his beard and mustache. She loved the way it neatly framed his strong jaw line. This was the man she'd loved much of her life.

Again, she felt the warmth of his mouth on the scar on her knee, then his lips tracing a path along her thigh, further up past her rib cage, then finally up to her neck.

"Right here is where you wear my favorite perfume," he whispered. "Kiss me, Gwen. Believe in me again."

She leaned back and gave in to his lips on hers. It had been months since she felt the heat rise in her that way and it felt good. Before thoughts of insecurity could enter her mind, she held on to George as tight as she could. That night, she let him make love to her the way she knew only he could. And for the first time since the previous summer when a young woman had trespassed on all that was hers, Gwen didn't think about her. It never even crossed her mind how Vanessa had chipped away at the structurally sound marriage she and George had built or how she had tried to take away the only man Gwen had ever loved the way she did her husband. That person was gone and Gwen and George were still there. The way it was supposed to be.

C H A P T E R

3 *Here I am, the older supposed responsible sister, and I'm heading home to Gwen. Responsible is the exact word my mother, Beatrice used. The way she said the word was as if to say I've been irresponsible my entire life. I admit I've had some pretty bizarre escapades, but my intentions were usually good. Though 'good' is far from how the situations ended up. One thing is for sure, under no circumstance am I running to Beatrice and telling her my business. Never mind that she lives only a couple blocks away from the condo I've lived in for the past three years. She has no idea that right now I'm sitting on an eastward bound bus to E. St. Louis. In order for her to know that I planned to leave, I would have had to tell her about the third or fourth good job I've left. Fortunately, to my credit, I didn't quit this time. Downsizing took care of that for me. I'm thankful that I worked two years past my contract as a Systems Analyst with this last company. Hell, that was damn long enough for me. The good thing about being laid off was that it saved me from having to resign. I've become an expert writer of resignation letters and a going away bash connoisseur. My social gathering etiquette is impeccably unquestionable by any and all of Miss Manners' standards. I got my shit down pat,* Journey thought as she lay back onto the seat.

Journey's mind was occupied with more thoughts of Bea trying to intrude, but she shook them off as best she could. It just wasn't happening so she pulled Dana from her purse as easily as she could without waking the sexy brother beside her. She thought for a moment how some would consider her silly for naming a journal. It was of no matter since it was her secret and nobody's business anyways. Dana had been her best girlfriend throughout high school and college and was killed in a car accident on the way to their twentieth year high school reunion. Besides Gwen, Dana had been her truest friend. Since Dana's death Journey had kept a dialogue with her in a thick, leather bound journal. The pen she used had been a graduation gift from Dana and had been refilled countless times.

The stranger beside her awoke momentarily to share his blanket with her before she began to recite to Dana all the reasons why she was right in not calling Beatrice before she left.

My first reason is definitely the job thing. Twenty years in the United States Army prepared me for everything except being a civilian. Remember how you would tease me whenever I sent pictures? "You look like a soldier ", you 'd say. And I would quickly agree. I know I told you this, but there was some kind of magic when I put on that uniform. I'm glad you had the chance to see me in it, which is more than what I can say about my own father. As I write this now, I wish you could see me. I lost all my hair and get this, when it grew back, I let it lock. Yeah, weird huh? You're still the only one besides Sweetie and Aunty Cut who knows about the cancer and chemo. Thank God, girl it's been some time and it's still in remission. Oh yes, I finally did the things we talked about all the time. One thing you told me not to do was sell the house. I did and moved into a condo. I decided to take Gwen up on her offer and come home for a while. I moved some of my stuff into a friend's garage, put the rest in storage and got on the bus. Oh yeah, I sold my car too. If I decide to move home, I'm buying mostly all new shit. The stuff that I just can't part with I'll have shipped home and the rest I'll give to Bea. Some, I'll give to my sister, Tilly, since she would have a tizzy if I didn't. Then, I'll have no reason to go back to Colorado.

You know girl, it's not as if I even have to work, I left the Military with the rank Lt. Colonel hoping to make full bird (that's Colonel since you always fussed about not being able to follow all that Army lingo). I just don't know what else to do. Beatrice thinks that any job where Caucasian faces are plentiful and where you have to dress in a suit is a good job. Who can tell her different? Believe me, I've tried, and today I just couldn't handle seeing that disappointed expression on her face. It wouldn't be so bad if for once the 'you're a smart girl, Journey' speech wouldn't follow. I always get the impression that even though she goes no further than that, the rest of the speech would go something like, 'then why the hell do you make so many dumb choices?'

I wish she'd just say it already.

Then of course there's the relationship thing. It's no secret that I've managed to screw up every relationship I've ever been involved in. Not single-handedly of course. It just happens somehow. For instance, I ended my last relationship when I fell asleep with Steve on top of me and woke up with Derrick's face lodged between my thighs. I think I passed out right after. That experience alone was enough for me to declare celibacy and stick to it. Almost a year has gone by without me so much as having smelled a man other than my uncles and nephews. Thinking about it now, I feel like crying except that it's this sexy brother beside me reeking purely of essence of man. There is no mint on his breath, which suits me just fine since I remember that smell. As long as it isn't heavy with the aroma of last night's sex or early morning sleep, it's okay. I can hear the sleep coming in his breaths and am not offended in the least when he leans over slightly onto my shoulder. I'm just happy there's no way he can know how wet he's making my panties.

I hate to keep complaining about Colorado to you because it's not like I'm saying anything I haven't before. Besides, I feel like I'm beginning to sound like the sister straight out of Waiting to Exhale, what was her name? Sarah? Sahara? 'Seems that ever since that movie came out, that every black woman is more or less characterized by at least one of the sisters in one scene or another. Either from that movie or some other. If I hear one more time about how I remind so and so of Angela Bassett, Halle Berry, or Pam Greer, I'm going to sock somebody. How the fuck am I supposed to believe that when all of them are as different as night and day? Some blackfolk tickle me...always trying to look like some fucking body on TV. As if it makes a difference whether or not I remind someone of either of them anyhow. They're rich and I'm not. Only a few hours before I'm out of Colorado completely.

No more reassuring myself. I know I did the right thing especially after replaying the last conversation with my last potential date. Not two hours ago, I get this page from a man who tells me how Tilly's nosy ass has been passing out my pager number again. She's always playing the matchmaker. So I call the number to see who it was and this guy picks up. We got as far as hi and how are you before I asked with whom I was speaking. Knowing full well that I didn't know his ass from a paper bag, the clown wanted me to guess. That was the first stupid thing he did. Then, if he didn't tell me seventeen times how he looked like Jon B. my name isn't Journey Renee Butchard. I wanted to hang up in his face right after I yelled, "Who the hell is Jon B!" Instead, I frowned across the table at Tilly who was watching me like a freshly baked Thanksgiving duck. I knew I should have never stopped by her house. I hung up the phone promising to keep in touch with him when what I really wanted to do was slap her. When my niece got home, she hipped me to just who the heck this Jon B. character was. I was surprised the songs on the CD sounded pretty good since most of the young hip-hop doesn't appeal to me. I'm a Motown era diehard. I have to admit that it is kind of funny when I think about it. It just goes to show that Tilly doesn't know any-thing about me. She actually believed she was doing something special by hooking me up with some neon, light-skinned man. Nothing against light black folks, but my last two boyfriends were so black they could pass for eggplant purple and I loved every inch of them both. Light, dark, black or brown, I like men. Period. Which brings me to my point. Colorado's dating scene sucks unless you're female and any other ethnicity than black. Then you have it made. Most men will walk all over my feet for the chance to speak to some white or Latino broad. No shitting. If I had the energy to screw one of their men for every one of ours they landed, I'd be laid up for eternity. Hmmm. That's a thought. I hear Latin lovers are hot. I've banged a few gray boys in my day too. Listen to me; my mind is still in the gutter. Back to my point. I tell you. I don't know what the hell possessed me to move to Denver anyhow. Then I remember why. Beatrice. My decision to leave was easier than deciding whom to tell first. Beatrice was out of the question, which left seven aunts and uncles to choose from. It would have been an easier choice had it not been for my family's notorious fallouts, especially around the holidays. Every year at least two or three of Beatrice's siblings stop speaking. In turn, the children who are mostly adults, side with their parents and all hell break loose. By the next year, some will have mended the relationships only for the cycle to begin again. Since I knew I had to tell someone, I stopped by the pool hall ran by Bea 's only consistent siblings. My Uncle Shot, and Aunt Cut, the owners of the simple establishment that gave them their names. Aunty Cut, named for her excellent barbering skills and Uncle Shot, for running the most well loved pool hall in the neighborhood. The Cut and Shot Barber and Pool House is the only place where customers get a free game of pool with every haircut. I can think of absolutely nobody else who could have made such a combination work.

As odd as barbering and pool are together, so are the two owners. Uncle Shot and Aunty Cut are as opposite as opposites get. Uncle will give until he breaks and Auntie won't break until you give.

Uncle Shot, who shuffles his discussion topics like a chef's soup of the day menu, was in the middle of a speech when I walked in. The subject today was poor folk.

"You see if you got three men standing next to each other, but only one has got some money," he explained. "I'm talking more money than he could spend in his life..."

"Yeah?" Some of the regulars prompted.

Uncle Shot paused for affect.

"Now if the guy gives the man next to him a portion of what he has, let's say um ...half."

A chorus of whistles could be heard throughout the room plus a couple bullshits and a few hell naws. Uncle Shot raised his hand to silence them. "No, no, let me finish. So let us say the man with half gives the next man half of what he got, then everybody got something."

The man in the chair whose fade was looking good under Auntie's expertise put down his newspaper and asked, "Then what about the third man? Who does he have to give to?" Uncle scratched his head a few seconds. "Shit, nobody. I figure to only do it in three's 'cause there ain't enough money to keep on dividing. The way I see it, only about one outta three folk got enough to divide in the first place."

The customer shook his head before he retrieved the paper. "Don't seem fair to me. The second and third man ought to do what the first man did to get all the money."

Some of the patrons chuckled and waited for the next comment or criticism. A young man called Smiley spoke up. "Hey, Shot. 'We talking about white folk or black folk?"

Aunty didn't give him a chance to answer. "You know danged well we ain't talking 'bout no colored folk 'cause we ain't dividing up shit."

It never ceased to amaze me how she could still call us colored as if it were still widely used in our everyday vernacular.

Uncle dumped the last bit of hair from the dustpan. "Ain't so, Cut and you know it. A bunch of us will give the shirt off our backs."

"The dilemma might come with that same shirt that's prob'ly been washed an' ironed so much it ain't fit to fool wit'."

Uncle laughed a low grumble of a sound. "You right about that, Cut."

Uncle 's cheer was contagious. A low rumble of laughter floated through the shop. This was a typical day for my aunt and uncle. Good people, men gossiping more than women, good-natured jiving, and a numb butt by the time your turn came up. I was next for the chair.

When my turn came, I took a seat in the battered red leather chair. Aunty grinned widely and announced that her favorite niece was in the mix. I choked back a sneeze as the odor of Auntie's awful gardenia perfume mixed with hair balms and talcum powders raged assault on my senses. My nose and throat adjusted as always. I got a few hard stares from the men who no doubt were trying to find some resemblance. I could have saved them the trouble. Our family, like most families is a vast rainbow. Aunty is as neon as I am brown. If she wanted, she could easily pass for white. I felt the plastic cape snap around my neck.

"Hey, Aunty. You're never going to change are you? Must you embarrass me every time I come in here?" I teased.

"Ain't nothing changed in all these years has it?"

"Definitely not that perfume," I mumbled.

Aunty gave me a playful nudge. "I got the last two bottles of that expensive stuff you sent me from overseas. I wear it on special occasions."

I leaned back into the chair knowing full well those bottles were sitting on her bureau collecting dust.

While Aunty organized her station, Uncle swept up the little bit of hair he'd missed, a faithful ritual the two performed each time she finished one client and before she began on another. I once asked why she waited until the next person sat down before she did that. What she told me made sense. "If I keep them waiting, they might leave. But once I get they butts in the chair, being late for that appointment ain't so important."

I waited until I heard her voice over my shoulder before I sat up straight. I could tell she was frowning even without looking up into the mirror in front of me. She spoke loud enough for everyone in the shop to hear. "I hope you come in here to finally cut all these things off your head."

I wasn't the least bit offended. Dreads were much too big a pill for Aunty to swallow. She'd seen a lot of hair in her day and what she considered nappy went against everything she grew up hearing. Why someone would deliberately choose to go nappy was beyond her.

"Hecky-no. If I let you cut them then the past months will have been a waste of my time. I just need a lining."

Aunty clicked on the clippers and I could feel the vibration through the hand she rested on my shoulder. Twenty-three months before, I'd come in asking her to shape my unruly hair into a neat little Afro. After seeing my head completely bald from the chemo, I knew that she was reluctant to snip a single hair. After some fussing, and my threatening to go to the barber around the corner, she finally relented. For the Butchard family, going to another barber ranks right below cannibalism. One just didn't dare. The next time she saw me; tiny twists had replaced my Afro.

"Whatever you say, but if you ask me, it just looks like a bunch of cuckabugs."

The next comment I heard started me to grinning and my eyelids to batting like Olive Oil at Popeye. The sexy baritone was all I needed to make my day. "I think you look good, Sister."

I didn't once regret my goofy smile when I seen from whose mouth the compliment had come. The handsome gentleman was sporting a head full of well-groomed locks. I assumed the boy sitting next to him was his son. The child was engrossed in a comic book.

"Thank you," I blushed.

"It takes a certain attitude to wear your hair natural. I love to see women so bold. When my son here is old enough, I'll support him if he wants to lock his hair."

As he talked, my mind conjured up images of a few choice positions I'd have loved to experiment in with him. His smile was hot enough to melt butter. Aunty must have felt the heat rising from me because I felt a slight yank of my head.

"Matt, you're just saying that 'cause you got a head full of those curly fries. Not to mention Journey is pretty to boot."

"Cut, what's wrong with me complimenting the beautiful woman?"

"Nothing as long as it stops there. Don't forget, I been around a long time. I'll keep your business out the streets this time."

Matt winked at Aunty. I decided to wait until he left to question her but I didn't have to. Minutes later a wiry white woman walked into the shop. The little boy with his freshly cut hair stuck his hand in hers. Matt waved as they walked out.

"Damned men and these white women," Aunty mumbled. "Every week he comes in here and faithfully flirts with every sister who dots the door then afterwards his tramp trollops in to get him. I hear she won't let him drive hisself to the shop, too scared he won't come back."

I didn't comment until Auntie handed me the hand mirror so I could see the back of my neck. She pinched my cheeks and grinned proudly into the large wall mirror. "I guess I can't blame him huh, Journey? You know I can spot a pretty woman a mile away."

I couldn't help but to grin back. Nobody mentioned it aloud, but Aunty had never had much use for men. Over the years, she had shared her home with an assortment of ladies. The one time I questioned Bea about why the women slept in Aunty 's room, Bea had thumped me so hard that I had to bite my tongue to keep from yelling out. I didn't ask again.

"How about you and me play your free game since I'm due for a lunch break?" She asked.

"You know you'll kick my butt. I'm out of practice."

"Don't worry. I won't whip you too bad. Besides, I get the feeling you got a lot on your mind that Aunty might can help you get off."

Aunty was right and I was thankful she was so intuitive. I left after she whipped my ass good in a game of pool and pouring out all my problems. My head swam a little from the secret stash of Brandy she kept under the counter. It felt good to talk and I left believing that I was doing the right thing.

C H A P T E R

4 The space where Gwen waited was crowded with weary travelers. Her feet throbbed as she glanced over her shoulder.

Seeing no sign of another coach, she took a seat in one of the hard plastic chairs. Why in the world Journey would choose to travel by bus was beyond Gwen, but then she could never quite grasp Journey's reasoning for doing much of whatever.

To pass time, Gwen pulled her battered Sunday school learner from her purse, but couldn't concentrate. Someone behind her snored loudly while a child screamed from somewhere. The man seated next to her saw his ride waving for him and smiled as he exited. A young woman who Gwen assumed was the mother of the child screaming moments ago, sat down beside her. She bounced the child on her knee while she counted change from her pockets. It hardly amounted to seventy cents. Gwen guessed the mother's age at about sixteen and the child's around two years old.

Gwen gazed at the expectant eyes of the child on her mother. She instinctively pressed the fingers of her right hand to her temple recognizing that at any moment, the child beside her threatened to bawl again. Another squeal like the prior one would set Gwen's nerves on fire and her stomach to churning.

"I'm sorry, just a little longer, Jordan," the mother soothed.

The answer was apparently not one Jordan wanted to hear. Her bottom lip began to quiver as if the near nonexistent air-conditioning had been turned to arctic.

"Please don't. Not now," the mother pleaded.

"Please not now," Gwen's mind echoed. Gwen knew that neither her telepathic pleading nor the mother's bouncing knee would stifle the looming bellow. Jordan's hunger was definite. Her eyes followed every pair of food toting hands, before settling hungrily on the vending machine. The child's bottom lip quivered double time, and there was no time for Gwen to tactfully offer the mother money for food before the damn broke.

Gwen spoke up quickly. "How about you and me go to the concession stand and get the little one a bite? It might help to settle her down. My treat."

Gwen's voice distracted the child long enough for the young woman to gape at the concession sign while they walked over. She swung Jordan to the opposite hip and retrieved the pocketed change that Gwen had watched her count earlier. She shoved it at Gwen complete with candy wrappers, a piece of a receipt and a few lint balls.

"This is all I have left but you can have it. It'll help some," she offered.

Gwen smiled at her and waved the money away. She led the way to the counter then turned her attention to the scowling clerk in front of her. After ordering French fries and two hot-dogs for the baby, Gwen addressed the mother.

"What's your name?"

The girl eyed her suspiciously. "My name?"

"Yes, your name. Everyone has one."

The girl couldn't figure if she were joking or not, but laughed anyway. Her face brightened. "My name is Renita and my baby's name is Jordan. Her father named her after his favorite basketball star."

Gwen would pretend that she hadn't seen the desperation on Renita's face. She would ask if there was a food preference although she guessed the girl would eat anything. "Do you eat hamburgers, Renita?"

"Um…yes. I mean…yes ma'am."

Gwen directed Renita's attention to the menu on the wall. "Order what you want."

Immediately, the squared shoulders drooped in relief. Unsure of whether or not Gwen would stop her, Renita turned to Gwen who nodded after each selection. Instead of a hamburger, she ordered a whopping helping of nachos with cheese and peppers plus a foot long hot-dog. Gwen guessed that the hot-dog would be wrapped up for later.

"You forgot to order a drink," Gwen reminded.

Renita focused intently on the woman dishing hot cheese all over the tortilla chips. She barely heard Gwen.

"Oh, I'd like a medium cola."

"Large," Gwen called out. "And I'll take a large lemon-lime please."

When the order was completed, Gwen helped carry the food to the small eating area. Cheese dripped from the side of the paper boat onto her hands. She almost chuckled at the meal before her. Nachos and hot-dogs. A child's meal.

Jordan stuck her hand into the cheese and shoved her chunky fingers into her mouth. "Good," she cooed to her mother.

Gwen glanced at her watch. "I have a while to wait. Do you and Jordan mind if I wait with you?"

"No, we don't mind."

Gwen sipped her drink and thought about what it might feel like to have Journey home. Their lives had been separated by too many gaps and absences. Momentarily, her thoughts took her away from the child and mother across from her. She didn't bother to interrupt their noisy chewing until Renita caught a glob of cheese falling from her lips then licked it from her fingers. Gwen passed her a napkin then waited until the two slurped loudly from the last of the soda.

"So. Where are you headed, Renita?"

Renita reached between her feet and picked up a backpack. "Could you watch her please while I go to the bathroom?"

Her answer was a diversion tactic but still Gwen reached for Jordan. The child let out a loud belch and willingly curled her arms around Gwen's neck. She turned quickly to call for Renita to take the child for a diaper change, but she had already disappeared into the crowd. Checking the arrival board, she was sure she had time enough to meet Journey. She and Jordan headed to the bathroom where they found Renita crying and leaning against the sink.

"Are you okay?"

Renita wiped her face with the back of her sleeve. "I'm," she choked.

Gwen didn't quite know what to say. "I brought the baby in so she could be changed." Her words brought a fresh wave of tears.

Gwen hadn't noticed until Renita dropped to the floor and dumped all the contents of the backpack. She frantically dug through the clothes, toiletries, and stuffed toys. By then, her tears were a flood.

"She don't got no more pampers. I only had five and I came all the way from California. She's potty trained but after she got so hungry, she wouldn't tell me when she had to go."

Gwen winced at Renita's 'don't got no'. The teacher in her fought not to correct her, but this was not the time for an English lesson.

Gwen rolled off a paper towel and handed it her. "Here, wipe your face. Jordan sees you crying and she's about to start howling. Tell me, where is your last destination?"

"East Saint Louis where my granny lives. She sent me a ticket for I can come live with her. I been calling my uncle to pick me up, but he ain't made it home from work yet."

Gwen reached for Renita. "Com'on. It isn't so bad. I live in East Saint Louis myself. Call your granny and tell her I'll bring you home."

Renita looked up with fresh snot mixed with water on her face. A piece of the brown paper towel stuck to the side of her mouth. She didn't want to appear ungrateful but had to ask.

"For real? Why?"

Gwen thought it a strange question until she realized it was genuine. "Why not?"

"Because I don't just meet people like you. How do you know it's safe for me to get in your car?"

"I don't. Is it?"

"Oh yes ma'am. My granny says I wouldn't hurt a flea."

"Then I believe your granny."

Renita started shoving stuff back into her bag. When she had draped it across her shoulder, she abruptly slung it to the floor again. "I remember now!" she said, flipping the bag completely upside down, "I put a pamper in here!"

Renita pulled out a pull-up like she had been panning for gold. "See!"

Gwen passed the child then checked her shirt for a wet stain. Thankfully the mushy diaper had held on to its contents.

"Now hurry up and wash your face and put Jordan on a fresh pamper. I have my sister coming in from Denver and I don't want her thinking I forgot about her. Her name is Journey. You'll get to meet her."

"Lady, I want to say, well what I'm saying is, um thank-you. I thought I was gonna go crazy until you showed up."

"You don't have to thank me, thank God."

Renita wondered briefly if Gwen was one of those Bible toting fanatics her daddy always shut the door on. Gwen read her expression.

"Yes, God and no, I'm not going to preach to you. Your spirituality is your choice and your business."

"I know a little about God from my granny."

"Get to know Him and you'll find that He will always send somebody. Today, it just happened to be me."

Renita didn't seem so sure but she shook her head yes. "Okay," she mumbled.

Gwen felt her eyes still staring curiously at her as she pushed the door open. A voice blared from the speakers announcing the arrival of another coach. Gwen hurried through the crowd to meet Journey. She didn't want her panicking if she couldn't find her. When they were kids, it was always Journey who was the late one. Since then the roles had reversed. Gwen was the one always too busy to notice the time.

Journey stood waiting for her luggage and looking over her shoulder. She reached out her hand to take her bag when the driver let it fall to the ground at her feet. Gwen walked up just as Journey slanted her eyes angrily toward the bus driver. She hurried knowing if she didn't get to her sister first, there was sure to be a scene. Had she not been waiting on Renita, she could have met

Journey when she first got off the bus. Gwen wondered how the heck she managed to get herself entangled in other people's crisis situations.

Journey was trailing the bus driver to the other side of the bus. "Excuse me, but I have another bag on this coach."

The driver continued to ignore her until she spoke up again. This time, much louder. "Is there something wrong with your hearing? I said…"

Gwen stepped up between Journey and driver. Journey turned her wrath on her. "Why the hell didn't you tell me that this bus stopped in Belleville first, Gwen? Belleville is closer than St. Louis and I could have been off this damn bus!"

Gwen held her breath to calm her nerves. Guarding her temper, she spoke through her teeth. "You know that I rarely go to Belleville unless I have to. They don't want *us* up there no more than *I* want to be. Now, let's just find your bag and get out of here."

Journey stepped around Gwen.

"That's what I'm doing," she said surveying the mostly white faces around her. She remembered Sweetie telling her years ago not to behave the way white folks expected. Hell, she was angry and so what the driver just happened to be white. Against Sweetie's tutelage, she copped an attitude.

The red-faced driver continued to ignore Journey until one of the other travelers nervously pointed toward her.

"Lady, wait!" He snapped.

Having chosen the worst possible combination of two words in the English language, the driver and the entire situation was working Gwen's nerves.

Journey stepped even closer to him and pointed in his face. She looked like she would poke him in the eye. "You can ask me to be patient, but you damn well cannot ask me to wait. I've already waited while you slung two of my three bags to the ground." She swept her hand indicating the restless crowd. "Did any of you see how he handed all the nice white people their luggage?"

One guy stepped up. "I did, Miss. I'll help find your bag."

"No, you won't. I been on this damned bus all night, been nudged in the back by a fat man's knee and I'm not about to put up with this! Thank-you, but he is going to find my bag, or nobody else gets theirs until he does!"

"I wish you and your luggage was in Belleville," the driver mumbled.

Gwen gently squeezed Journey's arm praying that she would just shut up. The whole scene had taken too much time. Together they watched the driver go through each compartment looking for the bag. When he found it, he placed it on the ground. Gwen reached for it, but Journey stopped her. "I want him to give it to me."

The driver brought the bag to her. "Here you are ma'am," he nodded humbly.

Instantly, Journey was satisfied. She smiled and nodded back as if seconds earlier she hadn't been ready to evoke God's wrath or recite the *I Have a Dream* speech to the crowd.

"Thank you and have a nice day."

Gwen couldn't help smiling. They embraced warmly.

"Still the same Journey."

"In the flesh."

Gwen grabbed her hand. "I have someone I want you to meet."

Journey raised her eyebrows and stalled momentarily. "Gwen, you aren't still collecting people are you?"

If you only knew, was what she thought but asked, "What's that supposed to mean?"

"You remember how when you were little you would befriend everyone who didn't have a friend?"

"I did not."

"Did too."

Journey was too busy reminiscing about old times to notice Renita following slightly behind them to the car.

"Then if that's true, then you won't be surprised to meet Renita."

"Who?"

Gwen stopped long enough for Renita to catch up with her. She pulled her by her hand. "Journey this is Renita. Renita, Journey. And the little one here is her baby, Jordan."

Journey looked the girl head to toe before she said anything. Renita shifted Jordan to her other hip and extended her hand. "Hi."

Gwen was sure Journey didn't know how her brow had wrinkled then smoothed out. She took the outstretched hand. "You look like a baby yourself." Gwen nudged her and glanced at Renita uncomfortably.

"Please excuse my sister. You would think after all these years away she would have learned some tact."

Journey realized her rudeness. "I apologize. Nice to meet you."

Renita shrugged. "That's okay. I'm used to people saying that sort of thing when they see me and Jordan."

"No, it's not okay. It was rude of me and you shouldn't think it okay for people to be rude to you. Please accept my apology."

Renita smiled. "Accepted."

Gwen cut in to smooth the moment over. "The car is just right over there."

When they had reached the car, she did not wish the ride home to continue in the uncomfortable silence. "Renita just push all that junk in the back seat around and make some room. I forgot it was such a mess."

Journey was in the car. "Hurry up, Gwen. I forgot how hot it gets here. I'm sweating already."

"Don't rush me, Miss Thing. I got the air conditioner serviced just for you. Now put your seat-belt on and remember, it's always been this hot in the summer."

Journey looked at the pile of books in the back seat. "How can I forget? I still don't know how we survived it. What's with all the books and stuff in the backseat?"

"Oh that's some reading materials I've been collecting from here and there. Can you believe the library was going to just throw some of that good stuff away?"

"Probably, Gwen because they thought it was trash."

Gwen eyed Journey sideways. "Why are you so sarcastic today?"

"I'm sorry, Gwen. I don't know. Let me start over. What do you need the books for?"

"Remember I told you on the phone that I was starting a literacy program for the young people in my neighborhood? It's a shame, but the reason some of the children are having such a hard time is they have no one to help them at home. Some of the mothers can barely read themselves."

Journey turned to look out the window. In her mind, this literacy thing was just another way for Gwen to avoid going back to her first love, which was teaching. Her job was made all the better with her appointment to Principal of the small elementary school she went to as a youth. Journey knew Gwen missed it, but not enough.

After that incident, Gwen seemed to search more and more for a substitute. Thankfully, this is closer to teaching, Journey thought. She spoke wistfully when she sensed Gwen waiting for a reply. "That's good, Gwen. You always have been good with youths."

Gwen hit the switch to let up the windows. Jordan squealed in delight. Through the rearview mirror, Gwen could see Renita flipping through one of the books.

"Journey, you sound like you're not good at drawing a young crowd. Remember when you went off to college? There was a line of girls holding back tears with myself included."

"Girl, that was too long ago. I've been too busy chasing me and Beatrice's dreams to connect with anybody like that."

"All that can change. There's enough work to share. Besides, you're not fooling me. I saw how passionate you were about your soldiers."

Journey shook her head from side to side. "Uh uhnn, Gwen. Twenty years with Uncle Sam took a lot out of me. I don't have the patience I used to have with people. These days are so different. Back then when I was full of ideas of making a difference, there weren't all these issues. Now there are too many babies having babies and women dying of AIDS. We didn't have to worry about too much of that shit back in the day."

Gwen glanced in the mirror but Renita didn't seem to notice the comment. "That's the reason to do it. Right now."

"Maybe for you, but I'm not like you. I don't think I have it in me to help anybody but myself. Frankly, I don't know how you stand all the pain in the lives you're surrounded by."

"Sometimes, I don't either. All I know is that I put it in God's hands and He makes it work."

"I would comment, but I don't want this to turn into a discussion about how long it's been since I been to church."

"See, Journey. You've misread me already. I'm not talking about where you fit God into your life. I'm talking about me. I can truly say that my worse day with God is better than my best days without Him."

"Amen," Journey mumbled.

"Can I come?" Renita asked. "Come where?"

"To where you gonna be reading at?"

The question brought a smile to Gwen's face. "Of course you can. I'd be delighted to have you and if you don't have a ride I'll pick you up."

"Can I bring Jordan?"

"Sure can."

"Then I can catch the bus. I can get there if I know where the bus lets us off."

Jordan giggled as if she'd been in on the plan. Gwen grinned at her through the rearview mirror. Everyone was quiet until the car turned onto the street Renita's grandmother lived. A few houses away, an old woman sat rocking on the porch. Beside her was a little boy playing with the laces of her shoes. Renita pressed her face up to the window making foggy shapes with the wisps of breath from her nose and mouth. She gently grabbed Jordan. "That's my granny right there. Look Jordan, there goes Boopie."

"Boopie," Jordan repeated clearly.

The woman moved slowly toward the steps of the porch and a little faster when Renita yelled out, "Granny!"

She sprinted with Jordan in her arms toward the woman leaving the car door open. The force from her hug didn't budge the older woman since it was met with equal strength. Journey's eyes clouded remembering all the summers of visiting her grandmother in Mississippi. Gwen had told her that Sweetie would soon be moving in with their sister Jean in few weeks. She couldn't wait to see her.

Renita's grandmother shielded her eyes from the sun with one hand then waved them out of the car with the other. She easily lifted Jordan for a quick kiss. The family stood expectantly while the two women exited the car. Journey mumbled something under her breath, but Gwen didn't catch it. Just in case, she cut her a warning glance. Journey looked confused.

"What? Damn, I only said they look happy."

"Oh, sorry."

"Stop making assumptions, Gwen."

She was about to apologize again but the old woman cut her off. "I 'preshate you bringing Nita home t'me. Com'on in and get a cold drink."

The cool air from inside was as welcoming as the cozy house. The woman talked as she walked ahead of them. "M'name is Elizabeth, but y'all can call me Lizzy. Ever'body else does. What y'all think about this heat?"

Gwen chatted about the weather while Journey studied her surroundings. She couldn't recall if she'd ever seen a house so immaculate. The embroidered doilies were perfectly aligned on the arms of the furniture. The ones adorning the tables were starched stiff. Journey got the feeling that if she opened up the closets they would be as methodically organized as what she'd already seen.

The kitchen was silent and Journey looked up. She sensed that she'd been asked a question by the expectant expressions on the faces in front of her. "I was just admiring your home. I apologize I didn't hear you."

"Thankee. Would you like some lemon in your tea?"

"Yes ma'am. Please."

Lizzy went back to the refrigerator. "The secret to good tea is to seep the tea leaves overnight in the window. None of that instant stuff for me. Tha's what's wrong wit' everything nowadays. Ever'body wants what they wants instantly."

Both Gwen and Journey drank the tea while Lizzy watched their faces. The satisfied looks were enough to make her smile. "I was telling your sister when you was off in a daze how pretty you two are," she said sliding her palm down Journey's face. Wish I'da had me some girls 'steada six boys. They some good chirren though. At least all except one. God help'im."

Gwen savored the tea. "I believe this is the best tea I've ever tasted." Journey pointed to the living room. "Are those your sons?"

Lizzy nodded proudly. "Yep. Come and let me show'em to you."

Journey looked into the faces on each of the photos searching for Lizzy's features. Four of them had the same sienna complexion as their mother and identical smiles. The last two she pointed out made Journey's heart leap. Nearly as chocolate as the frame they were in, the two were what she classified as USDA choice cuts. The thick black eyebrows hooding the eyes gave them a mysterious look. "Twins," she stated dumbly.

"Yessum. Michael and Cameron. They good looking ain't they?"

"Yes ma'am. Married?"

"Only one of them. Michael is a truck driver. In fact, he come in from out of town last night. He ain't seen Nita since she was knee high to a duck's butt."

Journey pointed to the picture on the far end.

Lizzy's smile faded. "That's Nita's daddy. He the only one don't even come home. I get a letter ever now and again. Shacked up wit' some gal when he was 'bout twenty-five. I ain't seen'im since. Come to think of it, I got a letter from him yesterday." Lizzy pulled Journey into the bedroom by the arm. "Can you read this for me?"

Journey took in the bedroom with all its deep mahogany furnishings. The sun cast just enough light inside to make the room look alive and inhabited. Otherwise there was no other indication that someone had slept there the night before.

There were no stray shoes around or butt prints in the tightly made bed. The room was as sterile as an operating room and except for the very faint scent of lemon oil and liniment; there would have been no odors at all.

Her eyes rested on the colorful perfume bottles on the chest of drawers. Lizzy waited patiently while Journey studied her surroundings. She imagined that this is how it would feel if she'd had daughters.

"Everything in here 'bout old as me 'cept for those bottles. My son brings them from all over, but I don't put perfume in'em," Lizzy said sniffng loudly. "Stuff smells either too sweet or too spicy. This old nose'a mine can't handle it. I do like yours though. What kind you wearing?"

Journey reached into her bag and pulled out the bottle. She hardly wore it and except for it being the only one accessible to her on the bus, it would have stayed forgotten.

"The label has worn off, but here. You can keep it."

Lizzy took the bottle and sniffed at its top. Except for a tiny bit missing, the bottle was full. "You sure you wanna part with this?"

"Yes ma'am. Consider it a gift."

Lizzy sprayed a little of the perfume in the air then stepped under the mist. She placed it gingerly next to her bottles. "Preshate that," she said shuffing back over to Journey.

The two women sat on the chest placed neatly at the end of the bed. Lizzy pulled her reading glasses to her nose from the string around her neck. Journey unfolded the paper.

Dear Mama, it read. Don't believe nothing Renita says. You know the child is just like her mama. They both lie like rugs. I wouldn't never let nobody harm my daughter. Mama, you know me.

The words sent a chill up Journey's spine. She quickly folded the letter and handed it to Lizzy. "Maybe you should finish reading this. It sounds like a personal family matter."

Lizzy didn't answer for a moment, but when she did, fire burned in her eyes. "Cain't," was all she said.

Journey was confused. "Ma'am?"

"Cain't read."

Journey wanted to ask why she wore reading glasses swinging from her neck but thought better of it. All she knew was she didn't want to finish the letter. Lizzy saved her the discomfort by rising from the chest and storming into the kitchen where Renita and Gwen sat at the table. The volume of Lizzy's voice startled them both into silence. Gwen's glass rattled against the table as Lizzy cupped Renita's face in her strong hands.

"What did he do to you! Did he touch you? Answer me, chile!"

Water flooded the girl's eyes. Lizzy's face was so close that Renita could see the blue halo around the cloudy brown pupils.

"You hear me, Nita? Did that lowdown son of mind come to your bed?"

"No, Granny. I promise," she cried.

Lizzy pushed her face even closer. Renita could smell peppermint on her breath and tried to hang her head. Lizzy's grip was too tight. A line of snot ran from her right nostril. "No."

"No what?"

"No he didn't touch me, but she brought somebody to the house."

"She who? Your daddy's heifer?"

"Yes'maam."

"What'd she do to you, chile?"

Renita squirmed from her grandmother's grip. "She wanted me to do it with this man for them some drugs, but I promise Granny, I didn't do nothing."

"Oh Lawdy, Lawdy ha'mercy!" Lizzy wailed.

Renita's eyes met with Gwen and Journey's before she ran from the room. Her uncle caught her before she collided into him.

"Hey, pumpkin. What's with the tears?"

Renita squeezed him tight. He smelled of cigarettes and exhaust fumes, but she didn't care. She'd always felt safe with him around.

"Come now, Pumpkin. It's not so bad," he said leading her into the kitchen.

Renita could almost believe his words they were so soothing. Michael looked confused at the two women at the table then to his mother. The question in his eyes asked before his lips. "Mama?"

Lizzy looked up. "Hey, baby. These nice ladies brought Nita home."

Gwen and Journey found the perfect opportunity to leave. "We were just leaving," they spoke in unison.

Michael's statement was more of a question than comment. "Not without introductions I hope?"

Gwen held out her hand. "I'm Gwen."

Michael looked apologetically at his dirty hands. Gwen took his hand anyway. He smiled. Journey recognized the smile from the picture. He held onto her hand while Gwen turned. "This is my sister, Journey."

Journey rose, but Michael barely turned his eyes from Gwen. "Nice meeting you. Are you really leaving so soon?"

"We must be going. Journey has just gotten in from Denver and we haven't been home yet."

"That's too bad. I hope to see you, I mean the both of you again."

Gwen fingered her wedding band as a hint. Lizzy led them to the door.

"Sorry t'make y'all uncomfortable. I jes' got beside myself. I swear sometime I wonder if Nita's daddy is right in the head. Promise you'll come back."

"We will. We promise."

"Good meeting you all, and thanks for bringing Nita home. Mama must have forgot last night to mention that Nita would be here today."

Gwen wrote down her phone number.

"No problem. Tell Renita to call me by next Sunday. I'll start teaching the following Monday."

"Thanks," Renita, who'd been listening, called back.

Journey remembered her purse in Lizzy's room and returned to get it. As she passed Michael a second time, he breathed the smell of her.

"Boucheron."

Journey looked up at him quizzically. "What?"

"Boucheron. The fragrance you're wearing."

Journey tried not to show her nervousness at being so close to him. She was tempted to press her hand to his charcoal face. She was sure there would be lighter prints left where her fingers had been. His smooth skin seemed as solid and powdery as a charcoal briquette.

To take her mind off his good looks, she asked. "How'd you know?"

"A lady friend of mine wore it once. I never forget a fragrance."

At first she had felt a tinge of jealousy at the intensity of his eyes on Gwen. Now that the same gaze felt uncomfortable on her, she was sure that it was his eyes. Looking at anything they would have been equally as penetrating.

"Well again, it is nice to meet you." Journey smiled on her way out. No, there was definitely something minutely different when he had gazed at Gwen.

📖

Inside the car, Gwen adjusted her seatbelt. "Nice people don't you think?" Journey didn't answer.

"That Michael seems like a good man for you, Journey. Fine and single."

"How can you tell after only five minutes in his presence?"

"I can't. I just said he seemed like he would be."

"Any man that fine and over thirty five who's single? He must be an asshole."

"How can you say that after only five minutes in his presence?"

Journey laughed at the way Gwen turned her own words against her. "Touché. But really, Gwen, he was checking you out"

"No-o-o."

"Yes he was and you know it." Journey mocked Gwen's voice. "We'll be back. We promise."

Gwen blushed. "You think so?"

"I know so. And why wouldn't he? My little sister is a very attractive woman. You know you got it going on, girl."

Gwen slapped Journey's arm playfully. "He was looking pretty hard, huh?"

"Indeed."

After they shared laughs, Gwen turned the volume up on the radio. An oldies station played.

When Journey didn't say anything for the next several minutes, Gwen thought she was asleep. She looked over to find Journey staring out the window. "What are you thinking about?"

Journey spoke through her broad smile. "I was thinking how different men are here at home. You can always tell they're near and plentiful."

"How?"

Journey sniffed. "I can smell them. Like freshly cut grass. I love that smell."

"Eager to fall in love again?"

"You mean that perfect love like you and George have?"

"Only God's love is perfect. Definitely not mine and George's for that matter. I mean like fall in love love. You know what I mean."

The frown was quick but certain. "Nah. Last man I loved burned me."

"That's no reason to shut yourself off from love, Journey. I shouldn't have to tell you that."

"No, you don't understand. When I say he burned me, I mean he burned me. Like VD," Journey said this as if it were no big deal. The blunt finality of the statement stuttered Gwen.

"Well, wh-what about after that? Did you date?"

"Once. You know your sister Tilly is always trying to hook somebody up."

"Was he nice?"

"He was a Judge and he peed in my closet."

Gwen laughed so hard, she almost had to pull over. "How'd he pee in your closet?"

Hearing it from someone else, the whole memory was hilarious. Journey could hardly tell the story for laughing. "We went to dinner, got slopped and went to my place. By the time we got there, we were too drunk to get laid, so we passed out on the bed. I woke up when I heard water hitting the floor. I found him in the closet."

Gwen pulled into the driveway and leaned over the steering wheel. "On your clothes?"

"No, I'd just moved in and hadn't hung my clothes in the closet yet."

"Lucky for you, you hadn't."

"Even luckier he didn't have to shit," Journey laughed.

📖

Gwen and Journey were still giggling. Gwen could barely get the key in the lock. "Shh. Shh. Shh. We're going to wake George for real sho'nuff if we can't stop laughing. Now come on and stop looking at me, Journey. I'm going to keep on bursting out laughing and you know it."

"I'm not saying nothing. If you don't look at me, you won't see me looking at you. Hurry up with the door. I have to pee."

Gwen at last got the door open. "Hurry up, but be quiet. George is sleeping and I have to pee too."

Journey dropped her bags and started for the bathroom. George jumped from behind the door and wrapped her in a tangle of arms. Dizzy from the sudden full-circled swing, she screamed and popped George playfully. "George, you scared the shit out of me!"

"Thought I was sleep, huh?" George held his arms out. This time Journey jumped into his embrace. It felt good being held in his brotherly hug again and she told him so.

"You haven't changed a bit. Still the same crazy Big George from across the street. I tell you—sure feels good to see you."

"Same here. Gwen's been jabbering for days about you coming. I don't know if I'm glad to see you to shut up her mouth or because it's so good to have you back at home."

"Quit sweet talking my sister. You know it's both of those reasons. Journey, don't let him run that sweet talk on you."

"Long as he don't go trying to marry me off to one of his bowling buddies."

George looked pleasantly shocked. He held up his hands palms out. "No, not me. Not after the last time."

"Mmm hmmm."

"How was I supposed to know the dude was taking crazy medication? He acted normal when he was bowling."

Gwen stuffed her laugh back in with her hand. "You must be talking about the man who painted his car with house paint. I forgot about him."

"Me too until I saw George here."

George lifted Journey's bags. He tried to hide the strain in his voice. "No more match making for me. Dang girl! What you got in these bags?"

"Wouldn't you like to know?"

Halfway up the stairs, George called down. "I saw Douglas."

Gwen quickly looked over to Journey to note her expression. Her eyes clouded over before she answered.

"I guess you told him I was coming?"

"I kinda did."

"Either you did or didn't."

"I did. He left his number."

"Tear it up."

George wanted to say more but didn't. "Okay," was all he said.

C H A P T E R

5 Allison sat on the couch with cotton balls between her toes. She was careful to balance the fire engine red polish on her lap. Why wouldn't she when she had paid so much money for the imported leather sofa? It didn't matter that Malik had complained that it had cost way too much since she knew he would give in to what she wanted. Allison had not seen one piece of furniture like hers in all the homes of her friends or colleagues. There were a couple look-alikes, but Allison prided herself that they were fakes. She liked the idea of owning anything that was one of a kind and since she did, it was well worth the money spent.

Malik came out of the kitchen rubbing his stomach. His face was stuffed with pie.

"Um. Um. Umm. That Gwen knows she can throw down when it comes to some food. I ain't had pie this good since well, the last one she made."

Allison rolled her eyes. "Listen to you, Malik. You *ain't* what? You're starting to speak with more ain'ts and double negatives than George and Gwen together. Hard to believe it's only been a little over two years since Gwen left her job, and already she is sounding like she came from somebody's Southern back woods."

"You forget I am from the South. What's that got to do with anything?"

"It means you don't have to be so country."

"So what if I don't speak the King's English all the time. I'm at home. I have been working all day in meetings with uppity folks. I should be able to say as many ain'ts as I want to at home."

"I'm just saying."

"Don't."

"Easy on that pie. You know if Gwen made it, it has a million calories in it."

"That's alright. They're good calories."

"I wonder if you'll think so when you can't fit into all of your nice suits in the closet."

Malik took his plate to the bedroom. "I work hard enough to buy more suits."

Malik wouldn't know hard work if it walked in and sat on his lap. I bet George works harder in a day than Malik works all week, Allison thought. "Honey, warm my side of the bed for me. I'm wearing your favorite nightie," she called sweetly.

I bet Gwen don't go 'round telling George how much pie to eat and correcting his English all the time, Malik thought. *I wish I'd known the woman would all of a sudden turn scared of the kitchen after we got married. She could wear some old raggedy bloomers to bed and I wouldn't care as long as my stomach is full.* "Okay, honey," he called back.

📖

Janelle lay curled up on Anthony's side of the bed. No matter how many times he told her to sleep in her own room, she didn't listen. She had her own phone, but she tied his up for hours. She had her own TV, but she flicked recklessly through his channels. He was tempted at times to sleep in her bed, but wouldn't do that. The one time he'd crashed in her bedroom, she pouted the entire next day. When he asked why, she eyed him angrily and shut her door.

He shook her. "Jay? Why is it that you're not in your bed?"

"I like your bed, Daddy", she mumbled.

"How come you can sleep in my bed, and I can't sleep in yours?"

"Cause."

"Because what?"

"Because my bed is too small for both of us. I think you be running from me when you sleep in my bed."

"What if I sleep on the couch, then?"

Janelle popped her thumb out of her mouth and sat up. "You don't want me in here no more?"

"No, honey. It's not that. Well actually, it is that. I mean you're a teenager now."

"So? I used to sleep with you and mommy all the time."

"Yes you did, but you were a little girl then."

"I thought you said I was still your little girl."

"You are."

"Then why can't I sleep in here with you?"

Anthony pulled his socks off. "You're being manipulative. You know what I'm saying."

Janelle's answer was her thumb back in her mouth.

"Get your thumb out of your mouth. That's the reason you're being fitted for braces."

"Can I stay?"

"Scoot over. You can stay this time."

He couldn't see the smile, but knew it was there.

"I couldn't win arguments with your mother either," he mumbled crawling under the cover. He had to tug a little since his daughter was wrapped in the comforter. He gave up and padded to the linen closet in the hall. The cold of the wood floor sent shivers up his back. The phone rang on the desk in his study.

A man's voice didn't wait for the hello. "We need to talk. You've been avoiding me all week. You can't expect me to just disappear."

"Daddy!" Janelle called.

Anthony's voice caught in his throat. "Baby, hang up. I got it."

He waited for the click before continuing the conversation. "Didn't I tell you never to call me again? Dammit, my child answered the phone!"

"That's not my problem. She has her own phone. Tell her to answer it."

"Don't tell me what to tell my child and don't call me anymore."

"Maybe if you just tell her the truth, we could go on as before."

"Man, what the fuck are you talking about? There was no before. You seem to have forgotten, that I never consented to what you did to me that day."

"I think you wanted it as bad as I did."

"You're sick, Sean, you know that?"

"Is it because you're a so called church boy."

"No, it's because I am not a homosexual. If I were, I wouldn't have reacted violently. Don't ever call me again!"

"Anthony, you know I could press charges? You almost broke my jaw."

Anthony slammed the phone down and snatched the quilt from the floor. "You're lucky I didn't kill you."

He caught Janelle just as she was about to roll back to his side of the bed. "Daddy? Who was that?"

Nobody important, honey. Go back to sleep."

God help me. Please Lord, help me, he prayed before falling asleep.

C H A P T E R

6 Journey dragged hard on her cigarette. The evening humidity had yet to die down even a little. She searched for an opening in the screened in back porch. She didn't find it but knew it had to be there. Twice mosquitoes had bitten her.

Noises from the house drifted through the opened window. She could hear George bumping around upstairs and Gwen's hushed voice directing him here or there. It reminded her of how her mother would supervise while everyone got ready for either school or work in the mornings. Instead of the children, it was their father who could never get it together for any of the many jobs he held. Either Bea was waking him for the seventh or eighth time, or struggling to locate his uniform for him. Mondays were the worst. On Friday, Darnel would come in late, full of liquor, and drop his clothes wherever was convenient. With Beatrice working six days a week, there was little time to clean every nook and cranny during the weekend. Sometimes his shirt might be stuffed between the sofa's pillow cushions or his pants kicked under a chair. The sisters would learn these spots, as they grew older. Gwen and Journey would search them out on Saturday and since Jean was the oldest, she would do the laundry before their mother came home. Even with their efforts, the terrible Monday morning arguments continued. Darnel yelling at Beatrice for being what he considered a less than competent wife, and Beatrice's screaming mainly for him being shiftless and no count. So the argument would pursue and reveal much too much information for the girls. On those mornings they would learn of Jean's mother who'd showed up at the door a year after Darnel and Beatrice were married. From the fights, all that was known of the woman was that she wasn't raising no damned baby by a cheating nigger like Darnel—her words exactly. For all anybody knew, Jean's mother could be a million miles away or around the corner.

Hoping it would never happen again, Beatrice took to raising the child as her own even though everyone must have known since she was seven months pregnant with her first child. Jean was eighteen months old.

Some mornings they would hear about the whore two streets over who took care of what their daddy said their mother wouldn't.

"And you have the nerve to expect me to have sex with *you*?" Bea would yell at him. " You'd do better to buy a friggin' blow up doll! If not that then ain't a damn thing wrong with your hands!"

"I don't want your pussy no way, woman!" He'd yell back. "I wasn't the first to get it, and I won't be the last. Keep your old second hand shit. If I want some'a your pussy, I'll ask the niggers in your old neighborhood for it 'fore I ask you again!"

Journey could still hear all those insults and cringed on the inside. She wondered if Gwen remembered them as vividly as she did. She wondered if Gwen and Jean remembered the night when they along with Bea had finally gotten fed up. That morning, they had watched helplessly as their father pounded his fist into Beatrice's face. She was naked and wet from the bath he'd dragged her from. God only knew what he'd done in the bedroom before their mother ran down-stairs. Enough was enough. Jean was sixteen, Journey fourteen, and Gwen a scrawny soon to be nine years old. Tilly was only five years old.

Together they cried until they knew Darnel would not stop until he'd beaten their mother within inches of her life.

Armed with a small souvenir baseball bat, Journey struck the initial blow. Jean followed with the heel of her shoe. Gwen helped until Tilly started bawling at the top of her lungs.

While Gwen carried Tilly kicking and screaming to the neighbor's, the three of them whipped their father's ass. Afterward, Beatrice sat wrapped in a sheet rocking her two oldest daughters in her arms while they cried. One of Darnel's shoes lay in the middle of the floor where he'd ran right out of it. They would never speak of the incident as if by not talking about it they could forget it had ever happened. Though thankful that all the chaos ended with his leaving, the damage was done. Journey never would forget that she had split her father's head with a baseball bat that he'd bought her during the happiest outing of her life.

Unfortunately, that wouldn't be the last time the girls would see their father. Darnel moved in with the woman Beatrice had shouted about all the time. That same woman bore him three more children before he left her alone and her children fatherless. At night, the sisters would hope for some tragedy to befall him or that he would shoot himself as he had so often threatened. There was neither tragedy nor suicide; there were only the drugs and alcohol that got to him before a bullet ever could.

It was in that evening's heat that Journey thought at length of her last encounters with Darnel.

After having gone through college rarely visiting home, she had earned a degree in Communications only to shock everyone with her decision to enlist into the Army. Journey remembered that she had come home to attend Gwen's college graduation. Gwen had been so excited and to celebrate, Bea had planned a cookout. Realizing that there was no salad dressing for potato salad, the two of them headed to the supermarket. Journey still wished that she'd sent Tilly to the store in her place.

Gwen had gone through the entrance, while Journey had stood outside to finish her cigarette. Gwen was safely inside and didn't see Darnel wandering around the parking lot begging. He looked as grungy as Journey had ever seen him and his stench was much worse than his appearance. His hair was matted and clothes hung off him like a badly dressed rag doll. She recalled thinking that if he could see himself the way she did that day that he would indeed stand in the mirror and kick his own ass. He had stood a short distance from her with only a pair of black wool socks sheltering his feet. She remembered the one lone shoe in the middle of the floor.

Journey had wanted to stub out her cigarette and run for the safety of the store. She couldn't figure if watching her father plead to carry groceries for change pleased her more than it hurt. Her feet wouldn't move from the pavement as he made a plea to anyone who would hear him. "I ain't had nothing t'eat in a week. Please lady, help a brother out."

The woman pulled a bill from her purse surely just to get him away from her. Darnel hurriedly stuffed it into his pocket and didn't so much as nod a thank you. It was okay though since the woman had taken off with her cart so fast that she wouldn't have seen his thanks anyway.

Finally, it was her turn. Darnel was looking down at her shoes asking if she could spare anything. She resisted the urge to identify herself or call him Daddy. When she didn't answer, he looked up. There was no mistaking the half moon shaped scar on his right cheek where a shoe had once sunk in. And alas, there was no escaping the recognition in his light brown eyes, but this was no time for reunions, but pretending. He quickly walked away and she lit another cigarette. It hurt knowing there was a time when the voice that begged for a handout was the same one that once had brought squeals of joy from four little girls. Sometimes even from their mother when she wasn't so tired from working. Maybe her mind had played a foul trick on her, she concluded. The figure walking away from her had to be someone else. Yes, the man was just another junkie bum on the street and not actually the man whose sperm conceived her. Never mind that they had the same eyes and Gwen had his thick eyebrows and slender fingers. He wasn't real. Her mind had fabricated him. Too bad her heart knew differently.

Inside the store, Gwen searched each aisle for Journey. They met by the ketchup. Gwen was visibly worried about her sister's behavior and asked her repeatedly if she were okay. Journey only nodded and told her that she would meet her outside. When Gwen heard the alarm sound from a FIRE EXIT door, she had no idea that it had been Journey who set it off.

When the security guard had asked Journey why she'd gone out of that door instead of the front, she lied telling him that it was the first time she had been into the store. After all, what was she supposed to say? How could she tell a stranger that she couldn't go outside through the front because she didn't want to walk past her drug addicted father a second time?

A squirrel stared into the screen. Journey focused her attention on it hoping to divert her thoughts. She lit another cigarette and prayed that her eye faucets would run dry. The salt from the tears was burning her cheeks.

"Damn squirrel. Go away. Shouldn't you be asleep anyway?" She blew smoke its way.

Instead of running off, the squirrel stood on its hind legs, pointing to its chest as if to ask, "who me?"

"Go away, you damned rat with a tail!" She yelled a little too loud. "Shoo!"

Gwen stood behind her. "Who are you talking to?"

She was too slow wiping the tears away. "Just an old funky squirrel," she sniffed.

"You coming inside? Dinner is ready."

Journey felt the warmth of Gwen's hand on her shoulder and resisted the urge to push it away. She reached to touch the hands shaped like her father's. She squeezed the fingers lightly. "I'm all crampy because my period is coming," she lied. "I think I'll lay down a while."

"I've missed you," Gwen whispered but Journey's words were to herself. At first Gwen didn't know what the words had meant, but she was sure she'd heard Journey correctly.

"After all these years, I can't believe I still love the bastard," was what she'd said. It was clear to Gwen. The way she said the words so softly, there was no doubt the bastard she was talking about. There was no need to assume that she meant a past lover. Gwen had felt that way too many times to mistake. The particular bastard in the memory and tears on Journey's cheeks was one in the same. Darnel.

CHAPTER

7 The door to the guest bedroom spilled light into the hallway. George had called Gwen twice, but she didn't hear. He could hear their voices, but neither Gwen nor Journey was aware of his presence just doors away. They sat on the bed with their feet curled up the way they had when they were kids. It felt as if he'd known them his whole life.

George was hesitant to interrupt their catching up talk, but he couldn't find his lucky bowling tie. Both ladies looked slightly agitated when he stuck his head in. The heat from their eyes burned through him. Suddenly, he felt silly for intruding because of a silly old tie.

"It's in the bottom drawer on the left." Gwen waved him away.

He remembered then. It was always in that drawer but he'd forgotten as he always did. It felt strange to him that night putting on the tie himself but he did it. Under no circumstance would he go back into that room. Especially after seeing Journey turn away from his sight. He was sure he had seen tears on her face. Tears on a woman's face could wrench his feelings into knots. He had been that way even as a little boy, he could never stand to see anyone cry. Nothing could make him feel as powerless as streaming tears.

George fought feelings of exclusion and grabbed his bowling ball. He could be of no assistance to the two women he loved. The help they needed was in each other. There was no answer when he called to let them know he was leaving. He'd suspected there wouldn't be.

Gwen wasn't trying to be mean. She really hadn't heard George leave. She was too occupied with holding tears back. She was tired of crying but as long as Journey kept going, there was no use her trying to hold back.

Gwen tried to comfort her. "The only thing that helps me is I try not to think about the awful times we had because of him."

"How can you not?"

"I don't know. Whenever it pops into my mind, I block it out."

"Have you seen Darnel?"

Gwen dropped her head. Journey couldn't believe it. "You mean you've seen him?"

"I used to see him all the time. He's been over a few times."

Journey's eyes bulged. "In this house?"

The question was more of an accusation. Gwen tried not to be offended. "Well, he is our father. I thought I could help him."

"I can't believe you, Gwen. You never even told me."

"Only because I knew you'd react the way you are now. You know…like I betrayed you or something."

Journey shook her head in disbelief. "I can't believe you."

"What? What would you have me do? What would you do if he showed up at your doorstep?"

"I'd tell him to go to hell and slam the door."

"No you wouldn't."

"How do you know?"

"Because I heard you downstairs when you said you still loved him."

"I was speaking of someone else."

"Liar. You know I know you, so don't even try it. It's okay. I still love him too. I don't like him too much but I forgive him. You should too."

"I can't."

"You can and sooner or later you're going to have to. Hating him is not going to do you any good. It's like you taking poison and wishing he would die. I know."

"That's easy for you to say, but don't forget I am older than you. I understood what was going on long before you did. I was with Bea when she went from door to door looking for him. I was in the kitchen when she boiled grits to throw on him. I wanted her to do it, but she didn't."

"He's different now."

"Different from what?"

"Different from the last time you saw him at the market."

"I never told you that."

"He did."

"What else did he tell you?"

"Does it matter?"

"No. I guess not, but still. If you saw him you'd know what I'm saying. People really can change. God changes people."

"Gwen, the most religion that man ever had was when those funny looking people came to our door and gave him that prayer cloth. You remember? Even then it didn't work. The only reason he kept it was because he'd written his numbers on it." Journey paused and rolled her eyes back in remembrance. "Come to think of it, I think his numbers hit too."

"That was a long time ago."

"You always did believe in him, Gwen."

Gwen leaned her head back. It was true. She had always believed in their father; so had Journey once. It hurt to know the sister who'd sat at the table teaching Darnel to read, never would again acknowledge him as their father. Together the three of them would recite the words on the page.

See spot run. See Jane jump.

Gwen's job was to remind him of the new words they'd taught him the agonizing weeks before. She could still see her child-self at the kitchen table where she'd point to her father's head. "Did you put the words away up here, Daddy?"

Darnel would tap his head and smile yes. Except he didn't do it the final time. Frustrated with all the hard work, Darnel had forgotten the word hope. Each time he stuttered to sound out the word, it came out hop. Before the two girls could remind him of the silent e, Tilly looked over his shoulder and shouted triumphantly, "Hope, Daddy."

The shame of not knowing a word his five-year-old did was too much. Darnel flung the book to the floor and started yelling.

"Everyday, I do as you girls say! Babydoll says to me, put the words away in my head, but when I do, somebody come and move the motherfuckas! And you Dollbaby," he turned to Journey, "always bringing a different book home. Dick, Jane, Spot, and all them motherfuckas getting on my damned nerves. See Jane jump, See Dick run, See Spot shit in the front yard. It's all bullshit!"

Then he was out the door. He didn't come back until the next morning. Journey cut into her memory. "What does he call you when he sees you?" "Dollbaby, and you Babydoll."

"And Jean and Tilly?"

"Jeanie and Dumpling."

Journey snorted. "Did he ever learn to read?"

"I don't know, Journey since we beat his ass before we finished the book. I never had the nerve to ask him again."

Gwen pushed away the memory of the souvenir bat with Darnel's blood on it. She decided it was as good a time as any to change the subject. "How's Tilly? Still trying to marry you off?" Gwen guessed.

"You got it. Between Tilly working one set of nerves and Beatrice working the other, I don't have any nerves left."

"How is Bea really?"

"Smoking and cussing less, trying to quit both."

"I guess that's good for Bea, huh? You know she called earlier?"

"You tell her I was here?"

"Auntie Cut told her. She was worried."

"You tell her I'm okay?"

"Yeah, I told her."

"Good."

"So what made you decide on here? I have been pleading with you to come home for the longest."

"It was the last time you called. Colorado had begun to taste like shit on my tongue. I was curled up in my bed in an old funky tee shirt with not one pair of clean drawers to my name. Tilly was over spraying disinfectant and stealing whatever she thought I wouldn't miss out of my closet. She wouldn't shut up about this new guy she's seeing and I had the biggest headache. Thankfully you called and I had an excuse to put her out my room."

"And?"

"And you asked me to come home. I figured what the hell. Beatrice and Tilly were smothering me so I figured I should just come."

"I'm glad you did."

"Me too."

"Now com'on downstairs. I'll make a pitcher of your favorite Kool-Aid while you tell me all about your wild times in Colorado."

"I could use a glass of your mystery mix Kool-Aid. You know can't nobody make it like black folks."

"You know it."

Journey slid her half unpacked belongings to the side, then stood.

Gwen spotted the photo album in the clutter.

"Bring your album so that I can put a face to the men you've told me about. You always did keep good pictures."

"Yeah, but after you see them, we're going to burn them. I'm starting fresh in an old place with a new twist."

📖

The phone rang while Gwen poured her second glass of the purple drink. She had to strain to hear her niece's voice through the line. Yvette was whispering, "Aunty Gwen, could you come over and check on mom. She saw them again and has been shut up in her room since this morning."

"Who is it?" Journey whispered.

"Yvette," Gwen mouthed. "Okay, I'll be there," she said before hanging up the phone.

Journey sighed and drained her glass. "Cooper?"

"Sounds like it."

"What's he stolen this time?"

"Yvette said something about Jean seeing them again. I can guess the rest."

Journey slipped on her shoes. "I'm going with you. You would think that after eight years of this shit, she'd be done with his sorry ass. Maybe, along with that TV and VCR he stole a while back, her brain was with it."

"I know, but what can we say?"

"We can say the truth, Gwen. Once and for all, we can say the truth. And don't tell me to watch what I say. We've been doing that for too long."

Gwen looked at her with raised eyebrows. "Maybe you shouldn't come. The two of you are like oil and water when it comes to Cooper."

"I know that look. I promise to try to be good."

"I doubt that very seriously."

Journey didn't hear the last comment. She was on her way to the car.

Yvette opened the door and screeched when she saw Journey. They hugged and rocked in the doorway until Gwen had to pass.

"Girl, look at you. You've put on weight haven't you?"

Yvette looked down at her feet. "Mama didn't tell you? I'm pregnant."

Journey looked to Gwen who shrugged her shoulders.

"How old are you now?"

"I'll be sixteen next month," Yvette told her.

"You know you need your ass kicked don't you?"

Yvette shook her head. "Mom said you were going to say that."

Gwen wanted to change the subject. There was no sense in getting into the whys and hows about Yvette. What was done was done. "Where's your mama?"

Yvette pointed to the shut door. Gwen banged hard on it and waited.

"Jean, open this danged door 'fore we kick it down!" Journey yelled.

Gwen cut her eyes hard at Journey. "I thought you said you'd try to be good."

"You knew I was lying."

When Jean opened the door, Gwen's hands involuntarily flew to her nose. The odor of the room was a combination of grief and strong liquor. "It smells like a distillery in here."

Jean still held the source of the odor cupped in the crook of her arm. Journey and Gwen took a seat on the neatly made-up bed.

Everything including Jean reflected her expensive tastes. She was still clad in a crisp navy blue business suit she'd worn to work earlier. The costly matching navy pumps sat propped in the corner.

The front of her dreadlocked hair was swept up into a bun with the rest hanged down her back. Two ivory barrettes were clasped on either side. Jean, at age forty-six, looked great as always.

"You might smell bad, but you look damned good," Journey commented.

Jean turned the bottle up to her lips and took a long gulp before Gwen snatched it from her hand. Jean looked down at the small splatter on her shirt. "Damn, Gwen," she slurred. "You know how much this suit cost?"

"Have it cleaned."

Jean tried to sit up. "How long you been in town, Journey?"

"Never mind that. How long have you been in that chair?"

Jean glanced at her watch, but the numbers danced around. She hunched her shoulders.

Gwen, having enough, spoke up. "Tell me one thing. Does this have anything to do with Cooper?"

Tears sprang to Jean's eyes. "He brought that woman to my house. They told me it was over."

"And you believed that shit?" Journey snorted. "Where did you see him this time? In the grocery store or standing on her porch? Maybe out in the park with her kids? What the fuck is wrong with you, Jean?"

Jean pointed a finger. "Don't start with me while I'm too drunk to kick your ass. You don't know shit."

"You bet' not try it sober. You haven't kicked my ass since we were kids."

"Don't think I won't now."

"Both of you, quit it. We're not kids anymore."

"That's her," Jean accused. "She comes into my house talking about what she can't possibly know.

"I bet I know Cooper still screwing that red-bone in Missouri. I know it, Gwen knows it, and hell…everybody except of course you, know it too. I wonder why that is?"

"I know what I need to know. I also know that people who live in glass houses shouldn't throw stones. You're mighty self righteous for a woman whose gone through the number of men you have and quiet as is kept, I bet you still hot in the drawers for that brother Douglas who dumped your ass all those years ago."

Jean was right but Journey wouldn't let her know it. "Even if you are right, this isn't about anyone but you. Look at you, Jean. You're forty seven…"

"Six, forty-six," she corrected.

Gwen picked up where Journey left off. "Whatever, you're a grown woman who works for a successful law practice, and you're sitting here dripping snot on a suit that cost more than some folks mortgage."

"Gwen, you know how it is? I don't need a lecture. You're not single and don't know how it feels to not want to be alone."

"Don't give me that mess. Just because you don't want to be lonely, does not mean you have to settle for Cooper. Eight years is long enough to figure the man ain't going to amount to much more that what he is."

"I know, but I just get so confused," Jean whined.

"That is not confused. That is confucked up." Journey spat.

Jean stood up. "Gwen, would you please make her shut the fuck up."

Gwen was at the door. "You two make me sick. For you all to be the supposed older sisters, you sure as heck got a lot to learn. If I'm always in the middle of you, trying to solve your problems, then who the hell is supposed to help me solve mine?"

Journey looked to Jean. "I'm sorry, Gwen."

"Me too. Let me make it up to you. I'll do anything, just ask."

"You're drunk, Jean and I don't need you to do anything."

"I just thought maybe you would listen to my side of the story."

"I don't need to. I've heard it all a hundred times before. Your only side is your backside that you keep bending over so that Cooper can kick you dead center in. And one last thing before I go; if you insist on being Cooper's fool, then the next time you want to throw a drunken pity party, then go for it. Neither you nor Yvette call me. Better yet, why don't you get on your knees and pray to the only One whom can love you unconditionally the way you hope that man of yours would. That is, if you can remember God's name ain't Cooper."

Jean looked frantically to Journey. "She listens to you. Don't let her leave."

"Maybe she should leave, Jean. Gwen is younger than we are and yet sometimes she seems the oldest. She's angry right now. She will be back because that's what we do, right?"

"Will you stay?" Jean was whining.

"You know I will. How often have you asked me to stay instead of yelling for me to get the hell out?"

"You know I don't mean it. You just make me so mad sometimes."

"Just like when we were kids."

Jean laughed. "Yep, just the same. You were always in my bedroom, in my space."

"Stealing your clothes."

"Eavesdropping on my conversations."

"Watching you sneak boys in."

"Watching Bea whip my ass."

Journey laughed too. "Bea knew everything didn't she?"

"Yeah, because you told it."

Journey drank from Jean's bottle then passed it back to her. "Nope, uh uhgn. Not all the time, I didn't."

The room was quiet.

"You know what Journey?" she asked passing the bottle back. "I hate feeling like a fool. I hate wondering why it's so hard to let Cooper go. I'm not even in love with the clown anymore and believe me, the sex was never mind-blowing."

Journey smacked her lips. "Probably for the same reason I still think about Douglas so much."

"What reason is that?" Jean looked genuinely interested in Journey's insight.

"Because we have been successful at everything but relationships, and I think we both hate to lose at anything."

"I think it's because too that a bit of Darnel has been in every man I've ever loved. I've been trying to save him my entire life."

"I understand. I married a Darnel. But that doesn't mean that we should be stuck trying to do the same thing Bea tried to do for years. We watched her struggle to change our father and she never could."

Jean couldn't help chuckling. "And everybody knows that if Bea can't fix something then that thing is unfixable."

"You got that right."

Jean sat up as best she could. "Well somebody has to break this cycle, dammit! How about I start then you take over. How 'bout that?"

Journey leaned over and hugged Jean close. "Deal."

Jean was so proud of her sister. "You know you look good with your hair that way."

"Thank you. I only watched yours grow for seven years before I got the nerve up."

"Excellent choice as always…"

The aroma of fresh brewed coffee entered before Gwen pushed the door open. Journey didn't wait for the offer before she snatched and nibbled one of the cheese hors' d'oeuvres Gwen had hooked up. Laughter echoed throughout the room.

"We should have known Gwen was somewhere cooking. We should piss her off more often"

Gwen patted her chest lightly. "You know me. When the going gets tough, the tough heads to the kitchen. Microwaves are wonderful."

After two cups of coffee, Gwen lowered the lid on the commode top and sat atop it. The bathroom smelled of chamomile and oils as Jean buried herself in the bubbles. For a spell, it was like they were back in the days of their childhood when Bea would draw their baths for them. The four girls would take turns making sure that one didn't get preferential treatment with Bea's fragranced oils and bubble bath.

Journey flopped cross-legged on the floor reminiscing about their happier childhood memories. It was Gwen's idea to call Tilly and put her on the speakerphone. The night seemed even more like old times when Beatrice popped over to Tilly's.

After hanging up, Jean fell asleep first. Gwen and Journey tucked her in and closed the door lightly behind them.

C H A P T E R

8 The past played back in Jean's mind. The coffee and bath had mellowed her enough for her sleep, but not enough for her to hold onto the slumber.

Cooper's voice rang in her ears. "I love you," he had said just the night prior. "I promise me and Anna are finished. She means nothing to me. She wants to talk to you."

More lies from him and the woman who'd sat in her living room sipping from her coffee mug, drinking her coffee. Though a much younger woman, Jean felt no threat in her presence. Age aside; this woman was no more attractive than Jean knew herself to be.

"I'm leaving town," Anna had lied.

The words were just to cover their plot and give her false hopes and what had she done but fell for the well-laid plan? She had foolishly believed that the three weeks without her had been too much for Cooper to handle. She had done what he'd thought she never could—stopped seeing him. At first she doubted the woman's words until she began to wonder why this woman would risk humiliation to sit and spurt lies from her chunky, blood red painted lips? Jean had not asked for the confession—had not invited her. Had Jean not been so smug in seeing Cooper appear so desperate, she could have thought more clearly. It was too bad that she had begun to believe those lying lips until she hadn't gotten lost just today trying to find a client's house. Who did she see but Cooper unloading a rented truck of furniture charged to her own Visa for what Jean had thought would go to his apartment.

The alcohol interrupted her thoughts with words of its own. She obediently rose from bed, changed into all black clothing over her pajamas. She accepted what the liquor insisted was a good plan. Her hands were steady while she steered her sleek vehicle across the dark, winding roads. Her blood alcohol content was clearly high, but Jean didn't so much as swerve. The sweat on her brow was the only indicator of the many drinks she'd consumed.

Jean parked her car. She reached into the back seat for a pair of sneakers she kept for the workday's end when pumps came off and comfort was called for.

From the trunk of the car, she removed a gas can, a bucket, and a two by four she'd taken from her garage. She stuffed an old tee shirt into the bucket. A rock from the curb took care of the streetlight. The experience from her childhood days came in handy. She was still a good shot and not one neighbor peeked from their window.

The rest was mechanical. Jean was barely aware of creeping around the house to find the water hose. She was delirious but she really didn't want to burn down the entire house. Not really.

The lights in the house were out, but Cooper's car was parked outside—a car she paid the down payment for. He had laughed and hugged her on the parking lot of the dealership. "I've never loved anyone like I do you. Marry, me Jean," he asked. And like a fool she'd eagerly accepted.

The task ahead got easier with every memory. Particularly when a shadow passed the window, which she assumed was the bedroom. She didn't have to double check to know there were only two exits. One in front, the other in back where the French screened door opened outward. Her plan was more perfect than she expected. One of the heavy lawn chairs propped just right under the doorknob would seal that exit. It hardly made a sound thanks to the rubber padding on the legs.

With that out of the way, Jean smiled and placed the bucket under the window. Not knowing what to do with the plastic can holding the gas, she decided to leave it in the bucket. She was no expert in arson so she didn't know whether gas exploded or what. She tossed in the tee-shirt, lit it, then ran like hell.

Cooper's voice was the first she heard after the loud WHOOSH of gas igniting. He was yelling that he would grab the water hose Jean held. He slipped as soon as the hard spray of water attacked his nakedness. Jean stood just close enough for him to recognize her.

"You bitch!"

The fire was momentarily forgotten as Cooper was far too occupied with the thought of getting his hands around Jean's neck. She could still hear him yelling as she quickly rounded the corner of the house.

"You lousy bitch! I'm going to…"

His sentence was never finished because when he hit the corner, the two by four landed nicely around the area of his ribcage stuffing the words back into his throat. His muddy body crumpled to the ground. For fun, Jean swung it again, this time hard across his jaw. She was sure she heard something crack.

Anna's near naked body ran flailing after the fallen figure. Jean was out of sight but couldn't resist the opportunity. She waited until Anna leaned over a wailing Cooper and for fairness swung the board at her. It connected somewhere between her shoulder blades. She never saw what hit her.

If the neighbors saw anything, it was only a black clad figure disappearing down the alley.

By the time Jean pulled in front of the darkened house, all evidence had been properly disposed of. On the way, she'd taken off her gloves and sneakers. Her black overalls, skullcap and shirt lay somewhere at the bottom of an alley dumpster. She'd had to debate on the stick and whether she could safely keep it as a souvenir. No, it had to go too.

Jean had to struggle in the darkness to find a few pebbles small enough for throwing. This was the one time Jean could not appreciate Big George and Gwen's meticulous yard work. Hardly a rock was visible, let alone in the darkness.

She could feel clumps of mud clinging onto her socks as her feet sank into the earth. She cursed the neighbor's dog for its distracting barking. She tossed another pebble and willed for someone to show up. She was sure she saw movement and hoped it wasn't her imagination.

It was Journey who awoke. The pebbles against her window seemed too far away to be real. She sat up in bed with a start. "Where the hell am I?" she almost yelled.

Slowly her eyes adjusted to the surroundings. They hurt from squinting in the darkness. Then she remembered the packing, the trip, and Gwen. That's where she was, at Gwen's.

Journey tiptoed to the window, careful not to make much noise. Jean was waving madly. Journey's heart started its frantic beating again.

Once inside, neither woman spoke until they were back in the bedroom. Journey reached for the light, but Jean stopped her.

"No light. Not yet."

Journey, remembering her peaceful sleep, warned, "Don't start no shit, Jean."

"Oh, Journey. I'm not here to start no shit with you."

Journey couldn't help recognizing how light and cheery Jean's voice was. "Are you going to tell me what the hell is going on?"

Smelling of chamomile and outdoors, Jean leaned over and whispered, "I need a pair of your pajamas and after I shower, I'll tell you everything."

"Have you been drinking again?"

"Not while I was driving; only a swig after I pulled up."

"I got an extra toothbrush 'cause honey you need that too."

In the dark, Journey felt Jean's self-consciousness when she cupped a hand in front of her mouth and blew her breath into it. "Uhh! Sure do."

Journey waited a while before leaving the comfort of her bed. She was certain that whatever mystery had brought Jean there was something she might not want to know. Since falling asleep was not an option, Journey reluctantly trudged to the kitchen.

For the second time that night, coffee was made for Jean. She padded down the steps humming as she walked. "What time is it?"

"Two-thirty."

Jean picked up the phone and dialed her home. "Her dad must have picked Yvette up", she thought. Jean turned to find Journey in her path.

"Jean, what the hell is going on?"

Jean waved her off and leaned against the counter. "I did something I should have done a long time ago."

"That is?"

"Say goodbye to Cooper."

"What do you mean by say goodbye? Please tell me you didn't kill him"

Jean laughed. "No, I did not kill him. At least I don't think."

"Oh shit, Jean."

"Don't worry. I think I saw him move, but then again it was dark out."

"Tonight?"

"No, last week." Jean smirked. "Of course tonight."

Journey's questions were beginning to give Jean a headache. The weight of what she had done came crashing in on her. What if Cooper were dead? She answered her own question aloud. "I'm sure I didn't kill him, but just in case the police come, I've been here since five o'clock or so."

Journey grabbed her by the shoulders. "You're serious aren't you?"

Jean wasn't herself. She suddenly didn't care if Cooper were dead or not.

Journey set down a mug of coffee in front of Jean as the doorbell rang. "Remember, I've been here since five or so," Jean whispered.

"Who's at the door at this hour?" Gwen asked sleepily coming down the stairs.

"Shh." Journey waved for her to be quiet.

Gwen rolled her eyes to Jean who shrugged her shoulders. Journey smiled her biggest smile and opened the door wide. "Hello, officers."

Jean leaned innocently on the counter. The taller officer had to nudge the shorter one whose eyes were breast level with Journey. Journey took advantage by leaning to adjust a slipper. Gwen shot her a look then hurried to the door.

"Can I help you? I'm afraid there must be a mistake. This is my home, and I didn't call for the police."

Is there a Jean Butchard here?" The taller officer asked.

Jean appeared dramatically with a tray of steaming coffee. "I'm Ms. Butchard. Coffee?"

Journey patted the couch cushions where she sat. The tall one accepted coffee and pulled out a small notebook and pen.

The short police was sweating. "We've had a report from one Cooper Mason that you assaulted him."

"Little old me? Assault a man as big as Cooper? Impossible."

The three women laughed in agreement. Officer Short cracked a smile while policeman Tall leaned closer to get a better look at Journey's crossed legs. He chuckled softly. "It does seem a little unlikely, but we have to check all leads. He insisted it was you who broke his jaw."

Gwen gasped. "A broken jaw?"

"And then some," Officer Short offered.

Jean crossed her legs animatedly. "Officers, there's been some sort of misunderstanding. I can't tell you how much I wish it could have been me that broke Mr. Mason's jaw, but I've been here since early evening. I'm sure by now you know that Cooper's got a sheet a mile long. He happens to also be a habitual liar who is still very much upset that I ended our relationship. Believe me officer; I would never jeopardize my Law license for the likes of Cooper Mason."

Gwen couldn't believe her ears. Jean, who'd she'd never known to be dishonest, was sounding like a seasoned liar.

"It was about five, five-thirty when she got here. Right, Gwen?"

"About," Gwen said flatly.

Policeman Tall put away his notebook. "Sorry to bother you ladies. Like I said, we have to check. Mr. Mason gave us two addresses. We've been to your home and got no answer."

Journey swayed to the door while the shorter officer took some information from Jean. Gwen watched the two women flirt openly. It was embarrassing.

Gwen made eye contact with Journey. "Hussy!" she mouthed behind the officers' backs.

Journey smiled and stuck out her tongue.

After each officer had written his name and number down just in case either of them needed anything, they were shown the door.

George came downstairs. "Who just left?"

Gwen turned and pointed to Jean. "Did you do what the police said?"

George hadn't noticed Jean behind him. "Police?"

"Would you believe me if I said I didn't?"

"No!"

"Then yes."

"Did what?" George was confused.

"Broke Cooper's jaw," Journey clued George in.

"Ooh shoot! For real?"

Jean sat down. "Yes."

Everyone sat while Jean recapped her evening.

Gwen stared hard at her. "What made you do something as stupid as that?"

"You know Cooper is an jackass, Gwen." George defended.

Gwen threw her hands up. "That don't make it right, George." She got up and took the cups from the table. "You know you gonna pay for this one, don't you? And the way you sat there an lied! I wouldn't have thought..."

"Thought what, Gwen? That *I* could lie? Have you forgotten I'm an attorney?"

"Which makes it worse. You of all people should have more respect for the law."

"I'm not saying it was right, but it just felt so damn good."

"Mmm!"

"I know, I know, Gwen. Give me a break."

Gwen softened. "Somehow, I can't picture Cooper running naked in the night."

"I bet it was some kind of funny," George snickered.

Journey joined in. "Served his ass right. Now since everybody up, let's play some whist."

"And be the only man in this Blue Monday party? Noooo. Not me."

"Chicken," Journey taunted.

Jean flapped her arms like a chicken. "Cluck! Cluck! Cluck!"

George wasn't fazed. "Say what you want, but I am not going to be a willing participant in this chick party," he said kissing Gwen and sprinting back upstairs.

When they were settled at the table, Journey looked over her hand to Jean. "Really, what made you do it?"

"I guess I just snapped. I was sitting up in bed and I decided I was finally sick enough. Cooper brought that woman to my house."

"You should have kicked her ass right then. What she look like?"

Jean laughed hard when she thought about it.

"Like Cooper must be either blind or an idiot. Girl, she sat her fun looking ass in my favorite chair smacking these big red lips, and looking like she needed to be arrested for DWI."

Gwen hooted with Jean. "No she didn't get caught dressing without instructions!

 Honeychile, it was time to get rid of Cooper. I done heard everything."

Journey and Jean sat outside on the porch after Gwen had gone to bed. Neither was sleepy. Journey didn't want to look, but she was sure Jean was crying. She didn't look up from her tears while she talked.

"You know, the other night when I was watching TV, I heard someone testify that they woke up happy everyday and I cried. How dare I spend so much time miserable when our lives are so short? I wanna wake up happy," Jean cried.

Journey hadn't expected the laughter to end so soon. She changed the subject to keep from hearing the sound of crying. "You know, before the seventeenth century, the New Year started on the first day of spring. Yep, people would wish you Happy New Year on May 25th."

Jean was quiet while Journey rambled on.

"And another thing. On March 25th and August 1st, the sun is smack dab in the middle of the equator. Yep. There are equal hours of day as night. Isn't that awesome?"

Jean rolled her eyes. "Damn, Journey. Where did that shit come from?"

Journey snickered. "That was pretty messed up huh? I don't know where that came from. That's some stuff I fell asleep listening to so don't quote me on those dates. Funny how I remembered it. Sorry."

"Don't be."

"No, I am. It's just that I understand too well why you cry. When I think about how short life is, and how many days we waste being miserable, I cry. Surely, God doesn't bless us with a new day just for us to waste it tripping on madness."

"Yeah, you're right. That's got to be a sin."

The porch was quiet except for the night sounds. "Journey? Can I ask you a question?"

"Sure."

"Do you still look up to me as your big sister?"

"Sure do."

"Can I ask you another question and you won't get mad?"

"Yep."

"I smelled marijuana earlier. You still smoke?"

"Yep, and since I retired, I wake and bake."

"You're kidding right?"

"Nope. That's why I just ate that big ass bowl of cereal. In fact, I got a joint right now.

Can I ask you a question?" Journey asked not waiting for an answer. "Why did you quit?"

"Now you know I started smoking it in the sixth grade right? It was time for me to quit. That shit had me always thinking about next week. In college, I'd be sitting in class high as Kooda Brown and all I could think about was some test I had two weeks away. It's been ages since I smoked a joint."

"Want to smoke this one for old times sake?"

Jean thought about it before she took it from Journey. "Sure, why not."

CHAPTER

9 After Jean left, Gwen couldn't go back to sleep. It was early but she looked fresh in a bright pink shirt declaring *Jesus is my lifesaver.* Colorful circle candies were all over it. Journey staggered in grabbing at the cabinets.

"My, aren't you colorful."

"It's not the color but the message."

"Amen."

"Are you looking for coffee?"

"Bingo."

"Coffee maker wouldn't work anymore. I tried."

Journey looked panicked.

"Don't worry, I went out and bought instant because I didn't want you flipping out on me."

Journey mumbled, "Thanks. I have to get a coffee maker."

"Already took care of that. I asked George to buy a new one."

"Thanks twice. Sis, that's why I love you. You think of everything don't you?"

"I try."

Gwen was busy frying sausage and wasn't sure it was the doorbell or the TV she heard.

"That the door?" Journey asked.

"Could you get it for me?"

Journey peeked out the peephole. There was a woman cradling an infant. Beside her was a small child. Journey recognized Kathy, Allison's best friend and rolled her eyes hard.

When the door opened, Kathy shoved the baby toward her.

Journey held her hands up. "Who, whoa. Gwen!"

Gwen came from the kitchen. "Oh, you're early. Allison said you wouldn't be here until after twelve."

"Yes, but I thought she told you I might need you all day. I can pay you."

Gwen took the child. "No, we'll work it out."

Journey rolled her eyes at Gwen. The word we'll caught in her mind. "No, not we. You," Journey said aloud. She never liked Kathy.

The forgotten little girl started sniffling and tugging at her mother's clothes. Kathy kissed her quickly and headed to the door. Gwen laid the baby in the collapsible crib she'd brought out the day before. She'd bought it almost two years prior when she and George had been expecting. Since somebody was always dropping kids off for her to babysit, Gwen just kept it. She grabbed a cloth to wipe a gob of baby puke oozing down the L on her shirt.

"Look at this, Journey. This child is still in pampers."

"As uppity as Kathy acts?"

"Child, they some of the worst ones. The ones with the so-called money got the raggedyest kids. Check that bag for me and see what she got in there."

Journey pulled out a bottle filled with juice. The nipple was swollen to near double normal size and the pinhole had been bitten to expand it. Red juice oozed freely from the top. Meagan reached for the bottle confirming Journey's theory. "Looks like she still takes a bottle too."

"Apparently."

The little girl started sniffling again as Gwen took her hand. "Come on baby. What's your name?" The child's voice was a whisper.

"Meagan, what a pretty name. Why don't you come with Aunty Gwen to watch some TV?"

"A white girl's name," Journey observed aloud.

When Gwen came back, she was still complaining. "You see that child's head? And that nose! The girl almost three, she can blow her own nose if her mama would give her a tissue."

"Don't look like her hair been combed in days. She got hair just like her daddy. Remember that afro he used to wear?"

Gwen's palm flew up to cover her mouth as if it had been she who told a secret. Not knowing quite what to do with her hands, Gwen stuffed them behind her back. She leaned closer to Journey and narrowed her eyes. "How do you know her daddy wore an afro?" she questioned.

Journey realized her mistake too late. She could almost see the light bulb go on in her sister's mind. "Oops."

"Ooh! Ooh, Journey. Don't ell me…Ooh."

"You didn't know did you? Shoot! Me and my big mouth."

"Now that I think about it, that hair, those big old eyes, ooh, girl." Gwen whispered, "Malik? Who told you?"

Journey lit a cigarette. "Your nosy ass sister, Tilly."

Gwen sat across from her wide-eyed. "How'd she know?"

"Remember her last visit? He confided in her that some other woman was carrying his child. You know her mouth run like water. Her ass ain't ever kept a secret."

"Ooh."

"Would you stop saying that?"

"I can't help it. Does Allison know?"

"Girl, please. What do you think?" "Ooh."

"And you bet' not tell her either."

"I won't. Um, uuhn, umm."

When the doorbell rang that evening, Gwen thought it was Kathy coming to pick up her kids. She opened the door to find her friend, Aretha, and her son standing there.

"Hey, Retha. What a surprise. I wasn't expecting you to drop by."

"I wasn't expecting to drop by either. Omar and me was on our way home when my car broke down. Allison picked me up walking down the street. She's coming."

Gwen handed eight-year-old Omar a popsicle and pointed him to the den. She knew between the two kids there would be stains but at least the carpet was dark.

Journey walked in from the back porch. "Is that the cheap floozy, Aretha I hear?" she yelled passing Gwen.

"Journey, you smell like marijuana," Gwen whispered.

"So?"

Aretha rushed into the kitchen to hug her friend. They didn't let go until Allison came in.

Journey turned to see Allison scowling at her the way one would an unruly child. After sniffing the air, Allison looked at Gwen accusingly. "I smell marijuana."

"Don't look at me that way, Ally. Journey is twenty times two plus some. She can smoke a forest if she wants."

Despite her dislike for Allison, Journey acknowledged her presence. "Hi Allison," she said flatly.

There were no hugs between the two.

"You need to be ashamed of yourself. Still acting like some kind of hippie. Don't you think, Aretha?"

Aretha shrugged and looked up. "To each his own."

Journey sat down. "Gwen, check your friend. I'm not in the mood for her foolishness today."

"I seem to remember a time when we were all friends."

"No, you're wrong, Gwen. Journey and Allison only pretended for your sake," Aretha enlightened.

"Oh." Gwen sat on the couch next to Aretha. She was about to tell Allison how Kathy had left her kids when Meagan walked in. Allison lifted the child to her lap. "Hey precious. Don't you look pretty? Who braided your hair?"

Meagan pointed to Journey.

Allison turned to Journey. "You mean you came down long enough to comb hair?"

"Shut up Allison."

"Come on, Allison. Lay off Journey. She's at least trying to be civil. She doesn't owe anyone an explanation."

Journey bowed slightly toward Gwen. "Thank you, Sis."

"I'm being civil. I just can't understand with all those years of discipline the military must have taught, how you could retire and then revert back into the reckless teenager you were."

Journey scooted to the edge of the chair. She squared her body straight with Allison's. "How does it feel to be as miserable as you are, huh? Anyone who finds fault in everybody but themselves is one miserable individual."

Allison was taken aback. "How dare you analyze me? And wrongly at that. I happen to be very happy."

"Liar. You are the same as you were in high school. I didn't like you then or now. You were a miserable human being then."

"How you ever forged a career is beyond me. You haven't changed a bit, and the only reason you didn't like me was because of Malik. I bet you're still jealous because he chose me over you."

Journey laughed bitterly. "Is this what this mess is about? Tell me Allison. You can't possibly have been bickering with me for all these years because of Malik, because if it is then you're dumber than I thought. It's not me and Malik you should worry yourself about. In fact, if you would mind your own business like you do everybody else's you'd see what's right under your nose. Or on your lap so to speak."

Gwen cut her eye at Journey. "Can I talk to you in the kitchen?"

Journey tossed her head at Allison and followed Gwen. Their hushed argument hardly drifted into the next room.

Allison had become quiet. When Gwen and Journey returned, she was staring hard at Meagan. "I'm going to kill that sonuvabitch!" Allison bellowed.

Gwen hurriedly took Meagan from her lap back into the den. The door banged shut behind Allison.

Gwen wanted to choke Journey.

"Better call George to tell him to warn Malik," Journey urged.

Gwen shook her head. "You did that on purpose and I'm not getting into that."

Aretha's eyes widened. "I knew it. I knew it. The moment I laid eyes on that kid. Who's the woman?"

"Allison's best friend."

"Kathy? Ooh."

"Not you too. You sound like Gwen. Don't be so surprised. Malik isn't so innocent as everyone thinks. I was with him a long time ago."

"You ho!" Aretha laughed. "I thought I was the only one."

Both ladies looked at Gwen who couldn't believe what she was hearing. "Don't even go there. I would never. You two are disgusting."

Journey looked down at her shoes.

Gwen eyes bulged. "You're serious aren't you? How come you never told me?"

"Because Beatrice told me not to."

"You confided in our mother and not me?"

"Now Gwen think and then consider that question."

"Gwen didn't have to think to know the answer.

"I didn't confide in her. She caught us in the act."

"And you still didn't tell me?"

"Uh uhn. When Bea caught us, she beat the shit out of me. She said she'd beat me again if I told. You know she would have too."

Aretha leaned onto Journeys shoulders. She could hardly quit laughing.

"So don't blame me, Gwen. Blame your ma-ma. You know what Beatrice always said," Journey snickered turning to Aretha. "Some folks have the worst chirren," they laughed in unison.

"Go ahead. Blame Beatrice if it makes you feel better, but this one was on you Journey Renee."

"Gwen, can you come down off that high horse of yours for one minute. You know the only reason you wasn't hot in the ass like me and Tilly is because you had George sniffing up around you way back then."

"This is not about George and you know it."

"No it isn't. But that man loves your day before yesterday drawers. Always have."

Aretha spoke up. "Unless…"

"Unless what?"

"Unless Gwen ain't as innocent as we think. Maybe Gwen was one of those in the closet hot girls."

"If I were then I'm not telling now."

"Com'on, Gwen. Tell it."

"Gwen looked at them both and choked back a laugh. "Y'all must think I'm a new fool. Or an old one."

"Journey, you was wrong for telling Allison though," Aretha said.

"Shut up. Nobody asked you shit. You thought it was funny too."

"Ain't nothing funny about a married man screwing around."

Journey shrugged her shoulders. "He wasn't married when I screwed him, but he was about to be when Tilly did."

"Tilly!"

"Yes, Tilly with her colorstruck ass. You know all she used to talk about was light-skinned this or dark-skinned that. No way Malik with his good hair was getting away from her."

"Don't you think that's about the silliest mess?" Aretha asked. "Now we got whole books about light and dark. Who gives a shit?"

"Tilly!" Journey and Gwen stated.

"Well light with good hair or not, Malik got an illegitimate kid and Allison 'bout gon' kill him 'fore the day is over," Aretha snickered.

"I'd better call George and tell him. It won't be funny if Allison really does kill him."

Aretha stifled a giggle and rubbed her swollen foot. "You're right, Gwen. I shouldn't be giggling. Shit. That was my ride home."

Gwen didn't want to, but she couldn't hide her amusement at her friend's silly humor. The entire room vibrated with laughter.

CHAPTER

10 Sunday rolled around and Journey squirmed in her seat. She gripped the cardboard fan with the curvy wooden stick stapled to the tip. The words advertising Lovell's funeral parlor were a blur the harder she fanned.

"It's hot in here," she said a bit too loudly.

Gwen nudged her and stared stoically ahead at the choir. It had been much too long since Journey had been inside a church. Gwen had nearly dragged her up the steps of the huge building. Journey had finally relented. "Alright, Gwen. I'm going in but if they stop me at the door and ask for my ID then I'm going home."

Without her grandpa's presence, church had become a strange place for Journey—empty somehow. She still prayed every night and talked to God a lot but she was careful not to ask for anything. Since her bout with the painful chemotherapy she'd had to endure when cancer attacked her breast, she had not asked for anything. She made God a promise that if He would be so gracious as to spare her life, she would never ask for anything else. She'd even gone so far as to not let anyone but Sweetie know what she was going through and threatened to never speak to her if she told a soul. Her Aunt Cut found out by accident when someone she knew had known someone else in the same hospital as Journey. She had been sworn to secrecy as well.

Since Journey felt responsible for the cancer that afflicted her, she suffered her self-inflicted punishment alone. Whether because she continued to smoke, or had committed some unforgivable moral offense, she convinced herself that she had deserved it. She hadn't come near a church since her doctor announced that she was cancer-free.

From somewhere she felt the breeze before she heard the whir of the air-conditioning unit click on. She stopped fanning and let her mind wander to the roast slow cooking in Gwen's oven. She hoped George wouldn't forget to take it out, as he was known to do. Journey had witnessed in the past how the

Sunday football games dissolved his entire attention span. Her stomach growled in anticipation as the choir stood in their places. She remembered when she and Gwen had stood years ago in those same stands.

Gwen checked the usual pews to note who had made Sunday service. Allison and Malik sat stiffly beside one another and for the first time that Gwen could remember, Allison looked a mess. Her usual chic hair was frizzy and out of place and her eyes was puffy and bloodshot.

In front of them sat Anthony and Janelle. The child was smiling, as was her father. Who she didn't see was Monica sliding into one of the back pews.

Gwen felt her attention oddly drawn to the far corner where a woman sat. She couldn't remember ever meeting the stranger; yet felt somewhere she had. The woman was neither tall nor short, dark nor light, big or small. Her lips moved in what Gwen assumed was prayer.

Allison also noticed the stranger and appraised her appearance. Since the woman was neither attractive nor unattractive, she decided that only a little improvement was needed.

The hair, plaited in two braids down the side of the woman's head, should definitely be relaxed and left to hang. *A shame to have so much hair and leave it too kinky to blow in the wind,* Allison thought while unconsciously checking her weave tract to make sure it hadn't slipped. It didn't bother her wearing a weave since it was only to add volume, not length. Her hair was the perfect length, she felt.

Upon further examination, Allison noticed the parted lips and decided a light lip-gloss would greatly improve on the woman's looks. She could not see her eyes to note what could be improved upon; however, that dress was a complete no-no.

After the choir director lowered his arms indicating the choir could sit, a song, which came from nowhere, and everywhere rose above the crowd.

Why should I be discouraged, why should shadows come? The voice sang. Why should my heart be lonely? And long for Heaven and home? When Jesus is my portion. My constant friend is he…His eye is on the sparrow and I know he watches me…

Journey recognized the song and shut her eyes tightly against the onslaught of tears. The song was Sweetie's favorite. How many times had Sweetie sang that very one to her grandgirls? Journey could remember days in the hospital with Sweetie singing her to sleep to that hymn.

The voice was eerily touching to Monica as well. The words and melody slid down Allison's windpipe and began to consume her inside out. She forgot her mascara and leaned into the tears.

Monica wanted to leave, but couldn't bring her body to move. Often, her mother had sung that song to her and for that moment as the words rang, *I sing because I'm happy. I sing because I'm free. His eye is on the sparrow, and I know he watches me,* she could hear her mother's voice as clearly. That voice must be one of an Angel, was her last thought before the floodgates behind her eyes opened up and gushed salt water through her ducts.

Journey and Gwen held on to oneanother. When Gwen let go to pass another Kleenex, both their faces were dusted with the fine white cotton from the tissue. The tears on Gwen's cheeks accompanied by the singing were enough to make Journey want to run. She whispered something to Gwen then walked out of the church. Once she pushed her way through the heavy doubled doors, Journey breathed the outside air deep into her chest. She had to get away.

It had been too long a time for so many secrets, and Geneva felt drained as she sat down in her seat. She was unaware of the curious stares all around her. All she knew was that she was tired. Her voice, as resilient as ever, was all to remain strong. The pastor took his place behind the pulpit. Quiet sniffles echoed all around. Some of the choir members whispered among themselves. Geneva saw none of it. She'd fallen asleep.

The congregation turned their attention from the source of the melody to the pulpit. Gwen's mind wandered with only bits of Pastor Willard's sermon reaching her. *"The text of this Sunday's sermon comes from Luke 12:35. Be dressed and ready for our Lord! Take out your bibles and read along with me."*

Gwen had been thinking about all the Sundays Beatrice had sat with them on the first pew to hear her father deliver God's message. It was not difficult to envision Beatrice with the four of her starched, fidgety girls on the front pew. Peppermints were passed out to keep their mouths busy doing something other than talking. Such a stark contrast they were at church from who they were at home. Bea gave up on the charade when Darnel disappeared from the pew into the street. The arguments began and Bea, who'd always had a quick laugh, worked harder and laughed less. Grandpa would still call each Sunday morning, to remind them of service. When he noticed that Bea had begun to work most Sunday mornings, he faithfully stopped by afterward. When Bea got home from work, she would cook Sunday dinner as if they all had been in attendance. Darnel avoided those Sundays, so they were always good. Bea's laughter returned in Grandpa's presence.

After a short while, Jean took Bea's place on the front pew passing out peppermints. Easter programs and such were arranged and presided over by Jean. Their seats were emptied again when their Grandpa died. Not even Jean could stand not seeing him in the pulpit. Life took on a different path and the starched Butchard girls went about to forge their own identities and mend their own mistakes.

By the time her mind returned to the present, Gwen could hear the closing of the sermon by the rise and fall of the pastor's voice

"Brothers and sisters, how are you waiting for our Lord? Are you dressed or lounging? Or are you trying to fake him out by leaving your porch-light on while you hangin' out with the world. Don 't be deceived! Jesus knows before He knocks if you 're dressed and waiting. Let us all pray…"

As the church emptied, Gwen glanced occasionally at the still sleeping woman. She walked over and placed a gentle hand upon her shoulders. The woman awoke with a start.

"I didn't mean to startle you."

Geneva looked around at the near empty church and flushed with embarrassment. Gwen saw and soothed, "Don't worry about it. Pastor has members who sleep the entire service every Sunday." She extended her hand. "I don't believe we've met. My name is Gwen."

Geneva sat up. "My name is Geneva."

"Good to meet you."

"Has the church's van left?"

"I don't know, but I can take you home if it's not too far."

"Home," the word fell from her mouth like a foreign object.

Gwen didn't know how to read her expression. She took her hand.

"We won't worry about you going home just yet. How about a Sunday dinner?"

"That sounds okay to me."

📖

Gwen couldn't quite shake the feeling that she should know the woman in the seat beside her. She wasn't sure if Geneva was asleep or just lying back with her eyes closed. Just in case, Gwen chatted over the soft music on the radio and glanced over occasionally to her riding companion.

Geneva felt so deceptive riding next to Gwen. She couldn't help but feel it an odd twist of fate that Gwen had been the one to awaken her when in fact, she was the person Geneva had come to talk to. She and Darnel had planned that day many times, but each time her nerves had gotten the best of her. It wasn't that she didn't want to meet his daughters, it was only that she knew how much suffering he'd caused them all and in her own way, she'd contributed to it as much. She also knew that as they rode, Darnel was at Gwen's waiting. Although so much needed saying, Geneva thanked God that Gwen was not pushy with questions and especially that she seemed content only to send sideways curious glances her way.

Gwen hoped Geneva wouldn't notice the glares and think her rude for staring. At times, Geneva looked like a young woman while other times she appeared as old or much older than Gwen. By the time Gwen pulled into her driveway, she was sure Geneva was ageless. Maybe she'd ask her if she got to know her better.

Geneva turned to Gwen as she parked. "There is something I need to tell you before we go inside."

C H A P T E R

11 The voice yet rang in Journey's ears even as she had called George from the pay phone to come pick her up. She regretted selling her car but it was the last belonging that she and her husband had bought together. George had arrived shortly after and didn't question why she was sitting on the church's steps while Gwen was still inside. Journey had known that he wouldn't.

They had made idle chatter on the way home. Journey had not gone in but switched seats with George. All the while she had waited for him, she had thought she wanted nothing more than to go and climb in bed. It wasn't until they got there that she realized she couldn't make her feet move toward the house. She told George that she needed to pick up something from the store.

For a while, she just drove with no idea of her destination. She ended up parked in front of the Thrifty Shopper Supermarket where she'd last seen Darnel. Glancing around the parking lot, she spotted several men hustling change from customers. Each of them looked like zombies with their gray, ashen skin and hollow eyes. None were Darnel.

Journey lit a cigarette and leaned her head against the seat. She wished she could reach inside her head and unplug whatever it was controlling her memories. If not to turn it off completely, at least to press the pause button. Her brain felt like it was on overload. Too much Darnel, Beatrice, and everyone else. A joint is what she could use. She was sure that would slow everything down, but this wasn't her car. Her ashtray would have had a joint or at least a half one in it. George's only held a bunch of pennies. Her mind kept going.

From somewhere, another song played in her ears. It was Amazing Grace from her Grandpa's chest. Grandpa—the reason she and Gwen went to church, joined the choir, and collected cans for pennies to drop in the collection plate on Sundays. Grandpa in the pulpit beaming down proudly at his granddaughters. Beatrice next to them smiling proudly at her father. Grandpa, who told them how God would never leave or forsake them.

"Why didn't you ever mention how we'd leave Him behind?" Journey asked the empty seat next to her. "Why'd you have to die Grandpa?"

There was no answer, but even if there had been, Journey was crying too hard to hear it anyway. She didn't look up until she heard the 'thunk' up against the side of her door. A teenaged boy stood in front of the vehicle looking like he'd been caught stealing. The grocery cart that had gotten away from him rested against the door.

Journey could read the sorry in his eyes as he grabbed the buggy.

"I'm so sorry ma'am. It doesn't look damaged, but you can check."

Journey was too tired to get out of the car. She must have looked a mess to the young man. She appraised him and decided to let the incident slide. A small chip of paint wasn't worth the trouble of causing the kid more distress. He was surely sorry enough. She attempted a smile, but failed so she waved him away. He nodded his thanks and disappeared as quickly as he showed up.

Journey couldn't remember if she'd told George that she was going for cigarettes or snacks. She decided that it didn't matter because George had surely sensed her need to just get away for a while. She made a mental note to tell him thanks.

Journey put the truck in drive and turned it toward home. She didn't know what had brought her there in the first place. Had she wanted to see Darnel and if she had, would she have had the nerve to say something? If so, what? Maybe she would ask why had he taken her favorite piggy bank when Beatrice put him out.

Back at Gwen's, Journey could see Gwen peeking from the window. She hurried outside.

"I've been worried sick about you. You okay?"

"I'm fine."

"You sure you feel okay?"

"Yeah, I can't explain it right now. I just had to get away from that singing. I don't know why."

Gwen looked down and pushed a few blades of grass around with her shoe. "Yeah, it was something wasn't it?"

"Yeah. Let's go inside. I'm starving."

"I need to tell you something before we go in."

"It's okay, Gwen. We'll talk later. Let's eat now."

Gwen watched Journey go inside. "Shoot, I should have told her," she mumbled. "She's going to kill me."

Gwen tried calling to her again, but Journey's destination was set. She'd been anticipating the roast and oven baked potatoes. Gwen waited a moment more before she followed.

Journey was standing just inside the kitchen with her mouth gaping.

"Hi, Dollbaby," Darnel turned from the stove.

Instead of speaking, all she could do was think how ridiculous he looked in Gwen's pink apron.

"I brought your favorite dessert just for you."

Journey was aware of the words, but couldn't make the connection to them with Darnel standing there. She was sure she meant to say something neutral but what came out was, "You took my piggy bank. You bought it for my birthday, then you took it."

Darnel wrung the dishcloth in his hands. "Yes I did, Dollbaby."

"Don't call me that."

"It might not mean nothing now, but I'm sorry."

"Are you? Journey planted her feet firm for battle. "What else are you sorry for?"

Journey felt the tingly hand on her arm before she saw the person.

"I think his sorry is for every thing," the unfamiliar voice spoke.

Journey turned to the woman from the church. She wanted to hug her and push her away at the same time.

"How do you know?" The question was not one of anger, just curiosity.

"I know because I've lived with this man."

"So did I."

"Your father has changed, Journey. If you give him a chance, you'll see. Just like I did."

Seeing Darnel had jumbled her mind all up. Journey stared at the woman before her and tried to comprehend what she had said. Her mind would not unravel the words she had heard. *Just like she did what? Like she gave him a chance, or like she had changed?*

What she did know was that she didn't like the woman calling her name as if she knew her. Neither had she understood why Gwen hadn't prepared her because if she had then maybe words would make sense to her.

"This is Darnel's wife, Geneva. You hear me?" It was Gwen speaking.

Journey squinted at the woman. "Have I seen you somewhere? Do you know me?"

Geneva smiled the most beautiful smile. A smile Journey was sure she'd seen before.

"I don't think so, but maybe."

Before she could digest that whole scene, George's voice filled the living room. It was a welcomed distraction. Journey stopped in her tracks when she seen who came into the house with George. Douglas, holding a bouquet of white roses, approached her.

"Um, Journey...you remember Douglas?"

She cut her eye at George for asking such a dumb question. George, knowing that he'd stuck his foot in his mouth, hunched his shoulders apologetically.

"Yes, of course."

"These are for you. I heard you were in town," Douglas said.

Journey grunted, "Um."

"So how are you?"

Overwhelmed, Journey felt outside of herself. "I'll be upstairs, Gwen."

Before Douglas could open his mouth again, she was gone. Leaving him standing with the roses he brought.

Journey flung herself onto the bed and reached for her cigarettes. She did not care one way or the other if someone smelled the telltale odor of the cigarette she puffed on. The nicotine was soothing as it had been her constant companion. For twenty three years one brand or another had been her company. She'd tried quitting but each time it had felt like she'd abandoned her friend. Cigarettes soothed her when she was upset, hung out with her during phone conversations, called to her after a meal, and were always as close as the nearest drugstore. She would have normally gone outside but there were just too many people to pass on the way. There was too much going on downstairs for her to take. Darnel had a new wife who was impossible to hate and for a brief moment after she'd seen the pecan pie uncut on the countertop, Darnel had looked like the father she'd loved. Even felt like it too. Almost.

Then there was the sweetheart of her life walking into the door. For as long as she could remember, she'd loved Douglas, thought she loved him, and hated him. She was nineteen when they'd started to date. Douglas was one of the neighborhood thugs, and she was young and plenty naïve. Had he not pursued her, she would have written him off as another young man seeking the one thing Beatrice had preached to her not to give up. But as Douglas would have it, it was never to be that simple. Journey gave in and thus began years of roller-coaster rides courtesy of him. He was never consistent, or remotely as passionate as one who declared his love for her so vehemently. In the end, they loved without ever knowing one another.

Blowing the smoke through her nose, Journey went over the picture of Douglas in her mind. At six four, he was definitely looking more mature. Had there been some gray in the neatly trimmed beard she saw? She was sure it had been.

Because she'd once loved every inch of him, she'd noticed all of him. Like the fact that he'd let his curly hair grow out. His braids, twisted tightly to the back, lent to his bad boy persona but there was more. His expression was softer now, almost pleading. It was too much to imagine him becoming a man. Picturing him naked, she felt the familiar heat rise from between her legs. She cursed her body and closed her eyes.

When the knocking came, she knew it wasn't Gwen or anyone else. Her body had sensed him before he'd reached her door. She pretended to sleep.

Douglas eased the door open, as she knew he would and tiptoed over to the bed. He knew she wasn't sleeping since smoke still spiraled up from the ashtray. She felt his hand on her face.

"A long time ago, I hurt you didn't I?" he whispered.

Journey sat up and stared at him then slammed her palm against his cheek. Hard.

The sound echoed through the room while her hand print shown white on his cheek. His eyes flashed anger then went soft again.

"I guess I deserved that," he said rubbing his cheek and working the sting out of his jaw. "Will you talk to me now?"

"No."

"How about I talk then?"

Silence from Journey.

"You may not believe me, but I've thought a lot about you. About us."

"There is no us."

"I miss you."

"Get out."

"You don't mean that."

"Get out."

Journey saw defeat on Douglas's face. She felt powerfully in control as he shut the door behind him.

CHAPTER

1 2   For purposes of appearance only, Allison and Malik attended church together as they had nearly every Sunday since they were married. No one needed to know that all his clothes were packed in the trunk of his car. Allison had cleared his side of the closet the previous night. She hadn't spoken a single word since telling him she'd found out his secret and was especially hysterical about the way in which she found out. Aggravated as much by what he did as having been told by Journey, she resented the hell out of her for being the messenger. Malik was also angry with her but knew if not by Journey, then the truth would have come out eventually. In a peculiar way, he was relieved to have it out.

This was the one time since their marriage that Malik was scared. He hadn't known it would hurt so. Although he and Allison had been performing their role of the happily married couple for too long, it still hurt. It didn't matter how big their problems; Allison was his sworn lifemate and his wife. There would be no one at Anthony's house for him to turn over to and breathe the sweet scent of fragranced body soap. There would be no one to tell him which tie went best with which suit. At that moment, Malik would have given anything to be in his bed with Allison next to him. Never mind that she would scoot away more times than not.

Instead he left sitting in the church's parking lot long after he'd lost sight of Allison's car speeding away. He wanted so desperately to go home. "Home," he mumbled closing his eyes against the sting in his eyes. The word tasted funny on his tongue and left a horrible ache in his heart. He started the car and drove slowly to Anthony's house where he would stay until he could get his own place. The thought of living alone brought a fresh ache. The concept ping-ponged from his head, hitting every part of him known and unknown. Malik was sure he couldn't hurt worse if he were set afire. The pain was almost too much. All he could do was pray.

The night before was the worse night Allison could remember having since the night before she and Malik were married. On the eve of her wedding, she had prayed she was marrying the right man. Everything about Malik had felt right. He was young, ambitious and had proven willing to do whatever Allison asked of him within or without reason. He spoiled and pampered her the way she was used to her entire life. Mommy and Daddy adored Malik from the very beginning. The moments after she learned of her husband's unfaithfulness, she began to question all their years together. When she got home from Gwen's, her only mission was to rid herself of him and everything that reminded her of him.

Allison began packing Malik's clothes. Angry at his cheating, she was determined he would take nothing that they'd worked or paid for together. That included luggage. She stuffed his things in garbage bags.

All the time she packed, Allison tried to remember when she'd missed what had so obviously happened. A visual of her Malik's naked limbs entangled with those of her best friend flashed through her mind and sickened her. She swallowed hard to keep from vomiting. She and Kathy had gone to college together and were pledged sorority sisters. They'd roomed together; graduated together, and unbeknownst to Allison, shared the same man. Allison's tears were bitter on her lips as she headed to the shower. Somehow she had to scrub Malik off of her. Not only had he made love to her friend, but made a child as well. He'd given her himself, unprotected. This time Allison did vomit.

Had Malik stopped and tested the mood of his home, he would have known something was amiss. After work, Allison would have a glass of chilled wine to greet him with. There was no coaster on the designated spot and no soft music drifting throughout the house. The absence of music did alert him somewhat since it played whether he or his wife was there or not. It was set to a timer. But he quickly blew it off when he smelled the fragranced bath oils. He dropped his briefcase and hurried into the bedroom.

Malik paid absolutely no attention to the bags strewn around him. All he saw was his wife's glistening nakedness before him. He instantly hardened against his thigh. He could taste her on his tongue. Walking up to her, he held her from behind.

For a moment she let him hold her feeling the bulge of him against her back. Under different circumstances she would give in to him. How could his arms feel so good to her right then? She wondered. It had been months since her body had responded so strongly to his touch.

"I love you," he whispered before she pulled away.

"Did you love her too?"

Malik stepped back while Allison turned to face him.

Oh no, not now, Malik thought. Not like this when she looks so beautiful. "Her who?"

Allison reached for a towel to wrap around her. "Her Kathy."

Malik reached for her, but she pulled away. She'd felt she could fight him, throw something, or spit in his face. But seeing him only made her tired and light-headed.

There was no use coating his tongue with lies. He could not bring himself to lie. "I wanted to tell you but I was afraid you would um…"

Allison completed his sentence. "Leave you?"

Her eyes turned to stone as she waved her hand around the room. "Look around, Malik. Somebody's leaving and you can guess it isn't me."

Malik stood looking dumbfounded around the room. He picked up several of the smaller bags. "I'll leave, but we're going to have to talk."

"You should have talked three years ago."

"I made a mistake, Allison. I never loved Kathy."

The mention of her name from his lips enraged her. "A mistake is leaving the toilet seat up. Malik, ripping my heart out of my chest the way you have is a deliberate fuck up. You make me sick."

Anthony didn't know how the new living arrangements would work out. Malik had surely caught him off guard. "Of course you can stay here, man," he'd told his friend. He couldn't see saying anything but yes. Malik had been a good friend since they'd met through George. That was over twelve years ago. Malik had been there for him and Janelle since Jennie died leaving just him and his young daughter. Since Allison had as little as possible to do with kids, Malik had picked Janelle up from daycare, elementary school and at times from Junior High. Anytime Anthony ran late with one of his clients, he could leave a voicemail on Malik's pager. It was as good as done. Though he hadn't needed him so much since Janelle was older, there were times when he did. He had needed Malik just the prior week when one of the rookie basketball players he represented came to the hotel lobby escorted by two very blond Barbie types. Anthony had from the very beginning wished he'd followed his first mind not to meet the young man in the lounge since Marcus Derry had been a pain in the butt from the start. In the end, he regretted it more. Too much time was wasted. Anthony had felt like a guardian as he scolded and sent Marcus to put on something other than his bathrobe and to dismiss his entourage. Somewhere the line had to be drawn. He was a sports agent, not a babysitter. In the meantime, Janelle waited on the porch steps until Malik could open up the house with the duplicate keys Anthony had made for him. No matter how much he scolded Janelle for her carelessness, the "I forgot my key," scene played out at least twice a month.

Anthony replayed Malik's voicemail back in his mind. He had been too angry to return his friend's call immediately. He'd wanted to pick up the phone and ask what had possessed Malik to do something as stupid as cheating on Allison. Sure, Allison had her ways and could at times be a spoiled brat, but she didn't deserve betrayal. Of all the qualities she lacked, who she was amounted to so much more. Allison undoubtedly loved Malik very much and she was faithful as far as Anthony could tell. He picked up the phone's receiver and dialed Malik's cell phone number but hung up. He would have preferred to leave a message but he was sure Malik would answer.

Before that whole incident with Sean had clouded his judgment of everything, Anthony could have indeed told all these things to Malik. What could he say after what he'd done? He, Anthony, successful single father, financially secure before age forty, faithful church member and once devoted husband, had done the unthinkable. He'd put himself in a position to be molested by a man and a psychotic one at that. Not a man masquerading as a woman, but a for real man. A man who'd he'd considered a good friend until after…

It happened after a meeting he and Sean had regarding a football scout's proposition. They'd discussed the impending contract and later celebrated too hardy at Sean's chic apartment. Anthony, having never been more than a social drinker, felt the affects after his second glass of champagne. His words began to slur as his eyelids collapsed over his eyes. He remembered too late the antihistamines in his bloodstream. Coupled with the alcohol, Anthony's allergy medicine kicked in full force. It was not yet noon so Sean's invitation to the bed in the guest bedroom was quickly accepted.

The low lighting and light jazz never set off any warning bells. The aura of the apartment matched Sean's laid back manner perfectly. Especially since the man was a 6'2" easily 280 pound linebacker. Anthony had remembered thinking how he had to be a ladies' man with his easy spirit and boyish good looks. They'd discussed women often like guys do when they saw some fine body but never in a vulgar way. Mostly Anthony would find himself talking about how lonely he'd been without Jennie and how difficult it was not to compare every woman to her.

It was never meant as an invitation, but just a friend sharing his feeling with a friend. Sean was the perfect listener. Had Anthony known he was gay, bisexual, or whatever, he would have been cautious. But he didn't so he hadn't.

To tell anybody the truth of what happened would sound like a lie since Anthony had the damnedest time believing it himself. He had honestly felt nothing until Sean had started. For a moment, he remembered how good it had felt. Though a long time ago, he and Jennie had made oral sex oftentimes a part of foreplay. He was still remembering the sweet warmth of her mouth when the thought came to him. *Something is very very wrong.* He was not in his home, and Jennie was no more.

The shock of waking up to his friend straddling his legs with his mouth *there* angered him beyond imagination. Though he'd not had a fight since his turbulent youth, he swung. Sean toppled to the floor.

For his mistaken judgment, Sean suffered a broken smile from the force of Anthony's shoe smashing into his mouth. He claimed back injuries from the fall, but to date there'd been no calls from lawyers. There were only threats from Sean. Anthony's voicemail at his office was full of messages; all of them taunting and accusing him of flirting and leading Sean on. One claimed Sean's undying love then an hour later several swearing revenge. Anthony hoped the harassment would end but Sean showed no signs of wearing down. He'd finally had to change his office phone number, and his home phone number was due to be changed. Temporarily, his office had been moved to his home for fear of Sean coming to his job. Moving his office might put a strain on his business, but he reasoned it was necessary. He couldn't have Malik answering the phone as long as Sean was on the warpath.

C H A P T E R

13 Monica blew dust from a stack of videotapes and moved them to a clutter free corner. She held one up and read the title: *Mandy Monkey moves to Mobile.*

Gwen looked over her shoulder at the tape. "That's for the letter M. I have a tape series for each letter of the alphabet. My students would remember the phonics better if they sang along with the songs on the tape."

The subject of Gwen's leaving her job had become a touchy one since she'd stopped teaching. Monica didn't quite know if it were okay to bring it up but took a chance.

"Have the school found another Principal?"

"No, the Assistant Principal is standing in as Acting Principal."

"They still want you to come back?"

Gwen frowned unknowingly. "Yes, and I keep telling them I'm considering it."

"Are you?"

"Am I what?"

"Considering it."

"Sometimes and sometimes not."

"I can tell you miss it. You are or were a great teacher, Gwen. All the kids thought so."

Gwen grew suspicious. "Where is this going Monica? If it's not you then it's George or someone else. I'm getting tired of justifying my every decision."

Monica knew that she should back off, but she'd gotten this far. "Nobody questions your every decision, just that *one.* It is clear how much you miss it."

"I'll indulge you. Tell me, just how do you know?"

"Well, for one thing, you haven't been able to commit to anything else. I mean you renewed your cosmetology license, but you're all ready tired of that. You're getting ready to start this literacy program."

"And?" Gwen cut in.

"I'm just saying, you seem sorta restless since you've stopped teaching."

"Thanks for your concern, but I'll go back when I'm ready."

"You said that months ago."

"Drop it okay, Monnie."

"Sorry."

"Let's talk about something else."

"Okay. I had to tell you something anyway."

"Hold that thought. I think I hear the phone."

Gwen took the steps two at a time. She'd forgotten to bring the cordless with her. She snatched it from its base right before the answering machine clicked on. It was Allison inviting her to lunch. Gwen agreed although she had so much to do. By the sound of her friend's voice, she felt Allison really needed to talk. Monica came into the kitchen as Gwen hung up.

"I'm sorry, but I need to meet with Allison. Can you wait for me? I shouldn't be long. Maybe you can get Journey out of that room."

"No, not me. I'm not bothering Journey. What's so urgent that you have to meet Allison now anyway?"

"I'll tell you later."

Gwen was out the door before Monica could protest. Since Monica was not ready to go home, and she was curious as to why Gwen's presence was so urgent to Allison, she grabbed the remote and began flipping through the channels.

It seemed to Gwen that she hadn't made one green light from her house to the restaurant. At each intersection, she had time to reflect on the event that had led her to take a leave of absence. She could thank Monica for bringing the subject up fresh once more.

The day two years ago was in her mind. School was almost out for the summer and that morning was hot. Gwen remembered being in a good mood. She had scheduled meetings with the parents of the last two students in danger of failing the school year. The first meeting went well and Deidra Michael's mother had accepted the packet of make up work. Gwen sympathized with the child and her mother because Deidra was a bright child. It was just that her asthma kept her out of school so much that it was nearly impossible for her not to miss assignment.

On the other hand was Anthony Denny. His was a different story altogether. Though only in the sixth grade, he sported a diamond in each lobe and various tattoos on his body. He bragged incessantly about being in a gang and openly bullied other children. He was a pain in Gwen's side and as dumb as a rock.

Anthony's mother sat across from Gwen popping her gum loudly. She was full of attitude, sporting a blue bandana and at least six pair of earrings. Every time she moved her head, they clacked loudly one against another. The sound grated on Gwen's nerves.

Still, as she pulled Anthony's folder, she approached the young Miss Denny with the same professionalism as she did the more mature parents. Her experience had taught her that appearances sometimes, if not most, meant nothing.

Gwen poured herself a cup of coffee and offered one as well. The woman refused and for the next five minutes the woman ignored Gwen's report and let her eyes wander lazily around the room.

When at last Gwen got to the part of Anthony's failing, the woman who had up until then sat slouched in her chair bolted upright and glowered accusingly at Gwen.

"You ain't flunking my son. His daddy done bought his graduation suit."

Gwen was calm.

"Have you heard what I've been saying? Anthony hasn't turned in one assignment this year. I've sent letter after letter home with him with no response. I've also tried to phone you on a number of occasions."

"You ain't flunking Anthony," the woman cut in.

"I'm sorry, but at this point I haven't a choice. There's no way he can make up all the assignments. I suggest some extra work over the summer."

Miss Denny stood and pointed in Gwen's face. Instinctively Gwen stood.

"No, bitch! I suggest you change them effes into D's or somin' or I'm gonna kick your ass!"

Gwen reached for the phone to call the security desk when Miss Denny flung the coffee from the desk into Gwen's face. Thankfully, it had cooled some.

At first Gwen couldn't believe the woman was actually crawling over her desk at her. Before she could react, Miss Denny's hands were striking her face. In the mist of the chaos, she could hear Anthony who'd been sitting outside the door. He was shouting, "Mama, whoop that bitch ass good!"

It all was happening so fast, but Gwen managed to push the woman from her. Miss Denny was quick. She fell against the desk, but sprang right back at Gwen. This time when she pounced, her head met the coffeepot in Gwen's right hand.

There was an unnerving shatter and blood everywhere. Security found Miss Denny crying, cursing, and holding her head. The sight of her own blood was the shock she needed to back off Gwen. Gwen stood holding the handle of the broken pot.

Had it not been for one of the secretaries who'd run in seconds before to aid Gwen, the charges the woman sought to press on her would have surely stuck. She would have lost the job she'd worked so hard for.

One week later, Miss Denny pulled up beside Gwen's car in the parking lot. Gwen pulled off just in time. The only damage was a ruined suit from the coffee she'd been holding and a bullet hole through her rear window. Miss Denny had been caught and towed away to jail. Last she heard, Anthony Denny was in the custody of child protective services. The day of the shooting had been her last day at the school. Three days later she miscarried a child she and George had been praying for. Gwen still jumped at sudden loud noises, and hadn't drank coffee since.

📖

There was nothing on TV that Monica hadn't seen at least twice. She took the phone back to the room and began where she and Gwen had left off. She remembered when George had first started building the room onto the house. Gwen had needed extra space to tutor her students away from school. George, Malik, and Anthony had it completed by the end of that summer and she and Gwen had painted it. After the shooting, the room had been shut off from the rest of the house as if were an unwelcomed tumor. There had been no children knocking on the door that George had put in to allow access from the outside. All the posters they'd pinned up had wilted around the edges. She cracked the window and was about to search through another box when the phone rang.

Monica picked up after the fourth ring, positive by then that Journey had no interest in answering it. It was Janelle looking for Gwen. She'd gotten sick and couldn't contact her father to pick her up. Monica told her to hold tight and she would be there.

Monica found Janelle in the nurse's makeshift clinic. She was curled up on a cot with her head facing the wall. She had her knees drawn up tight to her chest. Monica placed a hand on her shoulder.

"Cramps, huh?"

Janelle turned with new tears on her face. "I miss my Mama," Janelle moaned.

Monica leaned down and held her hand. "I know, I know baby. Come on. Let's get you home."

The tears dried some as they climbed into Monica's truck. Janelle was still distraught over having gotten her period.

"Was this the first?" Monica asked softly.

Janelle dropped her head and began to sniffle. Monica reached over and lifted her head. "There is absolutely nothing to be ashamed of. Getting your period just means your body is preparing to become the body of a young woman."

Monica tried to remember if she had felt the same way. She hadn't. In fact, she and some of her fast friends had been waiting for their periods like

Christmas. Their friend Felicia had gotten hers and a pair of breast followed shortly after. Each girl had hoped that they would have the same luck. Monica shook off the thought.

"Don't worry too much. It's not the end of the world. We'll get you home to your dad."

Janelle looked panicked. "I don't want to see him right now. I feel so gross."

"Sometimes it can feel icky but don't you think you should tell him you're out of school?"

"Not yet. If I tell him why, he'll only look scared and try to tell me about what's happening to me." Janelle looked over to Monica. "Believe me, he won't know how. He'll get all weird on me."

Monica laughed at the observation and Janelle cracked a timid smile.

"Okay. I don't see any reason for us to panic him," she said pulling into the parking lot of a store. "I bet they gave you one of those big mountainous school pads didn't they?"

Janelle shifted in her seat and laughed. "It feels more like a pamper."

"I remember. Come on, let's get you something a little less bulky."

Monica picked up two packages of Ultra Thin pads, a couple pair of panties, and a bra that Janelle needed. She blushed as Monica instructed the clerk to ring the items up then hold at the counter what they didn't need right away. She paid and they headed to the bathroom.

"Here are some feminine wipes and a pair of fresh undies. Keep the other pair in your locker just in case. This bra should fit you fine, and I'll be waiting out here for you."

Janelle came out fresh and contented. The ibuprofen she'd taken at the school began to work.

"How about lunch before you go home?"

"Burger and fries?" "All you can eat."

"Cool."

Anthony was home when Monica pulled up. His smile spread as Janelle stepped out. He hugged his daughter and waved Monica out of her vehicle. It was the only time she had seen him in lounging clothes. He looked relaxed in his shorts, sleeveless tank shirt, and sandals. His baseball cap sat atop his neatly cropped hair. There was a shadow of a beard growing on his usually clean-shaven face. He'd also grown a mustache since she saw him last.

Anthony couldn't help notice Monica's long legs. In fact, he'd been distracted since she'd stepped from her truck. She was wearing his favorite color green with high-heeled sandals to match. The rest of her looked just as good as she approached. Her dress barely came past her thigh. He couldn't recall ever seeing her in attire other than jeans.

Anthony was immediately aware of the dirty garden gloves on his hands. He snatched them off wondering how could he have not noticed this woman before. He quickly tried to devise how to keep her from leaving right away.

"Hi, Anthony. How are you?"

"You're fine…I mean, I'm fine."

Monica blushed. "I can see that."

It was Anthony's turn to blush. "Thanks for dropping Janelle off. How'd you come to be by the school?"

"I didn't plan to be anywhere near the school, but Janelle got sick and called Gwen. Gwen was gone, so here I am. We tried calling you but the number has been changed."

"Oh shoot! That's right. We just got the new number today. I have to check on her."

Monica reached out and touched his arm. "Maybe you shouldn't just yet."

"Why not?"

"She got her period," she whispered.

Anthony let go of the doorknob. "So soon? Isn't she too young for that?"

Monica shrugged. "Unfortunately not. Girls menstruate at different ages."

Anthony felt embarrassed having this conversation. Monica could tell and tried to smooth over the subject. "Don't sweat it. We had a girl talk and she's going to be okay."

Anthony arched an eyebrow.

"Don't worry, I didn't get into the whole birds and bees thing. I just told her that her body was reacting normally and that she's growing up. The rest I'll leave to you," Monica assured.

Anthony breathed a sigh of relief. "Thanks. Would you like to stay for a while?" He could have kicked himself as soon as the words were out. "I mean, I got some lemonade freshly squeezed."

"Sure, why not."

Five hours later, Monica still sat in Anthony's den watching the last of a movie. By then, they'd swapped their respective lemonades for a light wine. Janelle stuck her head in. She had changed into her nightclothes.

"Night Daddy."

"Good night, baby."

Monica looked over to say good night, but Janelle tiptoed quickly over to her and gave her a hug. "Thanks, Miss Monica. I had fun. We should do it again."

"Sure Hon, anytime." Monica could scarcely believe those had been her words once they were out. *Anytime* was never reserved for children.

Anthony was pleased how Monica handled the time spent with Janelle. He had tried to involve other women in his daughter's life to no avail. She had taken to no one except Gwen and since then, Monica.

He got up to put another tape in the VCR.

"How did you like the movie?"

"I thought it was good."

Her answer was a little too pat for him. "You okay? Something on your mind?"

"Nothing much except for that movie reminded me of a comment my cousin made popped into my mind."

"Want to talk about it? I'm a good listener."

"It was about my weight although it's not that important."

"Does it bother you? Your weight I mean?"

"Honestly, not often. It has never caused me any health problems and I just like who I am."

Anthony patted her knee. "Good. It doesn't bother me either. I must admit I think it looks especially good to me today."

"Why is that?"

"You're wearing my favorite color."

Monica blushed like a schoolgirl. "You're looking handsome today yourself."

Anthony blushed. "I didn't think you ever looked at me. I did however notice your interest in Sean."

Monica giggled. "You always seemed so reserved."

"Anal?"

"Yes."

"Is that the only reason?"

"Honestly?"

Anthony refilled their wineglasses while Monica pondered her answer. "I'd never seen you with a woman, so I assumed you might be gay."

Anthony choked on his drink. "Gay?"

"Don't take it personal. I realize how narrow-minded I was, but now that we've spent some time together, I feel bad for having thought that of you."

"Don't. I asked for your honest opinion. I just didn't expect that."

"What did you think I would say?"

"Maybe that my having a teenager bothered you."

Monica sipped from her glass. "I never thought of it," she lied.

"Okay now that we've had somewhat of a first date, what now?"

Monica wondered if it were the wine. "Are you always this forward?"

Anthony raised an eyebrow. Monica thought he looked so sexy.

"Sure, I am."

She sipped her drink and stood. The timing was bad, but she had to get away from him. Sitting that close made her heart pitter-patter.

"I'll leave my number with you and you can call me."

"I will. Please, let me walk you out."

Anthony took her hand gently at the door. "Thanks for spending time with us."

"Anytime," was all she managed to say. There was that word again. The evening was ending so much better than her morning had.

Janelle peeked her head around the corner and smiled. Monica waited until Anthony reached for the door before she winked at the child. On the way out, she and Anthony brushed shoulders.

Oh my goodness! He smells so good too! She thought as she stepped out of the door.

CHAPTER

14 Allison never made it inside the restaurant. Gwen had sat in the passenger seat of Allison's car until the tears had slowed enough for Gwen to feel comfortable enough with Allison driving herself home. Lunch with Allison had turned out to be nothing more than Gwen sitting on the side of the bed alternately passing tissues and holding Allison while the tears and snot kept coming. Gwen had thought she would go mad if Allison's tears would not run out. She had driven to her friend armed with prayers and the most comforting words she could muster, but Allison had depleted Gwen's arsenal within the hour. Pulling the covers up over Allison, Gwen almost felt insulted. She should have been the one sleeping angelically instead of Allison. Yes, thank God Allison had finally felt better, but not before transferring all that anger and mush onto Gwen.

"Maybe if I could just grieve. Cry away all the held up tears, bottled up fears," Gwen thought as she slammed on her brakes. She had almost run through a red light. In the rearview mirror, she could see the disapproval on the face of the driver behind her. "So what," she mumbled pulling into the drugstore's parking lot.

In the store, she bought a cup of hazelnut coffee, the first cup she had bought since the incident. She carried her three creamers and two Equals to the counter and paid the cashier. She grabbed a book of matches and headed to the car where Journey had left a carton of cigarettes minus two packs on the back seat. Menthol lights like the kind she used to smoke until she found out she and George were expecting their first child. After years of silent hoping, it was happening.

She and George had been a happy couple before the pregnancy but even moreso afterward. If ever there were such a thing as a match made in heaven, theirs was it. They had known each other since the day George's family had moved across the street from them.

Gwen and Journey had stood watching George and his little brother for the better part of the morning until Beatrice caught them and shooed them away from the window. Gwen was six years old.

Marlin, George's younger brother passed nails to his brother who hammered them into the wood of the garage. The basketball goal they constructed was but a mere blue plastic milk crate with the bottom cut out.

George was a tall, lanky eleven year old and his brother a shorter but no less gangly nine year old. Darnel walked over offering a hand, but George had politely but firmly declined. His pride was plentiful even then.

Gwen could still remember when only her diary knew of her secret crush on George. She was nine years old when Journey found where she had written: *Roses are red, Violets are blue, I love George, and he loves me too.*

Journey had thought it hilarious to give George the note and because she did, she and Journey had fought like strangers until Beatrice beat them both. Gwen didn't think it was fair for her to get a whipping since Journey had won. Darnel, who usually declared the winner, said he couldn't tell.

After that day, Gwen had to avoid George for weeks, which proved difficult since he played basketball in his driveway every day after school. She would have gone on avoiding him except for one day he was waiting by her back door for her. She nearly peed her pants.

Back in the present, Gwen took a sip of the coffee and lit a cigarette. The combination was as settling as she remembered. She smiled thinking of how sweet George had been to her that day.

"Hi, Shorty," he'd said to her.

Gwen had stood there with her voice caught in her windpipe.

"I liked your poem."

Still no words from her throat.

"You hear me?"

She nodded dumbly.

"Just wanted to say thanks and to tell you that since you too little to be my girlfriend, you can still be my friend."

When Gwen's tongue came unglued from the roof of her mouth all she could say was, "I'm not that little."

George took her hand. "I'ma look out for you. Like a sister okay?"

"Okay."

Gwen was happy to follow George to the front door, but she was the only happy one. Marlin, who'd been standing across the street waiting on his brother apparently didn't appreciate the camaraderie. He picked up a smooth rock and launched it at Gwen. She felt the sharp sting right above her left eye before she felt the warmth on her skin and the salt-rust taste of blood on the corner of her mouth. She dropped George's hand and ran over and punched Marlin square in the nose. George wouldn't let him hit her back since it was only fair that she hit him back. She may have had a bloody brow, but Marlin had a bloody nose to match.

Gwen reached up and stroked the spot where her eyebrow stopped abruptly then continued smoothly to the end of her eye. That tiny scar served as a reminder of that day when George promised to take care of her. And indeed he had.

It seemed before she knew it, George was eighteen and gone off to college. Three years after, he'd come home. His mother had fallen ill.

By then, Gwen was sixteen with crushes on boys her own age but she would see him all the time with some of the older girls in the neighborhood. Sometimes she would catch snippets of Jean and Journey's phone conversation the summers they visited. They would talk bad about some of the girls Gwen would see hanging around George, who had during his high school days, gone from plain George to Big George.

It wasn't until Gwen's senior year of high school that he took notice of her. After her prom, Gwen's date, a popular boy name Bryce drove the rented Camaro to the Lane. The lane was where the fast girls went with their boyfriends to make out. Gwen knew this but decided she would go with the flow. She'd come close to sex but never as close as Bryce was getting. At the last moment, she couldn't fake it. She was scared out of her mind and definitely not ready. Unfortunately Bryce didn't see things her way. He cranked the monster engine and left her walking toward home in her fitted lilac dress with the shoes dyed to match. She thought she would cry but didn't. Instead, she smoothed the wrinkles from the dress that moments before had been up to her hips. She prayed with each step that she safely make it the two miles home.

Gwen's prayers were answered when George ran up toward her.

"I thought that was you. Why in the world are you walking?"

Gwen had to laugh. "My choice was to put up or get put out."

George smiled awkwardly and wrapped his jacket around her. "So you never?"

"None of your business, George."

"Aw'right, aw'right. You don't have to look at me like that. Let me take you home."

Gwen agreed and climbed into his truck. The girl he was with whose name he called Shena rolled her eyes when George made introductions. Judging by the steamy windows, Gwen could guess why. They rode in stony silence until George pulled in front of his date's home. Shena was pissed.

Gwen reached for the door, but Shena couldn't wait. She climbed over Gwen kicking George in the process. She slammed the door and didn't look back at Gwen who was climbing out of the truck. Gwen chased her up the walk until Shena ducked inside. George caught up with her and had to carry her back to the truck.

He was out of breath trying to stuff her back into the seat.

"Sit down, girl. How are you going to fight with that party dress on?"

Gwen was distraught over her entire night. She began babbling. "This night is supposed to be special," she wailed. "Journey told me not to go with Bryce and here it is I end up almost walking home on MY prom night! And look," she shouted pointing to the footprint in the lap of her dress, "do you know how much my mama paid for this dress? Beatrice is gonna kick my ass when she sees this."

George frowned at her. "You look too pretty to be talking like that."

It could have been the way he complimented her that calmed her, although she felt embarrassed by the way he stared at her.

"Besides, Beatrice ain't home. She and Tilly left about an hour ago. I saw Douglas sneaking in the back door with Journey."

Gwen knew if she went home, what she would find. Journey would no doubt be *borrowing* her old room to entertain her company. The same room Gwen inherited fair and square once Journey left for college. Gwen was in no mood to hear her sister's activities. With Beatrice gone, she would no doubt hold nothing back on Douglas. There would be banging and hollering all through the hallway.

George read her thoughts. "You can hang out at my house. Since Mama died, it's just Daddy and me. He don't care."

📖

"Daddy! I'm in my room!" George shouted when he opened the back door. George Senior called for him to lock the door and that was it. She followed George to his room where he passed her a pair of his shorts and a tee shirt. They watched TV and ate popcorn on the bed.

During a commercial, Gwen looked around at all the photos of George with dozens of smiling girls.

"Dang. You sure keep a lot of girlfriends."

George chewed a handful of popcorn. "All of them girls aren't girlfriends. Even if they were, none of them are as pretty as you."

Gwen was ready to tell him that plenty of them were but he had moved next to her with his breath close to her ear.

"You're beautiful. You always have been," he whispered.

Gwen blushed and leaned against his strong chest. One of his hands made its way under her shirt. The heat from his palm and her body made her gasp.

From that point on, he was gentle with her. Gentle kisses, soft touches, warm tongue in her mouth. He was experienced where she wasn't and she was bold and unafraid where he thought she wouldn't be. George covered her mouth with his hand when he entered her and removed it when her teeth clamped less tightly down on his fingers. She rocked with him until it was over and he lay panting beside her. When he was sure she wouldn't cry, they did it again.

Afterwards, Gwen sneaked across the street, shoes in hand, and dress dangling over her arm. George watched her the whole way.

When she got home, she laid in Tilly's bed thinking about how George had filled her with himself. She lay there until Journey peeked in on her.

"I saw you," she accused.

"So, I heard you and Douglas."

Journey looked hard at her, unsure if she was comfortable with this more assertive Gwen. Gwen thought her eyes were almost sad when she spoke again. "You're not a kid anymore are you?"

"I'm seventeen, but you're still my big sister."

"Good night, little sister."

"Good night, Journey."

A month or so after prom night, Gwen left for college. She and George continued sleeping together whenever she was in town. She had other boyfriends but sex was the best with her first love. Foolishly she expected it not to end, didn't even think about it until she entered her junior year. That was the year George got a steady girlfriend. He'd been so kind while telling her how much he really liked the girl. Neecy was her name. Things were getting serious.

Gwen couldn't figure why, but she was angry. So angry that she fell into the arms of one of George's good friends. Two months later, Jean took her to abort the child she carried. Thinking that it was George's child, Jean wouldn't even speak to him. Gwen had let her believe it too. Afterall, she'd done the unthinkable. The man whose arms she'd fallen into had been no other than Douglas, the love her sister's life.

Gwen's secret had shaped so much of her life afterward. The guilt she carried from the having slept with Douglas then even worse having the abortion was an ever constant souvenir. It was because of this that Gwen had taken her miscarriage as a sign of punishment. She further punished herself by leaving the job she loved. Anthony Denny's mother had given her the perfect excuse to exercise the punishment she deemed due her. Someday she would tell Journey her secret and beg her forgiveness because it was the right thing to do…because Douglas loved Journey and was at last capable of loving her. Finally because Journey still loved him. Yes, she would tell, but only if she had to. It was just that the burden had grown too heavy. This wasn't like any old boyfriend. This was Douglas. The same man that she and Journey had staked out to find his whereabouts. The same Douglas she had stood as lookout for as he and Journey sneaked under the porch to make out. The one who slipped her promised dollars as they both came out muddy with twigs and rocks in their hair. How many times had she stood watch for Beatrice for them?

It was selfish of her to want Journey to know only so that Gwen could hope to absolve herself of the guilt she carried. The exchange she knew would not be a fair one. Guilt for her sister's pain. There was no scale in the world to balance that.

Gwen stubbed out the cigarette and went back inside the store. She bought two over the counter home pregnancy tests and received a bargain. They were buy one get one free. On the way home, she smoked another cigarette realizing that if the test were positive, it would be her last.

George was home waiting outside for her. She could tell by the look in his eyes and the way he stood rocking from his toes to the balls of his feet that he was excited. She wished she felt the same with her nerves running amok. He scooped her in his arms and kissed her deeply.

Confusion registered on his face as he tasted coffee and tobacco smoke. He didn't question her though.

"Baby, guess what?"

Gwen wanted to hear but she had to get to the bathroom. If she didn't, she would lose her nerve.

"Sorry, baby. Hold that thought. I have to pee."

George's face drooped like a child holding a ruined surprise. *That woman has to pee at the most inopportune times,* he thought as she passed him.

Gwen tore open the package and peed in the designated spot. The urine seeped slowly over to the plus and minus sign. It took less than a minute before the plus sign began to turn darker blue. She didn't bother with the other test since the one confirmed what she had felt. Three times that week she'd vomited during the light of the early morning before anyone woke up. Her period, which came every tenth day of every month, was a no show. She estimated her pregnancy at about ten weeks. Until that day, she had been too chicken to use a pregnancy test. Both scared to know, and afraid to jinx it.

Gwen hurried and washed her hands and slipped the test into her pocket. She pondered a while for a reason to stall for time. Again she glanced the second test then dismissed it. The coffee had gone through her like a freight train leaving her with no pee left in her bladder.

To George, those few minutes were like ten forevers. He heard her footsteps and got excited again. Gwen shared his excitement for an altogether different reason.

"Okay, what's got you so excited and hurry because I have something to tell you too."

George tried to stall too. "You first."

"No, you."

"Okay, okay. I registered for school today. I'm going back to finish up them last few semesters to get my degree."

Gwen wrapped her arms around his neck. He squeezed her tight.

"I'm so proud of you!" she squealed in his arms. He didn't let her go right away.

"Now, you," he whispered in her ear.

"You're going to be a daddy."

George pulled himself from her embrace and looked down at her. "I'm sorry. Did I squeeze you too tight? How do you know? Are you sure?"

She laughed and pulled the square box from her pocket. "It says right here we're pregnant."

George punched his fist in the air. "Hot damn! We did it!"

Gwen hooted as he danced her around the front yard. There were curious glances from passing motorists.

"Oh my God. Thank you Jesus. Oh God thank-you. Please let it be a son!"

Gwen kissed him full on the mouth. They stayed that way for a long time. When their lips parted she saw a tear roll from her husband's eye. She knew they were happy tears but wanted to hear him laugh for reassurance. "God has truly blessed us with a miracle, but I'm telling you now. If the baby is a boy, we are not naming him George."

George's smile covered his whole face as he lifted her over the threshold. "Baby, you can name our son whatever you like."

C H A P T E R

15 Although Allison spoke nearly every day with Gwen, she avoided going to her house and limited calls to the mornings and late night when Journey was mostly out. In the past weeks, when she needed Gwen's encouragement more than ever, she didn't care if Journey answered the phone or not. She finally realized there was no danger since Journey ignored the ringing phone. The day of Allison's first visit to the doctor brought a new wave of depression. Without Malik beside her to share her feelings of having a life growing inside her, she needed to talk to someone, but not just anyone. She needed to talk to Gwen.

Journey opened the door and for the first time ever she didn't have an icy look or a salty comment to offer. Allison looked like hell and Journey knew she ought to apologize.

The words tumbled all over each other. "I'm sorry for what I said and the way I said it."

Allison waved her off. She had thought she hated Journey but standing there listening to her attempt a genuine apology; she knew she didn't hate this woman. In fact, since she'd had so much time to herself to think, it was she who'd provoked the fire in Journey that day. At first she couldn't admit to herself that she'd always been jealous of Journey. As far back as high school and especially after Journey forged an extremely successful career as a military officer.

Journey had always commanded respect as much in uniform and as a civilian. Journey had something Allison herself wanted—respect without whining or manipulation. Amazing also to Allison was how Journey had done it all without becoming snobbish or condescending. People still loved and drew near to her. Even yet, she suspected Journey knew of her jealousy but what she didn't know that along with the jealousy there was surely a mingling of high esteem and admiration.

"I must really look like hell for you to be apologizing."

"You want me to answer that?"

Allison glanced at Journey then to the mirror on the wall. "No, I don't want you to answer that."

Allison found her feet glued to the place in front of the mirror. "Mirror mirror on the wall, who's the fairest of them all?"

Journey was surprised when Allison didn't flinch away from her touch. She allowed Journey to lead her to the couch.

"Choose your poison, Allie. I think over the past weeks I've bought some of everything. I got a stash in my room second to none."

"Anything strong, but smooth."

Journey disappeared and came back as Allison took off her light jacket. She shook her head. "I can't give you this drink. You're pregnant."

Allison smiled a crooked grin. "Oh, I almost forgot. Of all people, you would be the first to notice."

"I should have noticed before. You got that damned pregnant woman glow."

Allison snapped the elastic front of her skirt. "I bought this to get used to the idea."

"That elastic will give you away every time."

Journey stared into her glass then spun a tornado with the ice cubes and her finger.

The room was thick with silence. "Look, Allison. Again, I'm sorry. You didn't deserve what happened. Tilly let it slip about Malik and when you started in on me that day, I jumped smooth into bitch mode."

"I should have known. Tilly never could keep her mouth shut could she?"

"Not old diarrhea mouth."

Allison's bottom lip quivered uncontrollably and she began to cry. "You want to know something?"

Journey didn't but couldn't say so.

"Deep down, I knew."

Journey couldn't think of any way to console her so she gave her the drink. "Just a sip couldn't hurt."

That seemed to make her cry harder. Journey pulled her onto her shoulder for what felt like hours. She finally sniffed and pulled away. The moment wasn't as awkward as it could have been.

"Who would have thought you would be sitting here patting my back while I cry on your shoulder?"

Journey smiled and smoothed Allison's hair down. "You're a good person. Sometimes a little different, but you don't deserve to be in pain. None of us do."

"Pain? That's just the beginning. Try confused. Look at me. I'm pregnant and my husband is staying with one of his best friends. What am I supposed to do?"

Journey drained the drink half full. "If I had the answers I wouldn't be hiding out at my sister's house eight hundred plus miles away from my life."

"Hide? You? I can't see you hiding from anything."

"Me? Shoo-oot. I probably would have hid from you if Gwen weren't downstairs teaching her literacy class. You know how she hates to be interrupted."

"Well thanks. Eventhough I cornered you into it."

"Don't mention it. At least you made me feel useful. By the way, pregnancy looks good on you."

Allison looked at her mockingly.

"Well it does. I'm sure even better when your hair is all fixed and mascara isn't caked to your eyelids."

Journey hugged Allison while she smoothed circles on her back with the palm of her hand. "See, I got you to smile. Seriously though, I am here if you need me. And I'm not just blowing sunshine up your ass."

Allison felt better. "Me too. Maybe I can return the favor."

Gwen's voice came from the kitchen. "Whoever is passing out sunshine, I'll take some. I'm not sure I'll take it in the exact place described." She almost gagged on her orange juice when she saw the pair on the couch. "Tell me the world ain't ending."

Allison straightened her clothes and pulled out a pocket mirror with the logo: *Early detection is the best protection.* The mirror with its pink painted on ribbon was given to her with her mammogram. The words meant early detection of breast cancer but seemed to signify so much more in her life. Where was the early detection in her marriage? She asked herself and nearly started to cry again. The doorbell rang slicing through the emotional tension of the room. Allison opened the door for the distraction. She was met with a bouquet of flowers where a head should have been.

"Journey Butchard?" the flowers asked.

"One moment."

Journey reached for the clipboard in the gentleman's hand. Once one of his hands was freed, she could see the smiling face behind it.

"Someone must really love you. I've been out here four times but today you got two bouquets and a plant."

Journey smiled her best smile. "You married cutie?"

The question caught him off guard.

"No ma'am, but I will be soon."

"Good. Congratulations." Journey took the plant from the porch step and the card from his hand. "What's your name?"

"Kerry, ma'am."

"Okay Kerry. Take those home and tell…what's your fiancé's name?"

"Kathy."

"Tell Kathy how wonderful she is and give her those."

"Thanks ma'am, I will."

Journey shut the door.

"You should have told him to watch out for all Kathy's." Allison dropped her voice to a spooky alto. "They are ve-ee-ry dangerous."

Gwen slapped her arm playfully. "You a trip." To Journey she smiled. "From Douglas?"

"Probably."

"That makes every day this week doesn't it?"

"Quit grinning like a toothpaste commercial, Gwen. I'm not going out with him."

"Must be genuine. Look at all the flowers."

Journey passed the plant to Allison. "Here, for you and the baby."

"I'm just saying," Gwen interjected.

"I'm not discussing this." Journey walked toward the stairs. "Don't say any-thing Gwen. Not nothing."

"Okay, just don't retreat back upstairs. I need some cheering up and heard you were the sunshine lady."

"Very funny, but I mean it. I am not going to discuss you know who."

 "Alright. We're moving right along. What's this I hear about a baby?" Gwen asked.

Allison rubbed her only slightly swollen belly. "That would be me. I'm pregnant."

"Oh my goodness. Congratulations. Does your well you know."

"Does Malik know is what she's trying to ask."

Gwen nudged Journey hard. "I don't need an interpreter. She knew what I was saying."

"No, he doesn't. He's been calling every day but I won't take his calls."

"You going to tell him?"

"It isn't like I can exactly keep it from him."

"You know Gwen is pregnant too," Journey blurted out.

"You kidding right?"

Gwen smiled an answer.

"Oh my goodness. Our kids are going to be the same age. Congratulations. I know George must be ecstatic."

Journey rolled her eyes. "Beyond, if you can imagine that."

"Oh stop teasing about George. You're happy too."

"Oh I am very happy for you and George." Journey patted her stomach. "I'm just glad the shit isn't contagious."

"I think you would make a good mother, Journey," Allison commented.

"Yeah? In what life?"

"Don't tell me you don't think about it sometimes."

"Honestly, I don't. I guess I used to, but shit. I'm too old now."

"No you're not. I heard about this lady," Gwen started.

"Uh uhn, Gwen. Don't go telling me all about some ancient ass woman who decided to have a baby. If I were to have a baby within the next couple years, hell. He or she'll be grown just in time to change my Depends."

"You so crazy."

"Hey, have anybody seen Monica?" Gwen asked.

"I called that hussy yesterday and I got her machine."

"She didn't tell you?" Allison looked surprised.

"Tell us what?"

"That she and Anthony have been spending quite a lot of time together."

"Bullshit!"

"No, seriously."

Gwen shook her head. "Nope, not Monica. She would have hightailed it right over here and told me everything."

"Believe it."

Gwen was unconvinced. "How do you know?"

"Duh! Malik is staying there with Anthony."

"I thought you said you haven't talked to Malik."

"I haven't. I just take an occasional drive by Anthony's house and I've seen Monica's truck a lot."

"How occasional?"

Gwen pushed Journey's shoulder lightly. "Dang, Journey."

"Just asking. Is it like occasional twice a week, or occasional every day."

"The latter."

"I knew it. So why won't you just talk to him?"

"Why don't you talk to Douglas?"

"Touché. If I do, will you talk to Malik?"

"You make this sound like a game. This is my marriage we're talking about."

"I know what's at stake. I also know that Malik's a good guy albeit he was stupid to do what he did. I may be insensitive at times, but I could see you and he were happy at least most of the time. Am I lying?"

"He cheated on me, Journey."

"Yes he did. And now what? Do you still love him?"

"You just don't get over something like this just like that." Allison snapped her fingers for emphasis.

"Tell me this. If it's none of my damned business, feel free to say so. Are you worried about what people will say about you?"

"What does that have to do with anything?"

"I'm just curious."

"No. I'm worried that every time I look at my husband, all I'm going to be able to think about is him with her."

"Are you thinking of divorcing him?" Gwen asked.

"Honestly Gwen. Sometimes."

"What about marriage counseling?"

"I'm not the one who got caught cheating."

"What if you were?" Gwen challenged.

"I'm not."

"But what if you were. Would you want Malik to talk to you?"

"I don't know."

Journey was watching the debate with interest. She joined in, "Well why don't you go out and cheat and find out."

"Journey!"

"Hell why not? Oh I forgot, you're pregnant."

"Even if I weren't. I take my marriage very serious."

"Good. You should, but I bet there's a one somebody in that office of yours that makes even your snooty ass moist."

Allison cracked a small smile.

"Hah! I'm right aren't I? I see your ass smiling over there. How fine is he? I might want to meet him."

Allison and Gwen couldn't help laughing at Journey's antics. "You know, I don't know where Beatrice got you from. You are just plain crazy."

"Shit, I just thought you all need to laugh. Hell, it's too stuffy in here. I left Denver to get away from all the seriousness." Journey put her hand on her hip. "I done ate enough out of sorrows pots and pans!"

Monica walked inside the living room. "Dang, y'all in here laughing so hard you can't open the door."

"Child, Gwen just talked you up."

"Look at here. It lives. I guess you decided to come out of that room. And looking real cute today too. You got your hair done?"

"Yes I did. Gwen took pity on me and scrubbed my scalp and groomed me right nice today. Speaking of cute, you don't look so bad yourself."

"Thank you. I feel cute too."

"Well, you should."

"Now what I miss. I want to laugh too."

Gwen scooted over so Monica could sit. "Not until you tell us what got you out of jeans."

"I guess I can tell you. I've been seeing somebody."

"Would that somebody be Anthony?" Allison asked.

"How did you know?"

"Never mind how she knows. Is it?"

"Yes."

"I told you he wasn't gay."

"And I admit you were right."

"So?"

"So nothing. We've been just trying to get to know each other."

Journey was getting impatient. "Cut to the point. Do you like him?"

Monica was blushing. "I do. I think he's nice."

"Nice? That's all?"

"I don't know yet. Right now it's all kind of weird. All this time we've been seeing one another and now, it's different. I don't know. It's just too weird to describe. I just know I like him."

Monica glanced over at Allison then down at her hands. "There's something else. I know in the past, Allison that you and me haven't seen eye to eye on a lot of things, but Malik asked me to come over and talk to you. I told him I would be the last one you would listen too, but I just want to keep my word."

"Don't worry about it. Thanks though."

"I'm not trying to get in your business, but the man is a wreck. What you choose to do is your business, but just so you know."

"I appreciate your telling me."

"I also want to say, I'm sorry. I hate to see the two of you apart even if we don't all the time get along. I want to see you get through this. I wouldn't wish this situation on even you."

"Thanks, Monica."

"That's from the heart."

"We all feel the same way. I pray that your marriage will not end like this," Gwen added. "Believe it or not, I was nearly in the same situation and it took a long time for me to get over. Sometimes I still feel like I'm getting over it."

"Big George?" Every voice in the room asked.

"Between us, yes. I would never mention this except I want you to know that I'm not just all talk when it comes to your situation. I know what you're going through."

Monica sensed the gravity of what was to come and excused herself. She saw the barely visible nod of thanks from Gwen. Journey felt it too.

Monica pulled Journey into the kitchen. "We'll be right back."

Monica draped an arm around Journey's shoulder.

"What?" Journey asked.

"I just seen George at Anthony's."

"So?"

"So, Douglas was with him and I overheard them talking. He's coming over."

"Really?"

"Yes. The fight George taped last night should just about be off and I didn't want you to be caught off guard."

"Thanks, girl. I'm not ready to talk to Douglas just yet."

"Well, how about we go down to the VFW for happy hour. We can have a couple drinks and talk about whatever."

"Good idea. I'll get my purse. You drive since I'm already half drunk. Allison's been crying on my shoulder and the more she cried, the more I drank."

"Allison and you?"

"She's not so bad. It just took something like this for me to see it."

"You're right. She isn't. If you think she's a mess, you should see Malik."

"I'll meet you in the car."

Journey ran upstairs to grab her purse. "I think Douglas might be coming over with George, so I'm going out for a while," she informed Gwen on her way out.

"Did you eat something?"

"I'll grab something while I'm out."

"If you forget, I'll keep dinner warmed for you."

"Thanks, Gwen. Love you."

"Love you too."

"One question before you leave," Allison looked up. "Do you still love him? I mean Douglas."

"I'm afraid I do. See you later and take care of yourself."

"Thanks again."

"Anytime."

CHAPTER

1 6 Allison sat at the kitchen table chopping vegetables for the stew Gwen was making. Gwen wiped her hand on the dishcloth and sat down across from her. "Feeling better?"

"Some."

"Good."

"Gwen?"

"Yes?"

"I have a confession. I don't want you to stop me or look at me funny when I tell you this. Promise?"

"Sure, Allison."

"I didn't make Malik leave because of what he did. I did it because of something I did."

Gwen picked up the glass in front of Allison to refill it.

"No, don't get up. I need to tell somebody, and I trust you Gwen." Allison laid a hand atop Gwen's. "We've been friends for a long time, and never once have I felt I couldn't talk to you about anything. I don't know why I need you to know but I just do."

"Okay, Allison."

"I've known Kathy since college and I've always known how much she wanted Malik. That was partly the reason he appealed to me so much then. It was like a game except I didn't play fairly. She loved Malik, and I didn't. I was in love with someone else. A young man named Patrick. He was my true first love, but. Allison paused to catch her breath. 'There's always a but somewhere isn't it?"

"What's the but?"

"Patrick is white. White and everything else that goes along with the 90210 crap. He's rich, with a high social, and politically connected. Needless to say, I'm none of those. In a perfect world none of this would matter. It would simply be that two people fell in love. During college we swore that we would let nothing keep us apart. Foolish huh?"

Gwen was stunned. "But I don't understand. Interracial couples are marrying everyday."

"Yeah, but not us. His family would die if he brought me home and Mommy and Daddy wouldn't be too thrilled with me either. I'd be lying to you if I said I didn't love this man. I mean not because he's white or anything so superficial as that, but because I just did. And at times I believe I still do."

"Allison that was a long time ago, baby."

"That's not all. You know how we sit around and talk about all the lying, cheating brothers in this world? All you have to do is rent a movie, or read in a book all about the infidelities of our men. All our lives we've heard somewhere that men are dogs and it seemed the word dog was extra stern when describing our men. But what of us women?"

"What do you mean? Infidelity is no worse from either sex."

"Oh but it feels like it. You remember when you asked me earlier if it were me, would I want Malik to talk to me?"

"Yes."

"I couldn't answer because it is me. I didn't stop seeing Patrick throughout my marriage and it hasn't been easy with Malik trusting me the way he has. Secret trips, one lie after another. I wanted to end it so many times but I couldn't muster the courage until recently when Patrick divorced. He gave me an ultimatum. Leave Malik, or end our affair. With Malik gone, I thought this would be the perfect opportunity except I didn't count on missing him the way I do. Somewhere I stopped loving the dream and started loving the reality. I was not some Cinderella waiting for Prince Charming to realize he loved me more than any thing in the world and come to my rescue. My prince was here already—right beside me, trusting me, and loving me. While all the while I pushed him further and further away. I hated him for being who he wasn't instead of loving him for who he is. Kathy was simply an opportunist trying to get back what she felt I'd spitefully stolen from her. She had no right to sleep with my husband, but I had no right to sleep with someone else's."

"Dang."

"I know. It sounds so unreal to me now. I can't believe it was me. I don't even know if I could stand for Malik to look at me with that guilty look on his face. When all the time, I'm as guilty or more guilty than he is."

Gwen leaned back in her chair. "I had no idea."

"I know, and I don't expect you to pacify me and tell me it's going to be okay. I know that's not you. I just needed to tell someone I could trust and you're the only person I know that I could. You must think I'm an awful person now?"

"No, Allison I don't. I can't understand why it is that everyone seems to think I'm infallible. I've made mistakes; some of which will come full circle. But I can't keep punishing myself for what's in the past. To the best of my ability, by God's grace I try to live my life the right way. The way He deems me too, but don't for one second think I'm in any position to judge. George hasn't been the perfect husband but neither have I been the perfect wife."

"I'm glad I talked to you."

"Are you going to see this Patrick person again?"

"No. It's been over a year now."

"Then it's time to move on."

"And tell Malik?"

"Ooh, that's a tough one. I honestly don't know if you should tell him or not tell him. I suggest you pray over it and give it some serious thought. I'm sure when the time comes, you'll know what to do."

"You're right. I just appreciate you listening."

"As long as I got a pair of ears, you're welcome to them."

"I think I better go home before it gets too late. This baby in me has me tired all the time."

"Call me tomorrow?"

"First thing."

"Okay, and remember you'll be in my prayers."

"And you in mine."

The friends embraced at the front door. "Thank you, Gwen."

"Don't mention it."

📖

Anthony leaned against the chest of drawers. He decided to try at least once more to talk some sense into Malik's head.

"Man, I'm not saying don't go. All I'm saying is it might be too soon."

"It's been long enough. I have to go over there and talk to Allison before the both of us are too stubborn to say anything at all."

"I just think you might be being a little hasty. It's not like you all's other arguments. This isn't about who didn't balance the check book last month."

"Believe me, Anthony. I appreciate all you've done for me. I don't want you to feel like I have to do this because I'm in your house. I would go over there just the same if I were staying in a hotel."

"I know that. It never crossed my mind that you felt unwelcome here. You can stay as long as you need to."

"Thanks, but it's time."

"What are you going to say?"

"I don't know. I guess I'll tell her I'm sorry and I want to come home."

"And if she says no?"

"She can't say no."

"Com'on man, you don't really believe that do you?"

"Anthony, it's my house too."

"Yeah, but."

"No buts. If she says no, then I'll just make her see things clearly. I'm not leaving my home. It's just as much mine as it is hers. I shouldn't have left."

Anthony stretched his neck from left to right.

"Don't do that."

"Do what?"

"You know that silly habit of yours that you do when you're biting your tongue."

"What silly habit you talking about?"

"How long have we been friends, Anthony?"

"A long time."

"Then if you got something to say then say it."

"Okay then, I think you're setting yourself up for a big let down. I don't know how I'd feel if I'd ever found out Jenny cheated on me. I'd be angry for a long time."

"That's right, you don't know. Allison isn't Jenny."

"She's a woman who has been cheated on."

"Stop using that word. It makes me sound like some kind of player."

"How about a nicer word, like maybe betrayed."

Anthony slammed the suitcase shut. "You don't know everything."

"Then tell me. I'm not judging you, I'm just trying to understand where you coming from. Maybe you should think of how Allison feels instead of all about you."

"I know how Allison feels."

"How?"

"Because Allison betrayed me once upon a time."

"Naw, man."

"Oh yeah. And I didn't put her out of our house. In fact, I never even mentioned it to her. I just thought that if I waited it out, she would end it."

"Did she?"

"How the heck am I supposed to know?"

"The same way you knew she was cheating, you know if she's not."

"There goes that word again."

"Com'on man, cheat? Betrayed? What's the difference?"

Malik was exasperated. "What was the question again?"

"I asked if you think she ended her affair."

"How come it's an affair when Allison did it and it's cheating when I did it?"

Anthony started to stretch again but stopped. "I'm sorry, man. Do what you have to do. My door is open if things don't work out. I hope for your and Allison's sake, it does."

"Thanks. Now let's talk about something else."

"Aw'ight."

"So what's up with you and Monica?"

"Now you all in my business," Anthony joked.

"Don't be shame now. I hear the two of you carrying on in there. Laughing and giggling like teenagers."

Anthony felt selfish talking about himself amidst Malik's problems.

"So?" Malik pressed.

"It's weird right now. I can't really describe it. I just know I like her a lot. She's a lot of fun."

"She's attractive too."

"I think so."

"You should."

"I do."

"I'm just saying, if it's right…don't mess it up. You a good brother and as far as I can see, Monica's a good woman. She and Allison can't be alone in a room for five minutes, but I think she's cool."

"I appreciate that."

Malik lifted the borrowed suitcase from the bed.

"Okay, I think I'm ready."

"Let me help you with those bags. One thing."

"What?"

"You um, well you look like a man who is desperate."

Malik glanced at his reflection in the mirror. The shadow of a beard had grown in full. His eyes were red and puffy from crying. "Dang. I do look pretty bad."

"Yeah, you want to get her back. Not scare the heck out of her. I'll grab these two bags and take them to the car, then I'm going to go pick Janelle up."

"I'm going to try to beat Allison home from work. I want to be there when she gets home."

"Well, keep the key. See ya."

"Catch you later, and thanks man."

"You're welcome."

CHAPTER

1 7 Allison raked her nails from the crown of her head to the nape of her neck. The tracks slid out easily under the coaxing of the conditioner she'd soaked into her hair. The hot water felt good on her head and on her body. She leaned into the hard spray and shut her eyes against the stream. She felt her body relax.

On the side of her bed, Allison was careful to oil her skin entirely. Since Malik left, she'd neglected every step of her beauty regimen. Her toenails had torn right through a pair of her best pantyhose earlier that day and her skin felt like saran wrap stretched too tight. She lay back after she was done and enjoyed the cool air from the overhead vent. With her hair air-drying, Allison thought she could feel the hair on her head curling out of control. Years ago before she met Malik she used to love to wear her hair that way. Her head felt lighter.

Allison didn't remember falling asleep. She was awakened by the sensation that someone was watching her. She opened one eye slightly to find it was Malik's eyes on her. She wondered how long he'd been standing there.

It's too bad she isn't as innocent as she looks, Malik thought.

"You shouldn't sneak up on people this way."

"I wasn't sneaking up on anyone."

"You could knock," Allison said reaching for a robe.

Malik couldn't put his finger on why, but the anger swelled slowly from within. Then he knew.

"I shouldn't have to knock on my own door, Allison."

"You wouldn't have to if…"

"Don't."

Allison sat up and tossed the pillow aside. "Don't what, Malik? Don't say that you screwed my best friend?"

"Does it make you feel better to say it?"

There were tears in her eyes. "No, but I still think you should leave. I'm not ready for this."

"If you didn't want me here, you would have changed the locks."

"I didn't think about it."

"Yes you did."

"You're right I did."

Malik sat on his side of the bed. "I think we need to talk and I think you feel the same way."

"How would you know how I feel?"

"I'm sorry Allison, but it happened. I could tell you all about the how and where, but I don't think you want to know that. It was only one time. It never happened again and it never will happen again."

"How can you sit there so calm with your eyes glued to my breast telling me it just *happened*? How am I supposed to believe that it won't just *happen* again?"

"Because I'm telling you."

"Because you're telling me," Allison snorted sarcastically. I wonder if it were I sitting in your place, could I just tell you. What would you do Malik? How would you feel? Would you forgive me?"

"Yes. I love you."

"Would you? Are you sure about that?"

"How about if I told you I had an affair and repeatedly cheated on you?"

"I'd still love you."

"What if I told you it would never happen again? Would you believe me? Would you forgive me then, if the shoe were on the other foot?"

Malik's anger exploded. He paced the floor until he couldn't hold it in any longer. The wood of the closet door splintered as his fist slammed into it. "Why are you doing this!" he yelled at Allison. "Why do you want me to go those places. How dare you sit there and ask me if I'd forgive you when I have? I have forgiven you Allison because I know. I know that you've cheated on me, and I don't know how repeatedly and I don't want to know. That's how I know what I would do!"

Allison felt like covering her head with the covers or running out of the room, but it didn't make sense to do either. Malik was telling her with his own mouth that he'd known. She wanted to reach out for him but was too afraid he'd push her away.

"You knew?" she asked quietly.

Malik could only shake his head.

"Then why? Why didn't you leave me?"

Malik didn't turn to face her. "Because. Like I said, Allison. For better, for worse, I love you."

Allison stood behind him. "Can I?"

She took his silence for a yes and wrapped her arms around him. "I'm so sorry, Malik. I'm sorry for everything. How do we go on?"

Malik couldn't face her. "I don't know. I guess one day at a time."

"What about Meagan?"

"Nothing is ever going to change the fact that she's my child or that Kathy has a husband who loves her very much. I take care of her financially and if and when she is older and we decide to tell her, then we'll just have to cross that bridge when we get there."

Allison squeezed his shirt in her fist. "Can you look at me? Please look at me, Malik."

"I can't. Not now."

"Malik, please. I promise you, if you let me, I'll be everything to you that I never was. I promise."

"I married you because I loved you for who you are."

I know, but there has to be something. Tell me what not to do and I won't. Tell me what to do and I'll do it."

"You can stop trying to make me into him and love me for me."

"Oh, I do Malik. I love you so much. More than I ever thought I did."

"That's all I ever wanted from you, Allison."

She held him tighter. "I know, and I am so so so very sorry."

Malik gently pulled her hands from his waist. "I know. I'll be in the den for a while."

"I've missed you every minute. Don't leave me like this Malik."

"I just need a little time to regroup. I'll fix the door later."

Allison stood in the spot where Malik left her standing with the scent of him in her nostrils. How quickly the tables had turned. Nothing mattered to her in that moment more than Malik. He had known and yet never mentioned it to her. She had pushed him further than his limits and he'd forgiven her. How much more should she forgive him? It suddenly didn't matter so much to her that there had been another woman or a child. All that mattered was her husband and the knowledge that she never needed anyone as much as she did him.

Journey leaned back against the booth and watched the smoke curl up from her cigarette. She closed her eyes. She could always gauge how much alcohol her body could stand by how fast the room spun with her eyes closed. The room did not budge as she let her eyes focus to Monica. Monica cut her eyes sideways.

"Girl, no he isn't coming over here."

Journey followed her line of vision. "Oh yes. Mr. Powder Blue Poly & Esther Suit himself is walking this way."

Monica giggled. "He's coming for you, his long lost Journey."

"Nuh uhn. That's your man, honey."

"Oh wait. I think he spotted someone else."

"Nope, chile' that's his Mack Daddy pose. Com'on let's get on the dance floor before he comes. Hell, I'd even dance with him off this song."

Monica and Journey followed the line to the dance floor. Mr. Powder Blue Suit bobbed behind them. He fell in line as the speaker announced, "Right foot this time, left foot now stomp!"

The entire crowd followed the song's instruction when to step, stomp, or slide. Journey could feel the sweat by the time the song ended. Monica, knowing that another version of the same slide was coming, grabbed Journey's hand. "You staying out here?" she mouthed.

Journey nodded yes. She was having too much fun to stop. They'd danced nearly every song since they'd been there and at one point Journey thought Monica would never stop.

Monica would have stayed on except her bladder was calling for her to take leave. She pointed in the direction of the bathroom. Journey nodded understanding and turned her attention to the young smiling man beside her.

Like Monica had suspected, the next song was an extension of the first slide. She made her way off the crowded floor and watched everyone stomp and turn in unison. All those Black bodies sharing the same rhythm was beautiful to Monica. The slide alas ended and the D.J. switched to a slow grinding song. The young man beside Journey eased his way over. His movements were fluid with his pelvic area positioned for grinding. Journey smiled and winked her eye at him then politely declined. She met Monica at the table. Monica passed her a napkin to fan herself with.

"Girl, you see the body on that young brother? I can't believe you passed him up. Not you."

"No-oo. Some places, I don't even go. He must have been all of twenty-five. I'm sure he won't have any problems finding some young one to molest up there. 'Certainly can't have him thrusting an' rolling me into a hot mess. Especially when the bed waiting for me at home is empty."

"You know I know."

"Feels damn good to know I still got it. Whatever the *it* is it's still there."

"You didn't wonder where *it* was did you?"

"You know I'm too vain for that. *It* is something I'll never lose."

Monica watched Journey drain the last of her drink. It was getting late and she felt good hanging out with her friend again. They had been laughing like school girls until moments before. Journey reached for the pint bottle of Cognac.

"Maybe, we should call it quits, Journey."

Journey lifted the bottle. "The bottle's empty?" she asked surprised.

Monica tried to smooth things over when she was really worried about the amount of alcohol Journey could consume.

"Yeah, it was good while it lasted."

"There's more where that came from. You up for it?"

"I don't think you should."

"Am I drunk?" Journey giggled.

"If you aren't, you should be."

Journey placed the bottle flat on the table. She winked at Monica. "Am I drunk, or is Monica the drunk one?" she said spinning the bottle. She did a mock drum roll on the table with her hands. The mouth of the bottle pointed toward Journey. "Shit, I guess it's me. The bottle never lies right?"

The mood was turning quickly to uncomfortable. Monica had always looked up to Journey like an older sister and didn't know what to say.

"I'm just going to have one more, then we can go okay?"

"Are you sure? Maybe you shouldn't."

Journey waved the waitress over and ordered a double straight up. She cut her eyes to Monica. "Don't go getting all Gwen on me. You know a second ago, you sounded all gushy just like her."

"If I sounded like Gwen it's because we both love you and worry about you."

Journey waved her words away. "I know that, but I'm a big girl. Don't waste all that good worry on little old me."

"That's not what I meant."

"I know what you meant. Let's just talk about something else."

"Journey, you know me. What's going on with you?"

Journey sipped her drink, then nearly drained it. "I got problems."

"Meaning what? Everyone has problems."

Journey put her hand to her lips. "Shh."

"You are drunk."

Journey made a space about an inch with her thumb and forefinger. "Maybe a little."

"Whatever's eating you, drinking isn't going to solve it."

To Monica, Journey sounded surprisingly sober.

"How do you know?" she asked. "Ever tried drowning your problems in a bottle, huh Monica?"

"Yes, in the bottle and up my nose too."

"Ooh shit, well I guess you have. Tell me then, what exactly did solve the problem?"

"I talked to someone about it."

"That's all?"

"Yeah, you want to try it?"

Journey sat up straight and set the drink in front of her. "Okay, Dr. Monica here goes." She held up one finger. "One of my problems is I believe I've been bitten by the jealousy bug."

"Jealousy is not your nature, Journey."

Journey slapped the table. "That's exactly what I thought until I couldn't shake it."

"You want to tell me who it is?"

"Get this." Journey said motioning her closer. "It's my very own sister," she whispered.

"Tilly?"

"You're not very good at the psychology shit are you? No, it's not Tilly. Take another guess. I'll give you a hint. It ain't Jean neither."

"Gwen?"

"Bingo! I do believe you're catching on."

"Com'on now, Journey. You've got just as much going for you as Gwen does."

"Oh no. Gwen is absolutely perfect."

"Nobody's perfect. You should know that."

"Correction kid. Nobody's perfect except Gwen. She's the one with the husband, baby on the way, and the forgiving happy happy spirit."

"Look at you, girl. You're young and retired for crying out loud. You've been all over the world and have more colleagues who respect you than you can count. Not to mention you really don't have to work if you don't want to, and can buy a home anywhere you want to settle. So what you're not married. You have been."

"News flash. My marriage failed."

"Your marriage did, but you didn't."

"You don't understand, Monica. I married a soldier. You know like duty, honor country, soldier."

"He was also a man. You married a man, and a jealous one at that. You outranked him way before all the promotions. He was a smallminded asshole who couldn't compete with his wife."

"I never once asked him to because he didn't have to."

"I know that, and so do you. Besides, who was there every chance she got. Who was there to cheer you on when they penned the majority of those medals on your uniform?"

"Gwen."

"That's right. Because she loves you."

"I love her too. I just wish she wasn't so damned right all the time. I look at her and George sometimes and can't help but wonder if I should have chosen her life."

"Then if you love her like you say you do then you can't be jealous because love is not jealous."

Journey tilted her head in thought. "You might be on to something, because I truly do love her."

"Would you wish that all she has would disappear?"

"Never."

"Then you should think of whatever you're unhappy with her about because it's not jealousy. I can't believe that."

"Damn girl, you are good. Maybe I don't have no problems," Journey laughed. "Does this mean I can have another drink?"

"Ooh shoot!"

"What? What are you looking at?"

"If you don't have any problems, you're about to. Your brother in law and your ex just walked in."

"Shit. Don't look."

"Too late, they saw us."

"Okay, if I start to sound drunk, then rescue me."

"Better idea. Just talk as little as possible."

"Damn I must be really drunk."

"Hey there Sis, Monica."

"Hey Big George."

Douglas walked up seconds later. "Hi, it's Monica right?"

"Heck of a memory. Hi, Douglas."

"I try to remember all pretty ladies names."

"Flattery will get you everywhere."

Journey lit a cigarette ignoring Douglas.

"Hello, Journey."

"Douglas."

"Mind if we share a table."

"Sure. How about that one." Journey pointed across the room.

George pulled out a chair. "She's just kidding."

She wanted to say she wasn't but remembered Monica's words *as little as possible.*

"Can I buy you ladies a drink?"

Monica tried to rescue her friend. "Actually you guys caught us when we were just about to leave. Right, Journey?"

"Right."

Please don't let me stumble, Journey thought attempting to stand. Douglas steadied her.

"I don't need your help."

"Sorry."

"Excuse me," Monica said passing the keys to her truck to Journey. "I'll meet you outside on the passenger's side," she hinted. No way was Journey going to drive her around tonight. "I just saw someone I haven't seen in years."

Journey didn't want to risk standing but had to get away form Douglas's eyes on her. She stood soberly and began to walk briskly toward the exit.

George caught up to Monica. "Did she drive?"

"No, I did."

"Good. How many drinks did she have?"

"She just had a couple," Monica fibbed.

Douglas took the opportunity to catch Journey alone. He had to hurry. "I just want to talk that's all Journey. You can't run from me forever."

"Who says?"

"Please."

Journey stopped outside the door. "Okay, talk. What?"

"Right here?"

"Here is as good a place as any."

"Not here. Let me take you someplace."

"Just to talk."

"Promise."

"Douglas, you've never once kept a promise."

"This time is different."

Monica walked out a moment later.

"One hour is all I ask."

"I'll give you one hour, but not tonight."

"When?"

"Pick me up around seven tomorrow night, and I mean it. One hour."

"Okay."

📖

Monica pulled into the parking lot of her apartment complex. Journey had her eyes closed.

"I didn't think you wanted to go home with George looking at you expectantly and Gwen wondering if you've had too much to drink. This way, you can drink as much as you feel, talk as much or as little as you want then crash in my extra bedroom. Coffee will be the first thing you smell in the morning. We both will need it."

"I want you to know how much I appreciate this, girl."

"Not a problem. I know how it is when you can't talk to someone who understands. Think of it as a slumber party of sorts."

Inside, Journey sunk her bare feet into the plushness of Monica's carpet. Monica came from her room carrying a set of pajamas. "These will swallow you, but they should be comfortable," she said tossing them to Journey. "I'll make us a couple drinks and we can pour all our woes out."

"Only if you go first."

Monica folded one leg under her and sat in her favorite chair. "I can't say there isn't a whole lot going on with me, I guess it's just that I'm too tired of tripping to worry about it. A couple months ago, it seemed I just couldn't get myself together. I'm talking inside out tired. I just wanted to stay in my bed and let the world just pass me up. You know what I mean?"

Journey nodded that she did.

"I'd just come out of a relationship. This guy was the cousin to some character Devita hooked up with. I should have known then that it wouldn't work out, but I gave him the benefit of the doubt. You know how we do? Pick all the areas where the brother has potential then ignore the rest."

"Anyway, initially he was cool. Doing all the right things like wining and dining me. Finally, I gave him some and he went stupid."

"What he do?"

"Girl, he started wanting me to check in anytime I went somewhere and you know I am gone a lot. Most of the time I'm just hanging out or over to Gwen's, but I didn't feel I needed to tell him that. So after I told him I wasn't about to punch his clock, he started showing up at my job, my apartment, and a couple times at Gwen's. He started to spook me."

"Was he violent?"

"No, not physically. He would say hurtful things to get under my skin, but you know me. I'd come right back at him. The last straw was when he came over and I stupidly agreed to let him spend the night. We must have argued half the night until I just turned over and went to sleep. The next morning, he rolls over trying to get some. I ain't gon' lie I thought about it. The sex was that good."

"How good?"

"Like real good. In that department he was like king Ding-a-ling. Then I thought about it again and was like no. I told myself I could do better than this."

"What happened then?"

"He told me that if I couldn't meet his needs, then he'd find someone who could. I told him fuck him and his needs. After that," Monica shrugged her shoulders, "he called me a fat bitch and left." Monica refilled her drink.

"Now your turn. What's up with you and Douglas?"

Journey hugged a pillow to her chest. "Girl, Douglas is someone I've loved like forever. We just could never seem to get it together. You know how you can love someone and not like them?"

"Yeah, I've been there."

"Well that's how I felt about Douglas. Back then he had no direction, and no drive. He was so smart but he was just screwed up in the head. I say that now, but that's one of the reasons I liked him so much then. He was a bad boy type with that thug appeal. You know, cool as hell and fine as wine. I would get the biggest thrill when he said he loved me. We're talking somebody who was too bad to love anybody but he said he loved me."

"And you wanted to be the one to tame him?"

Journey had to laugh. "Isn't that funny. Me, trying to save someone? I wanted to be his everything and he was content to let me try. All the time he knew I would only get as close as he let me get. I must have looked like the biggest fool to everyone else."

"But that didn't matter did it?"

"No, not then and not even when I married my husband. I married a man who said he loved me but treated me like he hated me. You know the worst thing about my marriage?"

Monica waited until she continued.

"The worse he treated me, the harder I tried. I tried to make sure he was always alright. Whenever I was up for promotion was the worst. He acted like a number one jackass and everyone could see it. I could tell by the way people looked at me. You know that look like *what the hell is she doing with a twit like him*? No doubt they could see that he'd found a sucker and licked it. That sucker being moi. I knew I had to get rid of him when he nearly sabotaged my military career. He had the nerve to become what I hated most in the world—a junkie bastard. In the end, he blamed me for that too."

"I didn't realize. Gwen never talked about why you were divorced."

"Bless her. She's knows what I went through. I didn't leave right away. I stuck with Mitch through three stints in rehab before I gave up. Even then it took him to hit me before I would admit it was useless. Up until then I just hoped and drank."

"Where is he now?"

"Out of my life is all I know."

"You have any regrets?"

"No, except I shouldn't have tried to play the savior and marry him in the first place."

"Everything happens for a reason."

"I guess."

"So what now?"

"I don't know. I guess I'll just wait and see."

"Maybe you should give Douglas a try. It's been a long time."

"You're probably the only one I'll tell this too, but I think about him a lot."

"You think you can get past the past?"

Journey glanced over her shoulder out the window. "I don't know. Now tell me about Anthony."

Monica was blushing. "I think he might be the one."

"Well let's not jinx it by talking about it. Not unless you hiding something juicy."

"No, we haven't had sex and I don't plan to."

"Good, girl. Save that poohnannie. If he's Mr. Right, he'll be happy you waited. Just remember to invite me to the wedding."

"Nobody said anything about marriage."

"You didn't have to. I can see that gleam in your eyes. You've thought about it and don't lie."

Monica was all smiles. "He's surely marriage material. Turn that song up some."

Journey twisted the knob on the radio. McFadden and Whitehead's voice drifted through the speaker. She and Monica joined off key with the radio.

...We gonna get ourselves together, we gon ' polish up our act, yeah. And if you ever been held down before, I know that you refuse to be held down anymore, yeah yeah. Don't you let nothing, nothing, Stand in your way, And all we gonna do, I want you to listen listen to every word I say, every word I say. Ain't no stopping us now. We 're on the move...(You said it, we've got the groove)...

Journey suddenly stopped singing and turned the radio down. She turned to Monica. "Are you aware that there's some guy yelling your name outside your window?"

"Um hmm. You remember that guy I told you about?"

"King Ding-a-ling himself?"

"In the flesh."

Monica turned the volume back up and Journey had to yell over it to be heard.

"That nice ride must be the Ding-a-ling machine."

Monica laughed and threw a pillow at Journey. "You know you are a mess."

📖

The next morning as Journey stepped out of Monica's truck she couldn't remember when she had felt so good. She walked around to the driver's side and reached in to give Monica a big hug. Her friend squeezed her tight.

"You have been wonderfully therapeutic my friend. I think you missed your calling."

"At one hundred bucks an hour I think I did to."

"You know if you need me maybe next time I can be the one to talk to."

"I'm going to hold you to that."

"By the way, who was it you said you talked to?"

"I didn't say, but the answer is God. I talked to God. You should try it."

C H A P T E R

1 8 Gwen sat at the table preparing her lesson plan. It was only the fifth day since beginning what had seemed like a great idea and plan. The task of teaching teenagers and older to read was proving harder than she thought.

Though only five young people had showed up thus far, the class was challenging to regulate. Two of the four young women had a serious problem with authority, while Renita had yet to open up much. The one young man who showed up just seemed to be there to see how many of the girls he could lay before the end of the week.

Journey watched Gwen chew the paint off her second pencil of the morning.

"You gonna get lead poison if you keep that up."

Gwen barely looked up as she spit out the pencil. "Nervous habit."

"You? Nervous? That's a first."

"Yeah, for me to. Don't forget I'm used to teaching elementary age children."

Journey shrugged. "Children, adults, they're all basically the same. Don't pacify either."

"Not even sometimes?"

"Depends on the circumstances. If you think they're playing on you, then they are."

"Sounds like you could be of assistance, Soldier."

"Oh no. I'd only end up recruiting them into some branch of the armed forces. You know when I look at most young people, I see a soldier."

"That may not be a bad thing except everyone isn't military material."

"True."

"So will you sit in with us? Maybe another presence will be just the trick."

"You asking me?"

"Sure, you sound surprised."

"I just thought you would think of me as too brash for something like this."

"I'm not saying make them all drop and give you twenty, but I acknowledge all the teaching experience you've had. I've seen the way you took care of your soldiers. I'm certain some of them miss your guidance and direction. I know I did when you left."

"Really?"

"Absolutely."

"Thanks. I didn't know you noticed."

"Of course I noticed. Now, will you sit in with us?"

"If you don't think I'll run anyone away."

"If you run them away, then they don't want to be here. Besides, I don't pass out lollipops and baby bottles, Journey. I'm here to teach. I'm volunteering my time and my knowledge. They'll respect me or kick rocks."

"You should have been a soldier."

"Oh, but I am. Now will you?"

"Absolutely."

"Good. Get that for me, Journey I'm almost done."

Journey picked the phone up from its base. She recognized the voice right away.

"Doll-ling."

"Beatrice, Hi."

Gwen immediately looked up and mouthed the words, "I am not here."

"So how are you?"

"Fine, and you?"

"Good, except for neither of my girls were here for my grand opening."

"Tilly was there."

"Yes, but I have four girls, not one. You simply kont have forgotten."

"Beatrice, have you been watching Notting Hill again?"

"What is that supposed to mean?"

"With the doll-ing and konts. I see you're practicing your Euro accent."

"No, I've been watching *In the Heat of the Night*, and the accent is not Euro, But then again, I get my accents all mixed up. And you, my love are changing the subject."

"Bea, it's not like you opened a restaurant. You opened a Laundromat."

"So? And why don't you all call me Mom?"

"Gwen, Bea wants to know why we don't call her Mom."

"Didn't I tell you that I wasn't supposed to be here?"

"Oh yeah, Bea. Gwen isn't supposed to be here."

"What did she say?"

"Gwen, Bea wants to know what you said."

Gwen blew air. "Tell her that we don't call her Mom because she told us years ago not to."

"She said because you told us not to."

"Well, I changed my mind."

"Gwen, she says she changed her mind."

"Tilly calls her Mom."

"She says Tilly calls you Mom."

"Yeah, but Tilly is fake."

"She says Tilly doesn't count, she's fake."

"Tell her it's too late. *Mom* sounds as fake as Tilly is."

"Beatrice, she says it's too late. Sorry."

"Who are these people I call my children? At least I tried. Now, you still haven't told me why neither of you was here for my opening. This is a big deal you know?"

"I did."

"No, you didn't."

"Why don't you ask Gwen?"

Gwen rolled her eyes to the ceiling. "I'll get you back," she whispered. "Hi, Beatrice."

"Hi, Love. Are you all fat and jolly yet?"

"I'm pregnant, you make me sound like Santa Claus."

"No offense, but the way you cook I'm surprised you don't look like Mrs. Claus. I wish I could eat like you girls, I tell you everything I eat…"

"I know. Goes straight to your hips."

"Yes, and other places."

"You look great, Bea. The same as you did in our youth."

"You know me so well don't you? You know that's all I wanted to hear. Why does getting a compliment from you all feel like pulling teeth?"

"You want me to answer that?"

"No."

"So, how is Journey enjoying her visit?"

"Why don't you ask her, I've got to hurry. My class starts soon. Love you, miss you, and kiss-kiss."

Gwen shoved the phone back at Journey.

"Hey, I'm back Bea."

"So…have you seen Douglas?"

"I told you that isn't the nature of my visit."

"Yes, yes. I know what you told me. Have you?"

"No."

"Do I sense some hostility?"

"No it's your imagination as usual."

"Have you drank your coffee this morning? You're cranky."

"I'm drinking it now."

"And if you haven't seen Douglas, maybe you should. You know a good lay couldn't hurt you."

"Gwen, Beatrice thinks I would be less cranky if I had sex."

"Tell her I'll do my best to marry you off."

"Gwen is going to do her best to marry me off."

"Who said anything about marriage?"

Journey wanted to get off the subject of Douglas and sex.

"Anything new and different going on in the family?"

"No, everyone is as crazy as ever. Tilly is taking a masseuse class and your Auntie Cut has at last come out of the closet. Did she call Gwen? She said she would."

"Beatrice, can you hold?"

Journey held her hand over the receiver. "How come you're sitting here listening and can't talk? You know Bea makes me crazy!"

"I'd rather listen."

"I'm back."

"I hate it when either of you put me on hold. It makes me think you're talking about me."

"No, I was just telling Gwen how Auntie is out of the closet."

"Did she know?"

Gwen looked up from her pages. "Good. Now we don't have to be introduced to any more aunties. To date we've had about what, a hundred?"

Journey started to relay the message, but Beatrice was laughing. "Tell her I heard her, and she got that right."

This was typical of their conversations with their mother. Usually, they would click over and call Jean while Journey and Gwen each used an extension.

"If the phone cuts off, it's my phone card that just politely informed me that I have one minute remaining. I had to have the long distance cut off since Tilly and her kids keep running the damned bill up every time I turn my head."

"Well, I love you and I'll talk to you."

"No, no. Wait until it runs out. I still have to tell you that I'm thinking of coming for Christmas. Ask Gwen what does she…"

The phone on Beatrice's end went dead. Journey hung up the phone. "Beatrice is thinking about coming for Christmas."

"Must she?"

"You gonna call her back?"

"I'll call her later."

Journey sat quietly watching Gwen's eyes steady on her lesson plan. When Gwen looked up, Journey asked, "What are these students of yours like?"

"So far there's only five. You've met Renita who is mostly quiet and reserved. Then there's Lela who's Puerto Rican, real pretty girl. She does speak English but alternately substitutes Spanish in the same conversation. Depending on how frustrated she is, she curses in English. Next, there's Dominique AKA Nikki. Now Nikki is your typical high maintenance swapmeet queen. You'll hear her coming since all seven pair of gold hoops in her ears will clack and clang whenever she moves. Most mornings her hair gets bigger and her clothes lessen. She pops gum with a vengeance and worships Lil Kim."

"Sounds like a mess."

"Next there is Tony with a y who I suspect has a different birth name but prefers Tony because of it's masculine connotation. She dresses entirely in male attire and wears boxer shorts. I know that because her pants are always below her hips with one leg up to show off her Timberland boots. Her hair is worn braided in ghetto braids straight to the back. Contemptuous as heck."

"And last, there's Kion AKA K-Loc. He's a real piece of work. Considers himself an expert on pimpology, macking ho's and is quick to explain that he has a PHD in G."

"G?"

"I don't know, I didn't ask. My nerves couldn't take it. He's a good looking brother, around nineteen and so far has had some philosophical topic each morning which I suspect is due in part to the merry herb that he reeks of. All this while reading and comprehending at about a fifth grade level."

"I know that you can do what you need to. I believe that."

"Thanks, Journey. They are certainly a different group, but I like them for the most part. Today's assignment was to bring in a newspaper clipping to discuss."

📖

Journey added an extra chair to the long table that doubled as desks. She admired how Gwen had everything set up just so. Renita sat next to her staring hard at her hands. Journey whispered, "Relax," and she did.

The next one to come in was K-Loc who winked at her before taking a seat across from her.

"You like younger men?" He asked flashing what Journey guessed was his macking ho's smile.

She smiled back. "Why? You know one?"

"You looking at one, baby."

"You sure about that? You look like a boy to me. The men I know usually know how to tie their shoes."

She could see him thinking of a comeback line when Dominique and Lela walked in. He turned his attention from her.

"Hey mommi. Lookin' good as hell this morning."

Lela blushed while Dominique rolled her eyes so hard the blacks disappeared under her lids. Tony was the last to pimp in holding the crotch of the baggy khakis as if there were something there besides space.

Gwen cleared her throat. "Did everyone bring in their article?"

Kion leaned the chair back on its hind legs. "I don't got no newspaper, Ms. Gwen."

Gwen took a piece of chalk and wrote the sentence on the board. "Who can tell me what's wrong with this sentence?"

Nikki popped her gum loudly and took off her jacket revealing a red studded brassiere.

"Don't got no is a triple negative."

"Everyone agree? That's correct." Gwen picked up the chalk. "How do we correct it?"

"It should be, I don't have a newspaper." Nikki looked smugly at Kion and smirked. "Stupid."

"You can shut up, girl. You just mad 'cause you a ho and I didn't call you last night."

"You ain't never gotta call, 'cause you too broke for me."

"Don't front. You wasn't saying that the other night an' believe me you din't get paid. All you got is just plain laid."

"If you gon' be a ho you may as well get paid and laid. I would'a paid you," Tony offered.

Nikki popped her gum firecracker loud for emphasis. "I am strictly dickly and ain't nothing about me free."

Journey looked over at the group. " You mean to tell me it makes a difference whether or not you get paid?"

"Let me school you," Tony started. "The way I see it, if you gon' be a ho, you might as well make the best of it. It's so many females getting ran through for free, if you make them niggas pay for the coochie then at least you ain't no cheap ho."

"Kion is just talking smack. I am not no ho! He only wishes he could have some."

Journey twirled her pencil in her hand. "No you are not a ho, or a bitch, trick, cunt, or none of those things. Number two, it's just as degrading whether or not you get paid for having a man or woman use your body."

Tony sat up. "I don't agree. I still thinks it's better to be a ho that gets paid than a ho that gets laid."

Kion was up for the challenge. "What you know about it? Looks like to me, you just frontin' like you got the equipment."

"I use what I got and I bet I do a better job than you do. Another thang, I bet I got the equipment to kick your sorry ass."

"Don't fool yourself 'cause you a butch. You step to me, I'ma beat you like a hard leg since that's what you think you is."

Gwen sat at her desk. "Nobody is going to beat anyone. Now that we got that out of the way, I'd like you all to meet my sister, Journey."

Journey waved.

"Journey is a retired Lt. Colonel."

Kion whispered. "Damn, you too fine to be retired. How come you ain't all old an' shit?"

"You can do that in the military."

"You mean you was like carrying a gun and all in the desert and woods like we see on TV?" Nikki asked.

"Depending on what unit you're in. All the military is not like you see on TV. Soldiers have occupations just like civilians."

"So you a soldier just like the no limit soldiers with Master P?" That was the charming Kion.

"No, like a soldier with Uncle Sam."

Lela looked at her wideeyed. "You like?"

"Very much. Sometimes I wish I hadn't retired."

"You meet mucho Spanish people?"

"There's all races in the military. If any of you want to know about the military, I'll be glad to talk to you after the class."

"It beats watching Andy Anteater eating all the apples, or Busy Bee buzzing by," Kion commented.

"If you're unhappy with the curriculum, Mr. K-Loc, you don't have to stay. Why don't you go off and join the no limit clan."

"Good one, Ms. Gwen. Aw'ight. I'ma pay attention. My mama says if I don't get my GED she gonna put me out."

"Okay, let's surprise her by learning something. Who wants to start with their article? We'll start by reading it aloud and discussing what each one gets from it. Part of learning, is being informed. I'll start." Gwen pulled out her paper. "The title of my article is, **African Americans and other minorities among the highest infected with HIV**. *Since the onslaught of the AIDS epidemic...*

Since the Sunday Darnel had been over, Gwen had tried repeatedly to talk to Journey about him. She plain wouldn't discuss it and when Gwen tried to corner her, Journey was always too busy to talk. She was either going to Monica's, the skate rink, dinner, a movie, somewhere. Gwen's feelings were hurt that Journey felt she needed to avoid her. Gwen knew that this night would be a repeat. It wouldn't be the rink, or a movie, but Douglas who would provide her sister another reason to back away. Gwen found herself resenting Douglas's intrusion.

Gwen sat on the side of the bed-watching Journey pull different outfits from the closet. For a moment she was lost in the memory of that night when she was the one place she shouldn't have been. It was during the hour of their unbridled passion that she and Douglas heard the banging on the door.

"I know your ass in there, Douglas. Open the doggoned door!"

Gwen pushed him off of her. "Shoot, that's Journey. I didn't know she was in town."

Douglas stared at the door while Gwen searched for her underwear. A shadow passed through the curtains. Gwen was sure her sister had seen her.

"You lousy bastard! Open this door. Who is she?"

"Nobody, I'll call you tonight."

Gwen thought that was about the stupidest thing he could have said.

"If nobody is with you then open the door!" Journey had challenged.

"I'm not opening the door. You're just going to act a fool."

Gwen heard the loud thumps against the wood and peeked out the window. Journey was kicking the door as hard as she could. "You open this damned door or I swear I'll bust every window out your car."

Douglas looked at Gwen who shook her head. "Don't open that door. If she sees me here, she's going to kill the both of us."

The sound of glass breaking brought Douglas out of hiding. He slipped on his shorts and ran to the door. "Dammit, girl! That's my fucking car!"

Gwen snatched up her things and hid in the closet while Douglas ran outside. She could hear them arguing from where she hid. Minutes passed like days as she crouched on the floor of the closet. She expected any minute for Journey to storm in and find her.

After some time of sitting uncomfortably on a pile of shoes, Douglas opened the door.

"I'm sorry about that. I got her to leave."

Gwen looked down at herself half dressed and had a hard time comprehending how she'd ended up in Douglas's closet. She began to cry uncontrollably. "What have I done?"

Douglas helped her from the floor. "We'll never tell it. We just made a mistake. Right now, she hates me and there's no use her hating both of us."

"If she ever finds out, she's going to hate me and I don't blame her."

Douglas hugged her to himself. "Shh. She won't, I promise. Nobody will."

Now that Journey was home for good, Gwen wondered if Douglas would keep his promise. Journey stood in front of her.

"Hello? Earth to Gwen."

"I'm sorry, I was somewhere else. What did you say?"

Journey stood in her underwear holding up two dresses. "Which one?"

Gwen pointed. "The green one."

Journey looked at her watch and slipped the dress over her head. "Back in the day, that darned Douglas was a terrific liar, but he was always on time."

The doorbell rang.

"Told you didn't I? Seven on the dot."

Gwen passed her sister the shoes from the nightstand. "You look pretty."

"Thank-you. You think so?"

"Green was always your color."

"Still my favorite."

From the bedroom, they could hear George and Douglas talking about the game that was about to start.

Between the flowers and Douglas's calling everyday, Journey had relented. She stopped breaking dates with him and agreed to phone conversations. This would be their first face-to-face meeting since their paths had crossed at the VFW.

"It seems you and Douglas are getting along," Gwen observed.

"It's been a long time since well you know that incident," Gwen started. "You sure you've gotten over it?" Gwen hated herself for asking as soon as the words were out.

Journey scrunched up her face then quickly smoothed it out. "I guess getting along is what you can call it. Sometimes I feel silly still holding against him something that happened ages ago. I don't know if you ever really get over something that caused so much hurt. I try not to think about it. I'm just glad Douglas didn't let me into the house. I can't say what I would have done. I'm sure it would have been something to destroy my career. At least I busted up two windows on his car," she laughed.

Gwen stood up. "It's all in the past now."

"We're just talking a lot these days."

"Talk is good."

Journey stood in front of the mirror. "Okay, say a prayer for me."

"Of course. Stop fussing over your clothes. Go."

This is ridiculous, Journey thought walking down the stairs. I've known this man all these years and I'm nervous like we're just meeting.

Douglas stood up and stared at her. George had a grin on his face the size of Texas.

"You better treat my sister like a lady or else."

"I doubt if she'll let me get away with anything less."

George winked at Journey. "You 'bout right about that."

Douglas extended his hand. "You look good, Journey. I couldn't remember whether or not you like chocolate, but I thought it would be a change from flowers."

Journey took the box and handed it to Gwen. "Thanks." For some reason that evening, she didn't trust herself to get close to him so she walked toward the door. She could smell him behind her.

The silence during the ride was suffocating. Douglas drummed his fingers on the steering wheel while Journey stared out the window of his truck. Douglas turned down the radio.

"I hope you can see out of those windows. I meant to go to the car wash, but I didn't have time. I had to shop for groceries."

Journey grunted noncommittally.

She's not going to make this easy, he thought. "Hope you're hungry."

"Some."

"Good because the bread should be about ready to come out of the oven."

"I thought we were going out."

"I was thinking maybe it would be more cozy to eat a home cooked meal."

Since the two of them began talking again, Journey had wanted to ensure that all their dates were somewhere public. She could end the date right then but decided she'd wait.

"From the corner of her eye, she took him in. His hair was no longer in braids but pulled back into a ponytail. The ends curled wildly. Once, she had suggested that the reason his mother never revealed the identity of his father would be because perhaps he was something other than black. Douglas had looked at her like she was crazy then told her that wasn't possible. Glancing at him with his wavy hair and odd features to Journey it clearly was a possibility. Although there was much she wanted to ask, she didn't dare break the ice for him. They pulled into the driveway.

Douglas's home was a sprawling ranch style brick structure. She could see where it had been amended from the garage. It was apparent that Douglas had done well for himself. She wondered briefly if he were still in the military.

"This is home," he announced as if Journey hadn't figured that out. She followed him into the foyer where he took her coat.

The food smells were almost as overpowering as Douglas's cologne had been. The scent of butter and garlic tickled her nostrils. A slightly fishy odor wafted lightly in the air.

"Fish?"

"Seafood spread," Douglas explained as he led her inside.

His home was decorated in rich Mahogany. They had several pieces of furniture that were nearly identical.

"I see you've been to Germany also."

"Yes. Six years. You?"

"I was there from '85 until '88."

"I missed you by a year."

"You know, after I found out you had enlisted, I always hoped we might run into one another."

Douglas couldn't say how much he'd wished the same. "World's a big place."

"True."

"Here we are. This is my dining room. Please, have a seat."

Journey wondered if he would continue announcing the obvious.

"Where is your bathroom?"

Douglas couldn't remember when he'd been so nervous. He could have just pointed the way, but found himself showing her. In front of the door, he stood.

"I think I can handle it from here."

"Oh yeah, I didn't mean…I'm going back to the kitchen." Douglas had spoken the words but didn't move.

"You're not planning to stand here until I come out are you?"

He laughed nervously. "No, no. You go ahead," he mumbled backing off, "shit, I need a drink."

Journey shut the door. "Me too."

Journey found Douglas downstairs standing over the stove. Soft oldies played from hidden speakers. Two candles flickered on the table illuminating the place settings. He'd apparently taken time to set the mood. She had an urge to blow out the candles.

"You need some help?"

Douglas answered much too quickly. "No. I mean I'm good, thanks." Journey sat down feeling idle. He set a wineglass before her.

"Red or white?"

"White, please."

"Good. I guessed right. I prefer white too."

Journey sipped her wine. The music was making her uneasy. A song whose title she couldn't remember ended then another came on. The Commodores sang *Just to be Close to You*. She shifted uncomfortably.

Douglas didn't notice as he set the green leaf salad down.

"I hope you like the salad dressing. I made it myself."

When she didn't answer, he watched her expectantly. She picked up her fork. He smiled until she swallowed and nodded her approval. It was actually really good.

The salad dressing wasn't the only good course he served. There were lobster tails, shrimp, and the salmon was excellent. She couldn't ever remember him cooking anything other than Top Ramen and wondered if his wife had taught him to cook. When the dinner was down, Journey leaned back. "Did your wife teach you to cook?"

"Most of my recipes come from phone conversations with my mother. My wife couldn't boil an egg."

"Is that why you got divorced?" She hadn't meant to ask that question.

Douglas swallowed hard then drank from his glass. "After eight years of marriage, Rita, that's my ex-wife's name."

Journey knew that but didn't interrupt him.

"She felt like she was married to the military. Her bitterness was directed either at the Army or me. I tried to convince her to go to school, or do something that interested her, but she would always have an excuse. Finally, I got out the Army to save my marriage, but we found out later I was the reason we couldn't have children. I am sterile. She left me a year later, I re-enlisted into the Reserves."

"Oh."

"I retired last year, and Rita is happily married and expecting for the second time." He drained his glass. "That's life I guess."

"Yeah."

More time passed before they spoke.

"Dessert? I bought a cheesecake."

Journey couldn't hold out any longer. "Douglas, what am I doing here? Don't get me wrong, dinner was nice but we still haven't talked about what it is you want from me."

Douglas dropped ice cubes in a glass and poured Scotch over it. He sat down and smiled awkwardly.

"We're here because I always wondered what it would have been like if we'd gotten married."

"Are you asking me to marry you?"

"No, I mean not yet. Only that you think about giving us a chance."

"Douglas, I told you. There is no us."

"But there was."

Journey began gathering her things. Being with him so near her was making her nauseous.

"I think you should take me home."

She wasn't sure if he'd heard her and didn't care to look at him. She was her old self again, young and weak for him. She slipped into her jacket and turned her back so she wouldn't have to look at him. *That's it,* she thought. *Don't look because if you do you will fall apart.*

That's when it happened. She felt him. He was close, she could smell him. His hands were in her hair, caressing her neck, hands that she knew. She was falling.

It was his voice that made his touch burn her skin. He should have remained silent but he didn't.

"I will never leave you," he said.

Her anger surfaced raw and fresh. When he didn't stop, she had to yell it. "Douglas, stop!"

He was reluctant. "You felt it, I know you did. I felt you."

"We can't do this. We can't just start with some old feelings and make something new from it."

"Why not? People do it all the time. Why can't we?"

"Because our relationship ended with you screwing someone and me trying to bust out all your car windows. That's the man I remember. I don't know you."

"Then just try to get to know me."

"No. I'll only expect the same treatment. My heart or my pride cannot handle standing outside your door pleading for you to come out."

"That was so long ago."

"Not long enough. I needed you to be true, Douglas. Besides my family, you were the one constant in my life."

"I've changed, you'll see. I couldn't be what you needed. I couldn't be what I needed."

Journey faced him. "If you couldn't love me there, how am I supposed to trust you to love me here."

"Because I was just so angry then."

"I'll entertain your excuses, Douglas. What made you so angry that you could shut me out that way?"

"I can't explain the kind of anger I felt. I just know I was angry at God, myself, you, and the entire world."

Journey slung her bag to the floor. "What the fuck did that have to do with me!"

"Journey listen. I've thought about it and I know. I can't tell you how but I just dammit know that we can do this! You've changed, I've changed."

"And just how the hell do you know that we won't end up treating each other the same as we did?"

Douglas was frustrated but was determined not to give up. "I know because the woman you are right now would never tolerate the way the me-back then treated you."

"You damned right I won't. Take me home.

Journey could hear voices in the den. It took a moment to realize it was the TV. George had fallen asleep on the couch. She pulled the covers up over him and pressed the off button. The TV hissed off.

Gwen startled her from behind. "I came down to get him. I told George that the TV would end up watching him but as you can see, he conked out right here." Gwen sat on the arm of the sofa. "I didn't expect you home so soon."

Journey could see Gwen's lips moving but the words drifted into her mind only intermittently. *Watching, TV, conked out, so soon.*

Gwen touched her arm. "Are you okay? Did something happen?"

Journey wondered how she could tell Gwen when she wasn't quite sure herself.

"Journey, you look ill. Come sit down."

Gwen started toward the kitchen, but Journey couldn't follow. The comfort of the quiet darkness was too inviting.

"It's too bright in the kitchen."

Gwen looked puzzled for a moment. "Then we'll turn the lights down."

That seemed to settle it. The two of them sat in the darkness, two silhouettes in chairs against the moonlight. The hum of the refrigerator was the only sound.

"You want to talk?"

Journey shut her eyes and contemplated the question.

"There's nothing to talk about. I'm hurting like hell and I don't know why."

"I've felt that way before."

"All I know is Douglas isn't real to me. When I was younger, I would dream about the day when he would be the man for me. He would be this, not that, or he'd keep the traits that I liked and lose the ones that I didn't. I had him all rearranged to fit my dream then I fell in love with that made-up man. I fell in love with the made-up him because the real him hurt me so. I fell in love with an apparition, a ghost."

"What if he's no longer a ghost?"

"How would I know? Ghosts can appear in any form. What if I believe that he's changed only to find that one day he takes his original shape? I'll only feel hurt again won't I?"

"I wish I knew, but I don't."

"I don't want you to know. I don't even want to know because if I know then I would have to do something. I would have to stop being angry and I don't want to. Anger is easier."

"Anger is consuming."

Journey looked at the shadow across from her. "I know that, Gwen."

"Don't get aggravated, Journey. I'm only trying to understand."

"I'm sorry, it's just that this thing that I don't understand keeps welling inside me. I often wonder if I knew who the she was in that house that day if then I could divide the hate I felt for Douglas all those years. Maybe hate her some instead. Now, doesn't that sound silly?"

Gwen was quiet for the longest time. Journey stood up. "I think I should go to bed."

"You know her," the words were so low that they almost didn't reach her ears. "Did you say something, Gwen?"

"I said you do know her."

Journey at first didn't recognize who was talking to her. The quiver in Gwen's voice frightened her.

"It was me, Journey. I was there."

Journey felt like someone had punched her in the stomach.

"You?"

"Yes."

"And you pick now to tell me? You waited until I'm all oozy with hurt to pile some more on me. You, with your selfish ass actually thought I needed to hear that now?"

"If not now then when? Years ago, yesterday, tomorrow? You were right about one thing. If you knew everything then you would have to do something. Now you know."

"And just like that, that's it?"

"No, that's not it. Every day I'm sorry for what I did and I wish I could take it back. But every day it's still there—a mistake I cannot undo."

"That was no mistaking what you did. You were intimate with someone I loved more than breathing."

"Yes."

Journey whirled around. "That was around the time…the miscarriage. Tell me that wasn't…"

"There was no miscarriage, and yes it was. I had an abortion, and started to hemorrhage."

"Fuck! I came home to the hospital for you. You told me it was George's child."

"No, you assumed."

"How could you? I held you like a baby. I fed you ice chips for crying out loud!"

"I still needed you and I wanted to tell you but I was too afraid."

"You should have been. I have to go. This shit is just too much right now."

"You can't leave. Where will you go?"

"I don't know."

"Please, Journey it's too late to leave. Wait until morning."

"Stay over there. Don't come any closer to me. I don't trust myself near you. I'll call a taxi then I'm out of here."

George appeared from the shadows. "You don't have to call a taxi. Get your things and I'll take you wherever you need to go."

Gwen shut down when she heard him speak. He had heard, she could tell in his voice. Even in the dark she could feel his eyes burning through her. He spat the words out like hot coals. "I'll be outside. I can't breathe in this house."

C H A P T E R

19George sat like a stone behind the steering wheel. No radio played; no words were spoken.   He parked in front of Monica's apartment before glancing quickly to Journey. Missing was the customary, cheery, "Here we are," George would announce whenever he served as transporter. In its place was a hard yank on the gearshift from D to P. Journey sat wondering if words were appropriate. George licked a tear from the corner of his lips. "I don't know," he announced as if a question were asked. Not any question, but the questions. *What will you do? Where will you go? Are you all right?* He answered them all.

Journey reached awkwardly over to pat his shoulder before stepping from the vehicle. Garment bag slung across her arm, she spotted Monica's truck. George was gone by the time she turned around. She guessed he'd seen it also.

Please be home, she thought as she rang the doorbell.

The chime of the doorbell temporarily paralyzed Monica. She crept cautiously to the door. On the way, she picked up the newly purchased baseball bat. "Who is it?"

"It's me, Journey."

Monica unlatched the chain and twisted the deadbolt. Journey noted the bat and looked quickly behind her before stepping in.

"I'm so sorry to wake you, but I didn't want to spend the night in a hotel room."

Monica locked the door and carried the bat to the corner. "It's okay. I've been awake for hours."

"You always keep a bat by the door?"

Monica seemed disoriented by the question. "Oh that? I just bought it today for protection."

"Protection?"

Monica waved her to the couch. "Please forgive me if I seem a little jittery. Please sit down. I can't think with you standing over me."

Journey obliged. "I'm sorry, I can't stand that either. I was just startled and worried by your expression."

Monica tightened her robe for the third time. Any more tightening, Journey thought, she would cut herself in half.

"Some idiot has been calling here making threats."

"Threats? Have you called the police?"

"Yeah. They told me it's probably kids or a jealous ex."

"And you don't think so?"

Monica curled up in the chair. "No, I don't."

"Leroy maybe?"

"I thought maybe at first but crank phone calls are not his style. He would write me a poem and slip it under the door. Then when I tell him it's only the lyrics to an Isley Brothers cut from back in the day, he'd call me names then hang up in my face."

"What has this caller been saying?"

"At first, nothing. But now he seems to know stuff. Like when I'm home or have been out."

"That is too creepy."

"You telling me. Today he asked me if I enjoyed my walk like he'd been watching me. I called the police back and they told me to be careful of strangers and call back if I notice anybody suspicious. As if everyone won't look suspicious to me now."

Journey let out a long whistle. "What are you going to do?"

"I got a new telephone number today."

"Good. That will stop the calls, but what if this person is watching you?"

"I don't know."

"You should purchase a gun," Journey said matter-of-factly.

"I don't like guns."

"You don't have to like them. A gun will do a hell of a lot more than that bat."

Monica didn't answer but looked from Journey's luggage back to her as if seeing it for the first time. "What's with the bags?"

"Don't worry, I'm not moving in. I had to leave Gwen's house."

"What happened?"

"I don't know if I can talk about it right now. I feel like if I do, I'll crack all to pieces."

"Is Gwen okay?"

"We had a disagreement, not a fist fight. She was fine when I left."

"I doubt that if you moved your things."

"You're nothing, if not blunt."

"Look at the pot calling the kettle black."

"Touché."

"Should I be worried?"

"No, it will pass."

"Okay."

"But you'll call Gwen in the morning won't you?"

"Nope, I'm going to see her. She's still my friend regardless of your um...disagreement."

"You've always been neutral."

"Not always. Besides, it's what friends do and I don't want you talking no hotel business. I have a perfectly good extra bedroom."

"I've imposed enough."

"Bull."

"I can't."

"You can. My motives aren't purely noble. Maybe now I can get some sleep with someone else here with me. Think about it."

"Deal. I still think you should purchase a gun."

"And do what with it?"

"Learn to use it. What else? I'll take you to the range and teach you to shoot."

"I'll think about it."

"Okay, it's settled."

"I said think about it."

"Alright, think."

"See you in the morning."

"Okay. Don't let the bed thingies bite or whatever."

"Say your prayers."

"Yes ma'am."

"Don't get cute."

George let himself into his father's home, careful not to disturb any of the furniture. He could hear the TV in the den, the volume much too loud. He touched the bottle of Jack Daniels in his pocket.

Expecting his father to be sitting in his favorite chair, he turned quickly to him standing behind him.

"Hi, Son."

George tried to breathe normally as not to convey the panic he'd just seconds before felt. "You should announce when you're coming up behind somebody. You scared the heck out of me."

"Don't tell me a big man like you scared?"

George walked over and hugged his Dad close.

"Old man, you getting worse than that old cat of yours."

George Senior stood looking straight at his son. George shifted his weight uncomfortably before turning his head. His father's unseeing eyes pierced right through him. The older George felt his way to the cabinet and pulled down two glasses.

"What are you doing?"

George Senior ignored him and set the two glasses on the table. "Sit down, Son."

When George sat down, George Senior sat across from him and folded his hands. "You know, I haven't had a drink since your mother passed and I know you haven't either. You remember why?"

"Yes sir."

"Then why is it you have a bottle in your pocket?"

"I don't."

George Senior shook his head and smiled. "Never was much of a liar."

George pulled out the bottle and set it on the table. "You're not mad?"

"You a grown man, George. We both know what that bottle put your momma through. I remember that day like I remember every nook and cranny of this house. That day when you and me promised there would be no more liquor in this house. Ever."

"That was a long time ago."

"Yes."

George cocked his head to one side. "How did you know about the bottle?"

"Big George, I'm blind. I see everything," he laughed. "With my nose, hands, and mind."

"I didn't drink any of it."

"I know that too. Which brings me to my question. What happened so bad that you need old Jack there?"

"I don't need it."

George Senior took the bottle in his hands and walked it to the sink. "Good, then you won't mind if I pour it down the drain."

He didn't wait for the answer.

"I haven't wanted a drink for years now, Pop. Not even when we sat in that doctor's office listening to him tell us that you would go blind. Not even when I thought Gwen was going to leave me."

"And now?"

"I feel like leaving her."

"I don't believe that."

"You should because it's the truth. You remember when I told you about last summer?"

"'Bout that young gal?"

"Yes sir. Remember how shamed I told you I felt? I wanted to fall in a hole and never come out. I couldn't stand the thought of how bad I'd hurt Gwen."

"She was plenty hurt."

"It took her a lot of months to get over that."

"I 'spects so."

"I felt like shit, and there was nothing I could do, but pray she would forgive me."

"And she did, Son."

"Then tonight I find out that she not as innocent as she act, but a liar as well. Would you believe she's been with another man?"

"Heck no."

"Me neither except I heard it with my own ears. Not just any man, but my best friend."

"Douglas?"

"Yeah, him. That ain't all. She got pregnant by him and had an abortion. She told mostly everybody she had a miscarriage, but that was a lie."

"That's hard for me to believe, Son."

"Me too, but I heard it. Granted, it's been so many years but how does a man get over his best friend being with his wife?"

"So y'all weren't married then?"

"No, but so what?"

"So, I'm sure she thought it was best left back there."

"How do I know that? How do I know that every time she looks at me, she don't wish I was him? Or that each and every time he looks at me, he ain't laughing inside. You know how I dote on Gwen. Listening to me, you would think she was the holy virgin or something."

"And that bothers you?"

"Yes, it bothers me. When I almost cheated with that girl, Gwen looked at me like I was river scum when all the time she been acting like she could do no wrong."

"And now it's your turn to make her feel like she made you feel?"

"Whose side are you on anyway?"

"Nobody's. Just tryin' to understand."

"I hate it when you're right all the time."

"I'm not right all the time an' you know it. I came to terms a long time ago that I been wrong most'my life. I know it should be me in that ground instead'a your momma, God rest her soul."

"Pop, you loved Momma."

"Yes, but I took her for granted. I didn't cheat on her, but I cheated her out of the joys she should have had. All I ever thought about was working to take care of my family. I never once thought what my family would be like if Doris weren't a part of it. Not until it was too late. Now she's gone, and I'm as blind as a bat."

"I'm sure Momma knew."

"That's the point, Son. She knew, but I should have known. That woman knew me better than the grass knows the ground. It ain't often that you get somebody who completes the missing parts of you. I had that in Doris and I think you got that in Gwen. Forgiveness runs both ways, Son."

"Yeah, Dad but I'm in no forgiving mood. My head is not right for it. I need to be mad as hell right now because if I don't, I'm gonna hit somebody."

"Son, I'm not saying you can't be mad, I'm just saying that the more time you waste being mad is less time you got for all the good."

George glared hard at his father. "Daddy, quit being so danged logical."

George Sr. shook his head. "Don't get mad with me 'cause I ain't hanging no balloons and streamers at your pity party. You knew I wouldn't when you showed up. So go on, and maybe get yourself another pint 'cause I don't have it in me to feel sorry for nobody. I felt enough sorry for myself and I'm bled clean out."

"I didn't mean it that way. I'm sorry. I never meant to disrespect you."

"You did, but I forgive you. Best I can tell you, Son is pray. God will renew your strength."

"Will he?"

George Sr. felt around until he found the edge of the table then lifted himself up remarkably well for someone without sight. He walked toward the doorway. "Ask Him an' see. If you can't believe how blessed you is already then you more blind than I am."

Journey thought the strangest thoughts after she and Monica had gone to bed. She lay on her back spread eagle counting the roses on the border paper framing the mauve wallpaper. When the numbers went crazy in her head, she slipped out on the balcony. Fifteen minutes later, she lay in the same position.

Gwen lay in her bed also. She couldn't recall ever hating the sound of empty around her. She lay aching for the echo of footsteps, a drip from the faucet, or any sign of another human body inside the house. She hugged her arms around her tightly as if a chill had overcome her. She prayed her half-full bladder wouldn't force her to get up and walk the empty hallway but knew it wouldn't be long. She could almost feel the orange juice she'd drank snaking through her body to destination—bladder. She needed Journey to be in the room down the hall. She needed to see soft light seeping from under the door to Journey's room. That was familiar to her. Gwen could reach around the doorframe to turn the knob from dim to off without so much as a stir from Journey under the covers. She suspected it was a familiar ritual for Journey as well. Gwen recalled once when she had not awakened to turn off the light. She had no idea that it would be the topic of discussion the next morning. She'd walked into the kitchen to find Journey making coffee.

"You must have been tired last night," Journey had commented.

Gwen nodded a yes before trying to rub the sleep away from her eyes. Having tried both hot and cold water on her washcloth, she knew sleep was still upon her. Her lids were still heavy.

Journey watched her waiting for an answer Gwen had not known was a question.

"That light bugged me all night."

Gwen gave her sister that weird look Journey had grown so used to seeing. A smart remark would always follow.

"I didn't realize that I'd become the light keeper. Why didn't you just get up and turn it off?"

Journey's answer softened the slight sting of the comment.

"I just like it when you do it is all."

Gwen regretted her defensiveness. "I'll do it tonight."

That was enough to appease Journey and that night Gwen had in fact turned out the light—the same as every night after that. But that was before. Tonight was different. Without walking the hall, she knew that Journey's room was pitch black.

Gwen rolled over from her back to her side away from George's side of the bed. If she needed Journey then she needed George double. His side of the bed was like the black room down the hall. She couldn't help remember how each night George would pull her to him. Her head would rest perfectly in the crook of his arm right between his neck and shoulder blade. Other times she would snuggle her face against the soft down hair of his chest, but only when she was feeling especially snuggly. There were also the times, the ones she didn't much like thinking about, when every night she'd slept with her back to him. Even then George would scoot against her as she inched away from him. Months after what had come to be called 'the incident', he'd told her that he'd held on to her that way because he'd been sure she would leave. When that fear haunted his sleep, he would hold her extra tight on those nights. What started off as a gesture to spite George, who hated her turned back toward him, ended up being one of her most comfortable positions. George's breath tickling the nape of her neck with his strong arm around her waist—just within reach to softly caress her there. To add to her completeness was his muscular thigh arched over her hip accompanying his ever-hardening penis. It was enough to drive her mad with want.

Gwen had envisioned herself in that position earlier that day and wondered how they would lay when her belly was too big for even Big George's arm to fit around. Just the night before, he'd giggled while pinching and kneading the soft underbelly flesh.

Gwen crossed her legs tight to keep her hand from voluntarily going there, but it was like a magnet. She thought of George as she stroked herself to climax. The guilty feeling would come later, but for now her body was responding. Afterwards she would feel like a thief who'd stolen something, but…

When the last wave of pleasure rolled over her body, Gwen thought ever so briefly of the house void of the two most important people in her life. She needed them and resented the hell out of that need. She wouldn't remember even falling asleep the next morning.

📖

Journey covered her eyes with her arm. Like a projector, her mind began a sequence of scenes in her much too vivid recollection.

On her mind screen, Gwen sat in a highchair banging away at the mini table-top with her cup. Her wildly coifed hair bounced up and down with each bang. At any moment, Beatrice was sure to come into the kitchen, which wouldn't have been the greatest of things for Journey. Particularly because in Journey's pocket was a red Popsicle and in her hand was a blue one. Her plot to eat the blue one and smuggle the red one to Douglas was being foiled by her baby sister.

"Journey? Are you in there with Baby Sister?"

The question was typical of Beatrice who never called Gwen by her name when she was a child. For some years, Journey fumbled when strangers would ask Gwen's name. Everyone in the house but Darnel called Gwen Baby Sister.

"Yes ma'am," she called to Bea. She wondered if she sounded too innocent or not innocent enough.

"I'll be in there in a minute. Keep her company for a while."

Journey sighed heavily. A while to Beatrice could mean an hour since she was cleaning the house with the hi-fi blasting. Beatrice was screeching along with Aretha demanding R-E-S-P-ECT. Gwen seemed aware also that she was again a burden to her frowning big sister. She readied herself for a scream loud enough to be heard over the vacuum and Aretha.

"Shhh," Journey soothed. "Be quiet Baby Sister."

Gwen looked up at her with watery eyes. So sweet was that look. Of course that is until Baby Sister turned her big browns hungrily toward the last blue freezer pop.

Journey was determined to ensure that the melting popsicle in her hand stayed in her possession. Why shouldn't she be the one to reap the benefit of her successful snooping and swiping of the freezer?

Gwen's pooched out bottom lip made Journey's decision solid. Douglas would just have to go without the second stolen popsicle. She hurriedly bit through the paper and passed the popsicle to Gwen whose mouth worked as feverish as the loud wailing of the vacuum in the next room. Before long, the top of the freezer pop was gone.

Baby Sister looked up at her once again with her bottom lip now blue and quivery. Before she could whimper, Journey pushed the colored ice up far enough to be attacked by the child. She waited patiently until it was all gone, after a series of biting off the paper and pushing up the sweet ice.

Remembering all this, Journey could still summon the satisfaction she'd felt when Gwen dropped the stick and let out a big freezer pop induced belch. The blue drooled, gummy smile that came next would live forever engraved in the section of Journey's memory reserved for the happiest times ever. She remembered always wanting to be there for freezer pops and missing tooth smiles.

She kissed Baby Sister on the cheek right before Beatrice appeared in the kitchen. Journey didn't know how long she'd been standing there. She had been so engrossed in caring for Baby Sister that she had failed to register Aretha taking a break from the hi-fi . Beatrice snapped the picture just as Gwen licked Journey full on the mouth—a favorite picture amidst family gatherings. Later she had it copied and blown up so that each sister could have that moment preserved for all times.

The half melted freezer pop in her pocket, she gave to Douglas. Who would have known that years later, she would be making a choice all over between Douglas and Baby Sister? She fell asleep wondering if her love for Douglas was enough to end a relationship with the sister she'd loved since her birth. Sleep caught up with her before the mental question begged an answer.

Douglas had no clue as to any of what was going on. His thoughts were of Journey and how good it had felt to be near her. She had looked good, smelled wonderful, and felt better than he'd imagined—if that were possible. His body responded to his thoughts and he felt himself stiffening under the paisley print sheets. Most times he would concentrate on something less arousing when his nature rose in him that way. But this night, he didn't bother. Journey had left the scent of her perfume in his home, and that was enough. He let his mind fantasize about her in every conceivable and some not so conceivable positions. Although the night had not ended the way Douglas imagined, there was no reason he couldn't pretend. A sigh of pleasure escaped his lips at the image he'd conjured of Journey's exposed breast. He reached for her taking her nipple into his mouth. The rest was easy. He slept so intense that night and woke up with drool on his pillow and his juices dried on the sheet beneath him.

Gwen searched the bedroom once more, then sat on the side of the bed. She was sure her phone book had been in the middle drawer where she'd put it after she used it last. There was no way she could concentrate on teaching a class after the night she'd had.

Earlier she'd sat up in the living room listening to every car that passed hoping it was George. She'd awakened at about five a.m. She was up again at six. The thought of staying in an empty bed made her head swoon. There was just no point without George beside her. *This is not supposed to be happening to me. It's just not*, she thought slamming the door to the bureau shut. *George is supposed to be up making coffee and Journey is supposed to be tucked into the bed down the hall.*

Gwen reclined against the couch cushion and began to cry a slow stream of tears. Crying always had a soothing affect after the tears were gone. There would be no relief to the ache she felt since the tears dried up too quickly. It always happened without her knowing it. Somewhere inside, her tear ducts became one with her mind. She was seriously tired of crying, and just couldn't do it anymore.

Gwen got up and showered. She stared at the bulge in her abdomen that she hoped would be a son. Not that it mattered at all to her, but for George…What man didn't dream of having a boy?

Having completed the morning ritual of cleanness, Gwen did something she had been neglecting to do. She pulled out her journal and sat outside in the early morning sunshine. She began to write.

Dear Diary,

It seems that I've thought there was not going to be much use for you since Journey has arrived. She has always served as that release I need whenever something has gone amiss. She has been as always my confidante, my counselor, and my friend. But something has happened. Actually, someone has happened. Of course you remember all those pages back about Douglas. I must admit that the only memory of that evening and of him was left all those years ago under that entry of Dear Diary. I've since then seen much of him, since he and George are very much the best friends they were then. But never have I once looked at him in a way other than that befitting a wife of a man's best friend. Neither have I ever noticed anything strange in his looks at me. I'm sure I would have.

Last night the whole Douglas/Journey and Douglas/Me thing confused me. I wanted Journey to know the same as I am writing this down that it hadn't meant anything and that I'd made a mistake. She didn't want me near her, let alone hear any apologies I had for her. Looking back now, I never should have told her, for both of our sakes. Afterall, it was so long ago. Unfortunately, that's not all. George heard me telling Journey and now they're both gone. My heart is broken. I've never had both of them to turn from me at the same time. I'm used to functioning with at least one of them by my side. They both have been a part of me for too long to expect something different. Right now, I feel like I'm functioning without two members of myself. Like my legs have been chopped off. I'm glad that this is on paper because I'm not right sure if I'm making any sense at all. All I know is I miss my husband, and I miss my sister.

Gwen shut the book and squinted her eyes against the sun. Morning had come.

Something had changed Monica. Not just a little, but way deep down inside the territory in her that she avoided. The time she spent with Anthony was unlike any experience she'd yet to claim. There was no pretense, no heavy silences, or any of the silly awkwardness that often time accompanies a budding relationship. With Anthony, everything was just…easy. Yes, easy was the word. Not one thing was hard. And the easiness only worried Monica a little.

Though she had no way of knowing, Anthony felt the same. Of course he'd known Monica for quite some time, yet he was surprised to find he hadn't known her the slightest bit. A shame it took her beautiful legs for him to notice her that day. After the legs, he couldn't imagine how he'd missed her succulent lips and her ready smile. Gosh, she had such a nice smile.

Anthony would have gone on about all of Monica's lovely features—probably as far as an erection, had the phone not rang. He only answered thinking it may have been Janelle calling him from Monica's. That was another thing, Monica was so great with Janelle.

"Oh yeah, the phone", Anthony reminded himself. "Hello?"

"Anthony, don't hang up," Sean demanded.

Anthony didn't hang up. Instead he threw the shiny gray cellular phone as hard as he could against the wall. He didn't give a second thought to the chips and shards on the floor that used to be a phone. He tried to remember where he'd left off in his memory of Monica. He simply had to recall her face in his mind or be angry the rest of the night.

It was impossible. "Dang," he muttered reaching for the phone beside his bed. Monica picked up on the first ring. Her caller I.D. informed her it was the one person she wanted to hear from.

"Hi, Anthony."

"Hi, baby."

Oh my goodness, he sounds sexy, she thought.

"I just called because I was thinking of all the things I love about you…"

"Oh snap! Did he say love?"

"And the phone rang interrupting me. I only wanted to hear your voice so I could fall asleep with you on my mind."

Monica was struck dumb with silence.

"Monica? Are you there, baby? Say something."

"What would you like to hear?"

"Something sweet."

"How about, I miss you?"

"Sweeter."

"How about, I was thinking about you?"

"Sweeter."

"How about, I love you?"

"Bingo."

"Now what do I get for all my sweetness?"

"Anything."

"Tell me what you're thinking right now."

"How about, I wish you were here next to me?"

"And?"

"And I'm about to go to sleep now."

"Anthony!" Monica whined.

"Okay, just kidding." Anthony lay back against his pillow for a short pause. "Monica?"

"Did you mean it when you said you love me?"

"Yes."

"I love you more."

"Will you show me?"

"For the rest of my life. Promise."

"Well, until then."

"Goodnight, Love."

"Goodnight."

Monica's jaws hurt from smiling. She felt as light as cotton. Had Anthony said one more word, she was sure she would have floated from her bed, straight through her roof to oblivion.

Next to her, Janelle didn't even stir. She closed her eyes smiling as big and wide as Monica beside her.

CHAPTER

2 0 "This isn't happening," Journey thought kicking the covers from
the bed. With no one she trusted enough to talk to, she pulled Dana from her
garment bag. She began to write.

Dear Dana,

*I had a fight with my sister, Gwen a few weeks back. I had no intentions of
making up since I'd almost convinced myself that it didn't matter. And it
almost didn't since time has a sort of numbing agent—like Ambasol or Orajel.*

*I missed Sweetie's flight today and I'm halfway expecting her to ring the
doorbell. Sweetie, with her psychic powers must have known we'd had a fight
the moment she saw Gwen and Jean waiting for her inside the airport
terminal. Instinctively, she would know that there should have been three
idiotic smiling faces with six hands waving excitedly at her as if she were not
just old but blind as well.*

*I'd known about Sweetie's flight, but was due for an appointment. I could
have scheduled it for later, but at the time it just didn't make sense to. No
sense in stalling for time we ain't got. Remember, Dana, you used to say that
all the time?*

*Anyway, three hours ago, I was sitting in the crowded waiting room of the
clinic on Scott Air Force base. Around me sat an assortment of anomalous
injuries. I studied the people with gauze and wraps, limps and sprains
knowing nothing would look quite the same after this doctors' visit. I studied
them and studied them until I made some of them as uncomfortable as all the
wraps and bandages surely were. I stopped only after the illnesses coupled
with the brightest damn fluorescent lights in the world made my head hurt. A
fly buzzed near my ear and I wondered why it and I were there.*

*I checked my watch and noticed that forty- five minutes had passed since
I'd signed my name under a list of many.*

Ten o 'clock, exactly my appointment time—which everyone including me knew didn 't mean shit. Forty- five minutes and still no one had called my name. In the second it took to glance at my watch, I became fascinated with the small recorder of time. I ticked away the minutes along with the second hand tic-tocking my life's minutes away. Having got bored with watching the seconds tic away, I picked up my book but the words kept jumbling into one big word. I resumed my watch watching. Two more minutes passed before I heard my name being called only after the voice called out to Leann somebody and Georgette somebody else and Dennis—I think Jones. Yeah, I'm sure it was Jones. I'll more than likely never forget Dennis Jones for as long as I live.

Let me backtrack to before the clinic, before Leann or Georgette or Dennis Jones would ever be names I'd encounter. I need to go back even before the felt pen I used to sign my name on the list.

One morning last week, I think it was on a Tuesday, I woke up with that knowing. The kind of knowing you have without having to be told and not knowing how you know up until the moment you realize that you do. That's how I felt that morning. No reason, I just knew.

In the shower, I raised my left arm over my head and with my right hand I touched it. The thing that I knew was there.

Now on to this morning when I missed a call because I was still in the shower. I dressed while listening to the answering machine announce there were thirteen messages. Actually, I only had one since the other twelve were exactly twenty and twenty one days old respectively. The day of and after Gwen's and my blowup. Monica had understood without words regarding the messages. Neither she nor I erased them. This new message informed me that my labs were back from wherever they sent my blood, urine, and feces. I was told that I would see the same doctor who examined me the prior week, right before puncturing my breast with the longest, skinniest needle ever. The monotony of the voice did little to give me a clue as to what to expect, but then again I knew.

"Dennis Jones, Lieutenant Colonel Journey Butchard." The young 91 Charlie smiled as he said this.

I didn't rise right away, but watched him hoping he would be near when I came out of The Room with the doctor. I found his lovely body, beautiful smile, and broad chest quite wonderful to behold. I also liked the way my name sounded with my rank preceding it. Although retired, I missed being a soldier, which suddenly made me sad, since I was going to The Room.

My name he called again, well after Dennis Jones was changing into a paper gown that could by no means cover what his pants barely managed to.

Inside the room, the scenario played out this way:

Doctor: (Gesturing toward a chair) Please have a seat.

Me: No

Doctor: (Taking a seat, our roles having switched)

Me: Tell me.

Doctor: I think you know, Journey

Me: (Thinking now I really did know since we apparently were now on first name basis.)

Doctor: It's back.

Me: (Silent, but thinking how the IT can just fucking come back. I surely didn't invite IT back)

Doctor: The cancer is out of remission. I'm afraid it's also metastasized.

Me: (Dumbly) Metastasized?

Doctor: Yes, it's spread. Tests show…

End of scenario. I walked out cursing the damned tumor in my left breast. The voice called, "You forgot your purse."

I turned and saw him. His id tag swinging slightly around his neck identified him as Sergeant Everett. I stared at his picture while my legs turned to lead. He must have known I was a statue by then—the lead having coursed through the rest of my body.

Sergeant Everett took me to an empty room and let me cry all over his blue scrubs until there were no more tears. At least not until the tear reservoir could brew a fresh batch.

"Thank-you, Good Samaritan Soldier," I attempted to joke; my sense of humor straining under the weight of my diagnosis.

"Are you sure you're okay to leave? Is there someone to drive you home?"

I mumbled some crap about being just peachy and walked out the door. He offered to walk me to the car but I had the silliest thought while standing there. I couldn't have him walk me out. Afterall, who would call the names?

I turned to Doctor Vaserelli holding my book.

"Journey, we need to talk."

I ignored him. "You can keep the book. It only has cancer written all over every page."

"Journey," he called to my back but I didn't stop. I felt the fresh batch from the tear reservoir readying to erupt.

Only by God's grace did I make it home on the tear-bleared roadways.

That was the last sentence Journey wrote before she soaked her pillow and Dana with tears.

Journey's head pounded when the chime of the doorbell roused her awake. On the other side of the door stood Sweetie ready to pull her into the biggest embrace ever.

Journey fought not to cry again as Sweetie squeezed her hard enough to crack a couple of ribs. She only sniffed once, but Sweetie couldn't hear since she was talking like a windup toy that someone wound too tight.

"Come on, get your shoes. I stopped by KFC and bought a bucket of lunch. I have three movies too. I got one for you, Gwen and Jean. Hurry up, chile."

Journey didn't know why she didn't tell her, but didn't. She just smiled stupidly and slipped into her shoes.

"Now baby, you know I ain't got no business driving with this corn on my right foot, so here are the keys to Jean's car. Sho' is a nice car…"

Sweetie was still talking nonstop. "Yatta, yatta, yatta," is how it sounded to Journey. More yatta, yatta, yatta all the way to Gwen's.

At Gwen's, the hellos were awkward but welcomed. Of course Sweetie knew it wasn't time for talk. Instead they watched the first movie, which of course was a military film. While it played, each of them glanced sideways from the TV to each other. The rest of the time was spent filling their mouths with stale popcorn or rubbery chicken.

Before the credits could start rolling, Journey was heading to the back yard for a smoke. She quickly returned to the kitchen to grab a handful of cornmeal. Someone—she thought it was her friend Donna's ex-husband who had told her that cornmeal would kill ants. She thought it couldn't hurt to find out. Gwen's backyard was notorious for malicious red ants with stinging bites. *A real walking encyclopedia, that man is*, Journey thought.

She heard the door open. Instead of looking up, she concentrated on the ants scampering over the cornmeal she'd strategically sprinkled over their mounds. She thought how it must have seemed like an ant's Christmas except with the humidity as high as the temperature, it was apparent the tiny creatures would consume all the meal with not a drop of water in sight. Surely their little parched ant throats would choke. No Santa for them. At least that was her theory.

Still not looking up, she watched the millions of ants scampering over their mound houses. The chair squeaked but she still didn't look up. Didn't have to. Besides hearing the waddling steps indicative of pregnancy, she'd felt Gwen's presence before she'd lit the first cigarette. She lit another from the tip of the first one.

"You like the movie?"

"Yes, but I didn't identify with it much."

"It was about soldiers."

"Yeah but not me. It's not the same. There were no female soldiers in it."

"You're the smartest person I know. Maybe you should write a blockbuster hit movie about female soldiers. A GI Jane II or something."

Gwen wasn't just serving a big helping of lip service, she believed Journey could do anything.

"That's not what I meant. I meant there was nothing about the issues female soldiers deal with in the military. Like being passed up for promotions because you're black, female, in the wrong MOS, or all of the above."

Gwen wrinkled her brow for understanding. Journey answered without her question. "MOS means military occupational skills."

"But you retired a Lieutenant Colonel."

"It's not about that. There should be a movie about having to watch soldiers who I nurtured from rookie privates pass me in rank. Maybe about the insecure husbands, the support groups for every circumstance, the failed marriages, and the crafty uniform loving hoochies waiting at every station to pounce."

"Oh."

"Yeah. Oh is right. Stuff like that."

"You're bitter?"

"I'm tired."

"You sound like you regret it all."

"I regret nothing. I love the Army."

"See then? You made it through, Journey."

"Yeah, made it." Whatever *it* meant. To many *Its* in one day. Made *It…It's* back….

It was Gwen's turn to stare at the ants.

Journey realized that the weird had come. They were talking but not the way they talked. Their conversations never consisted of empty topics. Conversation that day was like making small talk about the weather. Who cares about the weather unless there was a storm or some other natural disaster coming?

"I'm sorry we argued," Gwen said. "We screamed at each other."

"I know," Journey replied, "and yes we yelled at each other."

"We screamed."

"Yelled, screamed. Tomato, tomotto."

"No, it wasn't the same. We both know it wasn't the same. We've yelled, but never screamed."

"That's true."

Gwen sniffed and Journey hoped she wasn't about to cry. She could never bear to see her cry.

"You forgive me?" Gwen asked

"Sure."

Gwen breathed out heavy air from her lungs. "I used to think that as long as you were smiling, I could see the world through your smile."

Journey looked up then. "And now?"

"Now, I know that as long as you're smiling, I can. You're my big sister and I never want to hurt you again."

"I know."

"You think we can go back? Like before the screaming?"

"I think so."

"Good, because I can't lose you, Journey. I need my big sister."

"Technically, Jean is the big sister since she's oldest." Journey didn't know why she said this, it just came out.

"I know that and I also need Jean too. Only it's different with us."

Her words popped the lock to the floodgates. Water gushed from Journey's eyes.

Gwen scooted over and pulled Journey's head into her swollen lap. She fought the tears but lost. "I felt something was wrong all morning. Jean did too. Please stop crying and let's talk about it. Nothing is that bad. Please just don't cry. I hate to see you cry," Gwen pleaded with heavy tear-laden words that barely got through her lips.

More wracking sobs from Journey. Gwen was sure her heart would melt away if Journey didn't stop.

"What can I do? Just tell me."

Journey looked up in desperation. "Buy me some time until I can talk about it. I can't right now. Just let me lie down for a while."

Gwen helped Journey up the stairs before she headed to face Sweetie and Jean. She washed her face and hoped Sweetie wouldn't look right through her phony smile. There was no such luck as Sweetie was standing at the bottom of the stairs just as Gwen was about to clear the last two.

"Sweetie, you startled me. My word, sometimes you sneak up on people like a cat."

"Never mind cats and such. Where's Journey?"

"She's taking a nap."

Sweetie maneuvered around her. "Go on in there and start the next movie. Get off those feet 'fore they look like big old sausages."

Gwen cleared her throat to stop Sweetie from going upstairs. Her actions rewarded her a stern look from over Sweetie's shoulder.

Journey wanted to ignore the knocking on the door.

"Damn," she thought she had muttered under her breath. "I'll be down in a minute."

Instead of Jean or Gwen, Sweetie strode into the room. "Don't damn me, chile'. I knew something wan'nt right way back at that apartment. Now tell me."

Journey fell into the warmth of her Sweetie's bosom, uncaring of the sobs now clogging her ear nose and throat. Sweetie didn't seem to care at all about the snotty tears on her newly starched shirt.

"I was seven years old when I saw your scar," Journey sobbed.

"You mean…?" Sweetie started.

For the first time in a long time, she concentrated on not the right words to say, but to say nothing at all. It was Journey's turn to talk.

"I remember it like yesterday. How I came into the bathroom while you were drying off. I didn't mean to walk in on you, but I had to pee really really bad. You remember?"

Sweetie nodded yes and rubbed her hand in circles around her granddaughter's back.

"I was so scared. But then, but then you explained to me what had happened, and I thought I understood 'cause I wanted to understand, but I never did until that time when I called you. When I heard the words breast and cancer referring to me. Oh Sweetie," she wailed. "I'm so sorry. When that doctor told me that, all I could think about was that scar slashed across your chest where a breast used to be. And now, and now, I wonder if my vanity is going to be my death. That's why you were the only one I ever told, and I thank you Sweetie for staying with me. I thank you so much."

"Chile', don't thank me. I knew what you was going through and you came out fine."

Journey looked around desperately shaking her head from side to side. "I'm not alright now and I don't think I can make it through again. If it weren't for you, I wouldn't have made it the first time."

"Nonsense. Chile' sit up, now. I know you hurtin' but we gotta get a second opinion."

Journey shook her head no. "No, Sweetie. I can't go to any more doctors."

Sweetie took Journey's chin gently in her hand and lifted her head. Looking her straight in the eye, she said, "Who said   something 'bout doctors. We are going to an authority even higher than those doctors. Bow your head chile', it's time to pray and believe God."

Inside that room, eyes closed in prayer with Sweetie, God felt more real to her than He had for a long time. So good and so real that Journey was more afraid than comforted. If He were there in that room, surely God would remember her plea to Him that fateful day. Yes, definitely. He had to because she did. Remembered it like yesterday—the exact words and everything. "Please God if you take away this Cancer then I swear, well promise to not ask for another thing. And she never did, except she wished she had made only one more amendment to her request. Her prayer should have instead gone something like, "Please God if you take this Cancer away *and keep it away* then I swear, well promise to not ask for another thing."

She must have fallen asleep because she awoke to nothing but quiet. Too much damn quiet. There should have been some noise but nothing. There was not one damned bit of creaking in a house so old and for some reason that pissed Journey off more than anything. More than the cancer.

She unfolded herself from under the light blanket where her long legs had been curled up into her chest in a near fetal position. She recalled some of the words from the support group when she'd gone through the battle with cancer.

There was mention of stages she would go through. She screwed her eyes up trying to remember them. Denial—well she was past that.

There was no denying what she felt. As she sat, she could feel the cancer trying to swallow her whole. Then there were the other stages. Anger, she remembered was one of them. Yeah, that would do perfect. That was exactly what the strange, tingly feeling pumping hard and furiously through her blood felt like. Pure, unchanneled anger. Now all she needed was a target. She would declare this night Journey's anger night and hunt for a target.

She walked down the stairs of the still too quiet house right into the kitchen. All around the table sat her sisters minus Tilly. Oh, but lo and behold, who did she spy at the sink, but the person who would become the ultimate object of all that hatred bubbling inside her? She would channel it all toward none other than DARNEL. She could have shouted and thrown her fist up in victory. Who would have guessed she would have her opportunity so soon? All she needed now was for him to say one word, just one. Foolishly, he did like she knew he would.

Humbly he turned and made contact with all eyes at the table. If he'd been smarter, he would have read the warning. Jean's eyes were saying, *oh shit, don't be stupid, and say one word.* Sweetie's calm eyes said, *this boy has always been a fool. This one time please don 't fool up and open your fool mouth.* Gwen's ever so briefly transmitted, *not now. Please not now.* And Journey's well they screamed, *I need this so bad! Say it, you bastard!"*

And he did. "Hello, Dollbaby."

That was it! Journey's words couldn't have been more vicious if she'd covered them with spit like a spitball and shot them through a doubled-barreled shotgun. "You have the nerve to call me that, you filthy gutter rat?"

Darnel dropped his head and bit down hard. "I'm so sorry you feel that way, but I understand. I'll take that."

"You damned well will take it. And whatever else I have to say."

Journey waited for a sign of retreat, but apparently that was the only thing Darnel had changed. He stood, with nerve enough to look up at her with those hateful, lying eyes.

"You hate me don't you, Journey?"

Sweetie looked up at Darnel and thought that was the single bravest thing he'd ever done. He'd known what would come next. Everyone did, but he stood his ground. Not for himself but because Journey's words were going to hurt him like hell, and right then it was what she needed. He knew she needed the victory of retribution. It was payup time, and his ass was on the table.

"You damn right I hate you and anybody who looks like you. I hate you for what you did to Beatrice, I hate you for what you did to this family, and I hate you for standing right there with breath still coming from your dog lips. The only reason you haven't turned and hightailed it out of here is because Sweetie no doubt told you I'm sick. And don't say that she didn't else everyone wouldn't be sitting around this table like it's a gotdamn funeral!"

Journey turned and made eye contact with everyone, no one even attempting a lie. Sweetie had indeed told them because Journey never would have. She would have made up some lie and pushed everyone from her life the way she always had when she'd needed them most.

"Shall I go on?" Journey asked.

No answer from anyone except Darnel who sucked in his breath sharply as if preparing to receive more word bullets from his daughter.

"Why aren't you gone yet?"

"I'm still your father, Journey. I have a right to be here even if it's jus' a small right. I don't care what hateful thing you have to say; I'm not leaving. I'm tired'a running."

Journey gestured around the room. "You hear that? He says he's tired of running. Darnel, you're a coward now, just like you were then. My God! You expect us to believe that all of sudden you possess some decency? And don't dare stand there thinking you're doing me a favor. Is that it? Are you standing there thinking, oh poor Journey. Don't you dare ever pity me!"

"Pity you? How could I ever pity you, Baby—I mean Journey. I love you. Hell, I even admire you. I wish I was half as strong as you but I wan'nt."

"You never once even said, Journey you can do anything. All I ever got from you was what I couldn't do. DollBaby, that's stupid. Girls don't do that. What kind of father never has anything edifying to say to his own daughter?"

"You're right. I put Bea and you girls through hell and I know it. Please, listen. Everything you say is true. I don't gotta excuse for that. The onliest way you responded to me at all is when I said you couldn't do somethin'. You think I didn't see that all I had to do was tell you that you couldn't do something and it was good as done. I know it was pitiful but that was the only way I could help you." Darnel began to cry and took one step toward Journey. "I'm so sorry. I was better off out of your life than when I was in it. But times wan'nt always bad. Remember I was your daddy. Whether you hate me or not, don't look at me that way. I still am."

"Lucky me, DADDY!" The words were heavy with sarcasmed sap. So heavy they dripped and threatened to glue everyone to the kitchen.

Darnel looked for a moment about to cry. "Don't you remember nothing good about me?"

"No. I remember candles when the lights got cut off because you fucked up the light bill money."

Her next words were so hard to speak that they nearly tore her throat apart. "I loved your sorry ass once. Oh God, how I loved you Darnel. All I ever wanted from you was to be Dollbaby again but you couldn't even give me that."

Darnel's tears flowed faster as his chest deflated. The quiet spectators around the table watched the air seep from his chest like helium from a balloon. Darnel was shrinking right before their eyes. He was pitiful when he spoke. "What can I say?"

"Nothing. It's too late."

"If only you would'a talked to me when I called. I been trying to say I'm sorry for a long time."

"Maybe you should have written me a letter."

Darnel knew his daughter could be mean, but not that mean. Her words stabbed extra deep because she knew he couldn't read and what few words he knew would have made a sorry letter. Besides, what kind of letter would it had been beginning with *Hi, see Spot run?*

📖

Jean couldn't stand any more of the pain in that kitchen. She wanted to run as far as she could away from it all. There was more pain still to come, but for that moment Journey had had enough.

Jean reached in her purse and slid her car keys to Journey. Go on, Sister. Take these keys and get out of here."

Gwen looked up to protest but Jean cut her a look that said to let her go.

Gwen didn't want to see Journey leave unless she was leaving with her. She'd tried to be strong like Sweetie had told them but there was no way she could keep from bawling like a baby when Journey walked out that door.

Gwen turned her head full swing toward Darnel.

"I'm sorry. I only pray that one day all'a yall can forgive me."

Jean, who'd remained neutral the longest, stood up and blocked Darnel's path. "Not so fast. Believe me, I want to see you so far from here as quickly as you want to leave. But since we're sharing all the shit on our minds, answer me this?"

Darnel didn't quite know what to expect since Jean had mostly showed the quietest of contempt for him when she showed any emotion toward him at all. She was so close to him that it was strange. He couldn't quite recall the last time he was so close to her. It had to be a long time because now she was taller than he. Funny, he'd never noticed how tall she was.

"Okay," he nearly mumbled.

"That woman I saw you with in the grocery store?"

Darnel had never wished for a hole in the floor. He wished the floor would open up right there and swallow him whole. Even if his tongue weren't glued to the roof of his mouth, Jean would have known the answer.

"You think I'm stupid and that I'd never figure it out? I look like my sisters because you're our father, but I always *felt* something. Even before the arguments and accusations from Bea who God knows I love. She is the only mother I've ever known, but still…I've been needing to hear you say it for a long time. That woman I saw…she's my mother isn't she?"

Before Darnel could finish a nod yes, he felt it. All the hate in the room landed right above his left eye. He'd known he hurt his children but enough for one of them to spit in his face was more than he could bear. Then he thought about it. Gwen. Gwen wouldn't turn her face from him. He sought her out with spit blinding him in one eye.

Jean laughed at him standing there but there was no humor in the sound. His sight was sickening to her and she could no longer stand being near him.

"It should be you with cancer instead of Journey," she hissed before walking from the room. But not before glaring at him with Journey's eyes.

Gwen was his reprieve. He could see her holding a towel. He knew he could count on her. He started to walk to her but something hit him in the face before falling to his feet. It took a moment to realize it had been the towel Gwen was holding. She was standing looking at him with Jean's eyes on her face.

"Get out of my house."

He could feel her eyes burning him. He imagined that all their eyes were on him setting every inch of him on fire. He wanted to speak or turn away but the eyes were too hot. Suddenly, all of his daughters had his eyes and looking at them was like staring into a great big mirror in front of his face. He couldn't look, but he couldn't look away. They burned so deep because their eyes belonged to him. Those eyes could be so hateful because they'd come from him. Each pair of them. Mostly everything else about his girls was Beatrice all the way. Except for those mirrors to the soul. He had to vomit, then he had to pee more than he ever had to in life. He all but ran out of house.

📖

Journey drove Jean's car without really thinking where she would go next. By then, she was beyond angry. She was downright reckless. She just knew it had to be somewhere other than at Gwen's. But first she had to wash Darnel from her.

Thankfully when she got to Monica's, the apartment was empty. Monica had left a note telling her she'd gone with Anthony.

In the shower was when everything began to close in on her. Her whole world was shrinking. By the time she exited her shower, Monica's apartment was the size of a dollhouse.

Journey stood in the middle of the floor—naked and dripping from head to toe. Her hand involuntarily moved from her side to her breast. The lump was the only thing that hadn't shrunk but instead grown a hundred times its size. She had to get out before the tidal wave of emotion worked itself up from the deepest pit of her stomach to her chest to her eyes. Jeanie's car was much too small at the moment. The key to Monica's truck hung on the nail with a colorful plaque spelling out *life is a garden* in connecting flowers.

Journey heaved ignoring the sure smell and taste of vomit with the promise of more. She wouldn't give in to her stomach's weakness. There was no time for that. She heaved once more before snatching the keys from their resting place. She ran to her closet and grabbed an orange tank top with the matching wrap around skirt. Her chest began to swell and there was no time to grab shoes or underwear. She left the house barefoot.

Inside Monica's truck, Journey listened to Matchbox 20 singing *Mad Season*. She turned it up as loud as it could go and lost herself in someone else's reality. When the next song began, she looked up to Douglas standing inside his door as if he'd been expecting her.

They stared but neither of them moved for a spell.

Journey walked by remote; unsure of why she was there at all. The closer she got the faster Douglas walked. Just as she reached him, the tidal wave pushed up through her esophagus and a sound somewhere between a moan and hiccup escaped. Douglas saw her tears before she felt them and lifted her from her feet. Journey closed her eyes.

When she managed to choke down the storm, her senses were again about her. They stood in the living room arms length away. Journey was aware of her shirt being yanked over her head and her back against the cold sweat of the brick wall. The chilled moisture felt good on her back and heightened her excitement. With one hand, Douglas cupped her breast—the breast, and slid to his knees. His head ducked quickly under her skirt as he sought her out with his tongue. He made contact just as she felt for the tie that would free her of the skirt. The orange material fell around his shoulders like a cape.

Douglas's face was wet with her when he came up. Journey snatched open the heavy starched shirt oblivious to the buttons. His shorts fell to his ankles. She paused taking in the ready erection pushing against the silky material of his boxer shorts. They too fell around the calf length black socks she'd known every man in the military to wear. Her husband had worn them but it wasn't time to think of him or socks.

Douglas never felt Journey's weight while carrying her to the bedroom but was aware of the acrobatics they performed trying to keep himself from sliding out of her warmth. They made it as far as the stairs. The rest of way, Douglas carried her up the stairs.

Journey could not say when the tears started but they did. She turned away from Douglas who lay on his back heaving from their frantic lovemaking. He turned to pull her to him. He felt the resistance but rolled her easily toward him.

He opened his mouth to say something but before he could, Journey shushed him. "Shh," she said and nothing else. And shush he did. Instead of allowing her to turn away as she started to, he kissed her tears until there were no more. Then he watched her while she slept.

Sometime during the lateness of night, the phone rang. A frantic Gwen went down a mental list of places Journey could be. She rang Douglas's number on a long shot hunch and was relieved that her sister was there. She wanted to hang up, but the desperation in his pleas to tell him what had Journey so torn up, made her not. She told him because he loved Journey. And Gwen felt that deep inside.

When Journey awoke, she glanced over at Douglas's sleeping face. Tears leaked from his left eye as if all the hurt he cried came from the side housing his heart. The right eye remained dry. Journey leaned over and kissed him to hardness and he woke up holding her almost too tight. The tear leaking stopped as they made love again. Slowly.

📖

The next morning, the sun was shining brighter than Journey had seen for a while. Dressed in a tee shirt and shorts, Douglas's clothes covered her body while his scent filled her nostrils. She felt strangely at peace except a small part of her. There was something she needed to do.

She drove on until she pulled into the parking lot of the little Catholic school she and Gwen had attended many summers ago. Every summer they would walk to the school where the rigid nuns were. There were several ones she remembered fondly.

From where she sat, Sister Carol saw the truck pull up and squinted her eyes toward it. She expected it was a parent readying to drop off one of the children who attended summer camp there. Instead she recognized one of her favorite students. She stacked some papers by the window and went to meet Journey. They stood hugging for the longest time.

"God is with you, my child." Sister Carol told her.

Journey sniffed only once and followed her into the chapel. On her knees behind the still familiar pew, Journey could see the rugged wood cross suspended from the ceiling high on the wall. She closed her eyes.

Dear God. I've been such a fool to run from you all these years. But you never could let me go could you? Thank you for that. She paused and took a breath. Lord, this is not easy but for some reason I just know that I'm not going to be on this earth much longer. The same way I knew the cancer was back. Once upon a time, I blamed you, but all I can do now is thank You. I feel free to love you because you loved me without my deserving it. Thank you for my life and what life I have left. Bless me to forgive in my heart so that when I stand before you one day, I can hear 'well done'. I confess now that I've done a many wrong things, but because of your son I can begin again. Father, again I thank you for being a father to the fatherless like your word says. Help me to do better. Amen.

CHAPTER

<u>Deliverance</u>

21 Gwen sat in the rocking chair where Journey's room used to be. She studied her cappuccino as if trying to deduce how hard or easy it would be to climb in and drown there. Baby Joshua stirred on her lap; drawing her attention from her coffee mug.

She picked up the heavy, leather bound journal Journey had given her. She plucked the top from the ink pen with her teeth before beginning to write.

Dear Journey,

This is the longest and hardest story I ever had to write but I promised to tell you everything. I finally got a chance to be still and I think I'm ready. So here goes.

I'll never walk into my kitchen and not remember that night. You, Sweetie, Jeanie, Darnel, and me. All the hurt in that one room was enough to wash away a small island. Strangely, it seemed after you emptied your hurt reservoir, mine swelled up. All the years of struggling to make peace with Darnel wasn't so important. I thought I never in life wanted to see him again after that night. He was even less than a thought in my mind. He was a peon.

Gwen turned to see George staring at her. He'd walked in and she didn't know how long he'd been standing there. He saw the tears falling and like the man that he was, he didn't question the tears or the journal she held in her hand. He kissed her and lifted his firstborn son from her lap. "I love you," he said with Joshua smacking his lips. Gwen had just finished nursing him from her breast and expected that Dad and Son would soon fall fast asleep in front of the TV. But that would be later. Gwen couldn't say anything for fear of all the feelings in her belly bursting out, flowing deep and drowning

George and baby. The feelings weren't for him but for Journey. She had to finish writing.

For a while, Journey your story became all our stories. For the entire six and a half months you lived, you grew and grew until you occupied every space in everybody. You didn't do it on purpose, but how could you not? You were dying and boy did I hate you for that.

We argued about it at times, you remember? You had resolved whatever inside you that you needed to, leaving me to grapple with the fact that you would not be here with me.

Anyway, after that night, everything changed. It's a wonder you didn't go crazy with all the activity centered on you. I was by far the worst and I admit it. That in itself was amazing since both Bea and Sweetie was here. Tilly tried to share some of my insanity but she was no match for me. Boy, did she yell and scream at me one day. Girl, she was crying and snotting Tilly-style. She kept talking on and on about you being her sister too. And she was right but that didn't matter to me. For as long as you breathed warm breath, I was THE sister. They could share you only when my belly was so heavy that I had to step back. Then like clockwork, Bea and Sweetie took over where I left off. By then, you were really sick. Tilly, who 'd gone back home, came back and I'm sure she still resents me to this day for being so overprotective and overbearing. Everyone else kind of blamed it on my being pregnant, but Tilly was right. It wasn't pregnancy but selfishness. If I weren't pregnant at the time she probably would have tried to kick my butt until I saw her as a real person. She'd always claimed I hoarded you and it was true. I took so much of you from everybody because you meant so much to me and I'd had the most to prove. I hurt you deeply and every moment I spent trying to make it up to you was worth it.

Before you got really sick, we did a lot together. I miss those times 'cause girl let me tell you. You, Sweetie, Beatrice, Tilly, Jeanie, and me we laughed a lot. A whole lot. Honey Chile' this house was always full of folks. A few times you disappeared and everyone could smell the telltale odor of marijuana and we knew you were in the sun-room. It's the room that George built for me to teach in, remember? We named it the sunroom when you made George and Douglas add more windows until the room was more windows than walls. Then when you couldn't walk up the stairs, we moved you into that room. You and Douglas had more privacy. He was in the sunroom with me, the morning you died.

Let me see. Where to start? I guess I'll tell you something funny. We're throwing a party for you today. It's been one month, two days, six hours since you left us and before everybody goes back to his or her own stories, we're going to have one more shin-dig as Sweetie says. Just like when you were here. Girl, we had a many 'just because' parties

Tilly had that one picture of us painted onto canvas. You remember that picture with Sweetie, Bea, Darnel, and all of us in it? I told her she could have it made into a portrait because I knew you wouldn't be mad. Darnel and his new wife, Geneva will be here since it would be okay with you. I'm glad you made peace with him before you left because I never could have if you hadn't. It was weird seeing the two of you drink coffee together those few times. Too bad he was too screwed up to change sooner but better late than never. Jeanie is going to be here too. I'm glad too because for while after you died she couldn't stand to be anywhere near this house. She has some stuff going on with her but I'll let her tell you all about it. And of course there's Beatrice. Would you believe she hooked up with that fine uncle of Renita's? Yes! Girl. That's what I meant to tell you. He came over one day to drop Renita and Jordan off and your mother went to work on him. You know Bea has always been hot. She is shameless!

Gwen cocked her ear toward the door. I guess I better get up and start greeting guests. I think Monica just walked in with Anthony. I'll be talking to you soon because I have to tell you all about Joshua. He has your smile and your appetite.

Gwen closed the book and cried. She picked up the pen and began to write through blurred eyes. *Isn't it funny how five minutes in a traffic jam feels like eternity and the forty five years you spent on earth seems so brief. Until later, I love you for always.*

Gwen shut the book and stood up. She took just one last glance at the bed where her Journey had slept and shut the door behind her.

📖

There was enough food on the table for ten parties. Gwen's home was busting at the seams with any and everybody Journey knew. Douglas was somber but holding up. He even managed a smile or two whenever anyone said something funny about Journey. He was the second to sneak away from the crowd into the sunroom. He sprawled out across the bed he and Journey had shared and held on to her pillow for the longest time.

"I finally got to see after all those years what it would be like to have you as my wife. Only you would whiz me away to Vegas to be married by a fake Isaac Hayes. I thought your family was plotting murder after we returned with you wearing my ring; especially Gwen.

"I miss you every day, baby. Some days I don't know how I'm going to get through it without breaking down. When I feel like that, I think of you before the cancer took you away. I dream about you a lot. The memories of the walks on the beach, you sitting quietly—just you period. You, existing.

"Sometimes I roll over and reach out to you because I could swear I hear you humming beside me. You know you used to do that at times, hum in your sleep, even though you'd never admit it. God, there are so many things I miss about you. Who's going to nudge me when I snore too loudly now?"

"I carry your picture in my wallet, but I don't need to look at it. I remember every detail about you down to that small mole right above, well you know where." Douglas had to smile. "Look at you, still making me blush even after you're gone. Gone

I hate that word.

It's hard to be in this house sometimes. That's why I stay away. You spent so much time here during your last months until we finally just moved in." Douglas leaned back sobbing for the longest time.

"Journey, I love you. I miss you. And you'll always be number one in my heart. I'm going to get back to your party before George or Gwen comes looking for me. Rest easy, Baby."

⊡

Allison waited for a while after she'd seen Douglas come back into den. She gathered the baby and headed toward the sunroom to say her last good-byes to Journey. She sat in the rocking chair and stared out the window.

"You know, girl. It still feels like you're here. It feels like at any moment you're going to walk up to me and check me about something stupid I said. You always did get a kick out of ragging on me didn't you? I didn't help any either did I? Even still I knew you liked me. Deep down you not only liked me, but also loved me. I'll never forget when you and me sat in that room when Malik and I were going through. You helped me, girl and I love you for that. I looked a funky mess didn't I?"

Allison pulled back the hat on the baby's head. "I've got a surprise for you. Her name is Journey. I always did love your name but it was Malik's idea to name her after you. Can you believe it? Me with a baby? I can hardly believe it myself. I'm a mommy and I love it."

Malik is at work but he'll be here shortly. He misses you too. We all do. I'm going to leave now because I'm getting ready to cry. I shouldn't be crying because it's a party right? Besides, I can hear you telling me to dry my ass up if I even looked about to cry. I miss that about you."

⊡

Tilly came into the room and flopped down hard on the bed. "I know you're probably frowning at me for about to eat this cake right in your bed but I'm going to do it anyway. I always did do things just to get you riled up. By the way, you know I hit your closet don't you? In fact, I got on one of the cutest suits of yours. I know you would have given it to me if I had asked. I look good in it too. There's this other one I like of yours too, so do me a favor and convince Beatrice to give it to me. It's the one she has on today."

Tilly put the cake on the nightstand. "I wish you were here to tell me you were going to slap the taste out my mouth if I dropped one crumb. It's not as much fun without you looking at me. I guess I don't have to tell you I miss you do I? After all those years of being jealous of you, loving, hating, missing, and then loving you again I'm okay. I'm just so happy I had you in my life for as long as the Good Lord seen fit. I'm glad you were finally happy and so am I. Oh. Tell Gwen I'm not really still mad at her, I'm only pretending to be so that she can keep making up to me. I'm working on getting that painting in the garage. It would look great in my den."

Monica stepped outside the sunroom and sat in the chairs she and Journey used to sit in. "Girl, it's a shame when a grown woman got to sneak around. You know how some things you tell your man and some things you just don't. Not that it matters because you know I'm still going to do what I need to do for me. Sho nuff. You know I'm just talking mess don't you? You could always tell when I was B-S-ing just like now."

"Girlfriend, I tell you, that old love bug done sneaked right up and landed right smack on my heart. That man out there, is the love of my life and I'm not telling anyone nothing different." Monica stuck out her hand. "Look at this, girl. I'm getting married. Yes, me heifer. The very one who talked all that do-do about never getting married. I'm glad I didn't let all that silliness from those prank calls scare me off. Girlfriend, no one could have told me that the high-pitched female voices on the other end of the line belonged to Sean. How the hell could he tell me that if I were a real woman then I would find my own man? What am I if not real? A robot or machine? And to think, I wanted him over Anthony!"

"God sure has a way of humbling us doesn't He? Always be careful what you say because it's not like you can suck words back in. I'm just glad we never had all that messy stuff between us. There is not one regret on my end. Everything I said to you was from my heart. Every I love you was for real."

"Okay, I've been serious enough. Now I'm going to pull out this last joint you gave me and it's going to be the last one I ever smoke. This one is for you. And maybe a little for me too because some of these folk at this party working my nerves a little bit. If you were here physically, we would take a ride down State Street and puff away. Remember we did that a lot when you were up and about? Now I just don't really have the taste for the herb like I used to. I quit the day you passed."

"Now hold on, let me shut this door." Monica drew hard from the joint and held in the smoke. "Ooh. I just about choked myself to death. I'm going to thump this thing as far away as I can. Maybe it'll land somewhere and grow a big ole' fat plant for you."

Monica had to laugh. "Gwen would turn blue in the face if she found a marijuana plant in her back yard wouldn't she?"

"Girl yes, yes. Like I was telling you. That man in there loves him some Monica. I never thought I would change or even want to change but love matures a person. He makes me happy and I want to make him happy. I must tell you though; I almost thought he wasn't for real. You wasn't here that day when I walked outside and seen the scariest thing in the world on my windshield. Girl, written in big red lipstick letters, somebody had written YOUR MAN IS A FAG. Now you know I was about to kill me somebody. I must have drove straight to his house and demanded an explanation. You should have seen him, Journey. I thought he was going to die right there. And the story he told me, at first I didn't believe him except he's just not a liar. Believe me, I know a liar because I've told a buncha lies. I knew he was telling the truth when he said he had been drinking wine with that psycho, Sean. That man still falls asleep after two glasses. Can you imagine, being molested by another man? And the nerve of Sean wanting to sue him for breaking his jaw. He should have broken his ass is what I say. I would have because you know I don't get down like that. Anthony still felt bad even after I said I believed him but I guess he still felt like he had something to prove. Ooh chile' let me tell you. That night…umm! You know it was some kinda good don't you? As long as it had been for that man! You know I can't wait for some more you know that don't you?"

"Anyway, that one hit got me all goofy, so I better go try to eat something and put these drops in my eyes. God knows I don't want Janelle to see me high. She adores me and I feel the same way about her. Oh man, I think I hear our song, girl.

I'm going in here to grab Douglas, and get my boogie on. Then after I boogie with him I'm going to boogey with my own man.

Hold on! Ain't no stopping us now! I'm coming!"

📖

Beatrice bumped into Monica on her way outside. "Girl, you scared me. I could have sworn I smelled Journey out here puffing away. Now gone on in there and spray on some perfume. Nobody'll know but you God and me. Then bring the perfume out to me even though I don't give a shit who knows."

Monica hugged Beatrice and closed the door. Bea sat down. "Yes, I'm sitting in your chair. I wish you were here so I can sit right here on your lap like you used to do mine." Beatrice's eyes began to tear. "You're my baby, Journey. What am I going to do without you? I've tried so hard but I don't ever think I'll be able to say goodbye. A mother simply "kont" truly bury her baby. I know, I know you're a grown woman but not to me. You're still that baby who I could count on to laugh at my jokes, and to make jokes for me to laugh at."

"I've been thinking a lot about some of the rocky times and I know it was just because we were so doggoned much alike. You're most like me. You knew what I was going to say before I said it. You knew which boyfriends would last a while and which ones wouldn't. Tell me, what you think of my new one? Fine huh? I think I might even marry that one since the last one 'bout ate me out of house and home. You remember me sitting on your bed and you telling me to tell you something funny? I remember because I tried to think of the biggest tale I could to make you laugh. You were hurting real bad, but you still laughed and laughed. I didn't have to make that one up. That dude really did eat up all my food and lawd, could he go through some juice! He thought he was slick by bringing me a little glass every time he filled his big one up. I finally had to ask his ass if he ever drank any damned water. I was sick of his snack cracker eating, juice-drinking ass. Hell, I haven't had to buy that many treats since my girls were babies. Being with that youngster was hell. It was like sticking an elevator in a outhouse, child it just don't fit. I'm getting too old for that shit."

"Baby I hope you're hearing me and laughing. I thought I was going to talk to you about Darnel and all that other bullshit, but I think you made peace with that and ain't no sense raining on a perfectly good parade. You be happy, doll-ing. I love you my baby.

📖

Jean opened the window wider and pulled out a cigarette. "I seen Tilly ass come in here and you know she beat me to that suit don't you? I should have stolen it from your closet when I first saw it."

"I guess you've heard huh? Geneva and Darnel got married for real. You know I didn't want to believe he would ever change but wonder of all wonders, he did. It's still a little awkward around him. Well, I did spit in his face."

"And Geneva, well you know. I don't feel for her the way I do for Bea, but she's alright. We have lunch sometimes, but Bea is all the mama I need or want."

"I hope you know that you were cremated just like you asked. You're right about one thing, at every black person's funeral there is that drunken uncle and somebody yelling, 'take me instead!' The latter would have probably been Bea with her dramatic butt. 'Probably would' a climbed in the casket and all."

"Geneva did sing *I'm Free* at your memorial service and everyone was crying their eyeballs out. I guess I know now where I get my voice from 'cause Beatrice can't carry a tune if you bundled it up and strapped it to her back. Speaking of Beatrice, she's calling me. I'm her Spades partner so I'll talk to you soon. I love you and you'll always be my girl. Oh, how could I forget, your niece had a little boy. I know... a little knotty head boy. He's so cute though. Girl, I gotta go"

"Hold on Beatrice, I hear you! Journey I love you and this hand is for you. We 'bout to run a Boston on they ass!"

📖

The sunroom was empty for a while. Sweetie and Gwen sat around talking about the good times they had with Journey. Everyone expected to see them disappear into the sunroom, but neither did. They had too much of Journey in their hearts to feel sad about. But George and Joshua went in.

"Hey, sister. I bet you thought I wasn't coming in didn't you? Now you know I can't miss talking to you. Anybody else but you."

"Looky here at my boy. Isn't he handsome like his daddy? I knew you would think so. I'm not going to stay long 'cause this boy hungry again. I swear he eats as much as you used to before you got too sick. We don't want to think about that now do we? We just wanna remember the smiles you brought and all these damned windows you had us build in this room. Damn room almost glass. But you know I didn't mind. I would've done anything you asked me to. If you had asked me to plant a tree in here I would've. And besides that, you brought me and my friend back together. I missed that old hard head."

"I want you to know that your beloved room won't be wasted. We plan on making it a playroom for Joshua here. And just in case Gwen didn't tell you, she goes back to work next coupla weeks. I bet she wanted to tell you, but so did I."

"This boy sure has some lungs on him don't he? Must have gotten those from you too." George laughed a low chuckle that Journey always got a kick out of. "Don't you worry though, Sis. Joshua is going to know all about his auntie, you can bet on that. Sho'nuff. I'm glad too that he smiles all the time because Gwen was just plain mean and ornery when she was pregnant," George laughed out the door.

📖

Darnel held Joshua. His nerves jangled all up when the baby began to whimper. He couldn't imagine himself a grandfather when he'd been such a poor father. He hoped the baby's whimpering would not draw attention to the corner where he sat. He had not moved since Gwen had opened the door for him. He had been trying to become part of the upholstery of the curtains behind him.

George lifted the baby from his arms and Darnel stood, sat down, rose again. His legs had fallen asleep and felt like they were no longer a part of his body. He wanted to walk toward Journey's room but his legs were working against him. Although he felt like everyone stared at him, he knew that they didn't. This was a celebration and Sweetie had made sure that no one sat around talking about Journey's death. They could only talk about her life.

Darnel made it to the room, and stood where he'd stood the last time he'd seen Journey. She had asked that he open the blinds, which he had. He cleared his throat, reached into his pocked, and pulled out a crumpled yellowed piece of paper.

"You told me that day in the kitchen that I should'a wrote you a letter. It took me all night but I wrote one the best I knowed how. Here goes."

Darnel read like a child reading from a first grade reader—thick tongued with every syllable sounding like the one before it. There was no singsong lilt to the words to draw them together. They hung separately suspended with nothing but space to hang on to.

Dear daughter,

I wish I could see you now but am glad I cain 't. cause I am scared. I am scared that you will see me an know I am not too far from that man you saw at the groc 'ry sto. That day I ran away from you like I done the last day when I hit Bea. I want to try to tell you how I feel inside our house wit all you girls. I feeled so little around yall. You girls kept getting bigger and bigger and to me the bigger yall got the littler the rooms got. Yall started filling up evry room with learnin. I new one day yall was gon' figger out why I tol yall to wait for bea or jean to hep with yall schoolwork. Any other daddy would a been proud but all I feeled was shamed. Thas when I tried to learn but it seem like I jes coudn 'nt get it so fast an I got tireda yall specting so much from me. Thank God yall got yall book learnin from Bea. Anyway you tried the hardess. An it was like you faild when I coudn 'nt get a word rite. You was always the one to try to outbeat everbody evn the boys. You got that from me. I was the same kinda way when i was a boy. I saw it that day you held that bat in you hand. I saw it that day in save more lot, an I sware I nevva want to see it a-gin. But I did. Rite in that kichen I seen it. I prayed to God that the nex time I seen you that you woodint make me feel so shamed or so nekkid and that day came when you called for me an I came. Baby doll stood in the doway reddy to kill me if I brethed too hard ova you. But I sat by yo bed an I wonted to hold you but you handed me yo hand. You coudn 'nt talk to good and that wooda made me glad once upon a time but I was sad. I'm jes glad u din 't cry cause I did enuf for both of us.

Darnel crumpled the letter. "I can say what I wanna say better'n I can read an write it. I gotta tell you I am glad you was my child. And as long as I live, I will never forget that moment—how you didn't look at me the way I always did remember. You looked at me like I was your daddy and I could'a took your place then an' there. I swear on my dead mama's grave I wished it was me an' not you."

Darnel pressed his fist hard against his eyes, so hard that he saw rainbow colored dots under his lids. He sniffed the tears back deep into his chest and waited to make sure that his fist had properly blocked the seepage of tears. He cleared his throat then looked ceilingward. "I jes' wanted you to know I never did stop loving yall girls. The one who was every thing I could'a been was you. You was my boy-girl chile. Maybe if you was a boy you coulda' understood me. But I guess I'm glad you was a girl too for Babydoll an'nem. I gotta go but I jes wanted you to know that I'm still trying till the day I die. I'ma make you girls proud one day you jes watch."

📖

When the house was empty and everything was washed and put away, Gwen flicked off the light to the sunroom. She stood at the door before closing it. "Big sister, the last words you said to me were, "Baby sister I'm free." Right before you closed your eyes, you said that to me. And I know you are."

📖

Sweetie waited until everyone was asleep before she went into the sunroom. She was fussing all the way to the windows. "Who closed these danged blinds? They know you didn't like it dark in here." She twisted the knobs opening up all the blinds. "Goodnight, Journey. Rest in peace. I promise to leave the shades open just for you."